The Mamas

Motherhood Not Required

Short Stories to Inspire Deeper Friendships

Bernadette Botz

The Mamas
Motherhood Not Required
Short Stories to Inspire Deeper Friendships

Cover art by Kailee Botz

ISBN 978-1-7334884-4-0

Note from the Author

Dear Friends,

I was sitting across a table from my pastor sharing some of my testimony when he asked what my books are about.

"Um…friendship?" I waxed eloquent.

His response?

"Yeah, Christians don't make very good friends, do they?"

Oh. How his words have bothered me!

How can we, as God's people, not be the best friends in the whole world? I've struggled to learn how to maintain my own friendships, have you? For years, I took the low road and abandoned dear and precious friends because I was afraid of conflict. Did you? I felt pinned by my pastor's words, and I wonder…Do you?

"Yeah, Christians [insert name] don't make very good friends, do they?"

I have come to believe that if we can trust a few faithful friends to stick with us no matter what, we can change the world. When I can lean on my friends in the bad times as well as the good, and when I can trust them to hold my humanity with tenderness - in their hands and especially in their mouths, it gives me unnatural courage. Feeling safe in friendship is what gave me the courage to write this book.

My friends love me even when I fail, fall, and blow it. They love me even though I still struggle to keep my face unveiled to them. They check me when I'm angry, correct me when I slip into gossip, and speak truth to the lies I believe. My friends, "The Mamas," (Motherhood is NOT required!) have advanced the Kingdom of God by helping me become who God created me to be in Christ. Honest friends help me live a life that's more oriented to the Cross. They help me have a deeper, more honest relationship with Jesus. My friends have changed my life! I want to be that kind of friend too, and we – The Mamas – are on a mission to change the world one friendship at a time!

The book you now hold in your hands is what I've deemed, "fiction-ish." Most of these short stories are based on actual events, but they've been altered to protect our valued privacy. I know you'll relate to some stories more than others, but I hope you find yourself in the characters somehow. I pray you find hope for your friendships!

Now…about that poetry.

I know many of you don't like poetry, and that's okay. I have come to understand myself better through poetry, so you're going to see some of it in this book. I think my life reads much like a fragmented poem, so I write in fragments. Johnny Cash wore Black. I write in fragments, and I hope you'll trust the broken poetry of my life to make sense. Please don't skip the poems.

I'm over the halfway mark in my life now. I don't have time to "get my act together" on my own. I need my friends to nourish my heart and challenge my soul. I must grow in Christ, and I hope this book will help you grow too. I hope it will inspire you to link arms with a few safe and faithful friends who will go "all in" with you. As we Mamas like to say, "It's simple, it's just not easy!" Set your face like a flint now because friendship like this is going to cost you. Iron sharpening iron is good for our souls, but it hurts our flesh. Just hang on. It's going to be okay.

We must follow Jesus and the example He set for friendship. I hope the stories in this book inspire you to do just that. Follow Christ. Follow Him all the days of your life and keep reaching back to take others on the road with you. Don't go alone! Embrace the awkward. Normalize the discomfort. Laugh a lot! Becoming close friends who do real, messy life together is awkward and uncomfortable. But oh, it's so worth it, and so are you. You're worth it!

This book is a call to a higher way to live. First, in Christ —always in Christ—and second, with each other. In a culture that so easily cancels, let's be a people who love each other no matter what. Grit your teeth. Lean in. Hope for your life, and let's change the world, one friendship at a time.

"The Mamas" have prepared a companion study to help you get started in this endeavor. It's titled *A Companion Study for You and Your Friends* and is available wherever this book is sold. There are inciteful questions in the study that can help you grow together as friends so you can experience the closeness we all need. We're cheering for you!

For the Joy set before us,

Bernadette Botz
March 2022
www.granberrybooks.com

P.S. You can *befriend* this book by leaving reviews everywhere books are sold. Please consider helping Christian authors in this way. They've been called to a long and lonely road, and you can be an encouragement to them by being generous with your words.

Acknowledgements

For my King. At your feet, Lord.

For my editor, Jennifer Crosswhite of Tandem Services. Thanks for holding onto my voice and encouraging me that everything would be okay. www.tandemservicesink.com

For Carli Milacci, for being my web support and prayer warrior. How wonderful it's been to work with you! How blessed I am in getting to know you! cjmilacci@gmail.com

For Eryn Dyke for early editing and coaching. (Boy, did I get derailed!) Thanks for being gentle and kind. Eryn.dyk@gmail.com

For Staci Daniel and all her rah, rah, sis, boom, bah. Couldn't do this without your honesty and the huge part you play in this process. Thanks, Staci!

For Zoe Ixthys. Sometimes, it's the silent partner that's felt the most. Thanks for praying and believing.

For Kathy Smith who keeps me laughing at myself which is always the best medicine. Her cover art for my first book is amazing, but her friendship is the sweetest gift! sixbananas@yahoo.com

For Kailee Botz, for cover art. You have been my right hand in so many ways, Kailee. Thank you for all your practical support.

For Tyler Black – the lone male on my launch team, and one of the most encouraging people I know. Thanks for reading, editing, listening, and being a friend to my writing. I can't say enough about you, good man!

For Ashley Botz for keeping everyone going with food and hugs. Ashley, what would our family be without you? My kids married well, and I'm thankful for the richness you all add to my life and to our family. I love you guys!

For Dr. Marianne Weaver and your long-suffering ears. Thank you for holding my life so I could write this book!

For Shirley Nelstead who prepares for and prays for me.

For the Paul Broyles Family, for all the little ways you've changed my life. Writing books isn't my favorite, but "I'll do it anyway." Wendy – thanks for a love that covered all my sin and shame. You showed me Christ.

For MaryLou Erfle who stood for hours at the other end of my kitchen counter reading and making sure some of these chapters were just right. I deeply enjoyed our times together!

For Ron and Monica Stone. My two biggest fans. I love you.

For those who read the early manuscript. And the middle manuscript. And the last manuscript! Laquita Andrews, Christine Bushnell, Jobey Eddleman, MaryLou Erfle, Kris Hart, Sandy Huston, Jennifer Montgomery, Marie Newman, Kathy Smith, Renette Steele, and Kathy Woods. You all are amazing!

For Karen Cox, my indomitable neighbor and friend praying her brains out next door. Thank you, Karen!

For Renette Steele. Thanks for cramming a reading weekend in for me and for sharing in this wonderful, terrible journey of writing. www.renettesteele.com

For Sandy Huston who helped me again and again when I switched the entire format of this book! You were a dear, patient, and organized friend who helped me up when I fell. (again)

For Christine Bushnell and all her help and heart. What a gift!

For Kathy Woods and all your faithful prayers. Thank you for walking through the valley with me, sistah!

For Marie Newman and all the things (as usual) but especially for giving me the shirt off your back in more ways than I can count!

For Kris Hart and all the years of faithfulness to my family and my heart. Your hand is a treasure to hold. I love you.

For the most amazing launch team in the whole world! Seriously – you guys deserve an award. (for patience!)

For Laquita Andrews, Wendy Broyles, Karen Cox, Staci Daniel, Jobey Eddleman, MaryLou Erfle, Paige Garcia, Kris Hart, Sandy Huston, Zoe Ixthys, Marie Newman, Jennifer Montgomery, Amy Roth, Ranae Wetli, Kathy Woods, and especially my sisters. Mamas, your friendship, in and out of season, has changed my life.

For Jobey Eddleman. There's no one like you on God's green earth. Thanks for being you – the most wonderful friend.

In memory of my parents and for beloved siblings. John, Rita, Monica, Colette, David, Alex, Maria, and Pierre. Everywhere I go; you are with me.

For the family of God and especially those who have given their lives for the sake of the Gospel. I owe you an unpayable debt.

For my kids and grandkids for making me the richest woman in the world: Joshua, Ashley, Tyler, Sarah, EttaBaby, Daniel, Kailee, CedarBoy, Andrew, Hannah, and Mary Elizabeth. You give me life, and you make me a better person. I love you.

For my husband Michael, a man of The Book and a student of my heart. Thank you for leading our family by example. It speaks the loudest, Love.

Thank you. All of you. I am rich in family, faith, and friends.

Bernadette Botz 2022
www.granberrybooks.com
Granberry Books

Dedication

"The hand that rocks the cradle rules the world."
William Ross Wallace

For all you Mamas – *motherhood not required,* but especially for my own.
I miss her every day.

Table of Contents

Prologue 1

Chapter 1 Silent Scream 11

Chapter 2 Freeze Frame 18

Chapter 3 Runaways 24

Chapter 4 Too Much Mama.. 34

Chapter 5 Puke in the LEGOs 45

Chapter 6 Autoimmune Disease 54

Chapter 7 The Untold 62

Chapter 8 Beauty Is Beast... 68

Chapter 9 The Humanity.. 73

Chapter 10 Wheels Off The Bus 78

Chapter 11 Scrub-a-Dub-Dub Grace in the Tub............... 91

Chapter 12 The Five Commandments 99

Chapter 13 Prayer Day 1.. 106

Chapter 14 MANipulation.. 107

Chapter 15 Beauty Is Fleeting....................................... 115

Chapter 16 Prayer Day 2.. 120

Chapter 17 Smoking in 'The Boys' Room 121

Chapter 18 Kneeling Nighty 128

Chapter 19 Drowning Day.. 135

Chapter 20 Pool Day.. 144

Chapter 21 Found... 159

Chapter 22 To the Brim.. 165

Chapter 23 Prayer Day 3 169

Chapter 24 Porn and Poetry 170

Chapter 25 Fragments of Loss 178

Chapter 26 3M 194

Chapter 27 Prayer Day 4 198

Chapter 28 Puberty Works! 199

Chapter 29 Prayer Day 5 205

Chapter 30 The Mamas Are Screwed 206

Chapter 31 Ghost Rider 211

Chapter 32 Single Saves Them All 217

Chapter 33 When You Love Someone 223

Chapter 34 Weird Uncle 227

Chapter 35 The Mamas Are Mad 237

Chapter 36 Shirts 245

Chapter 37 Prayer Day 6 252

Chapter 38 Bandits and Beggars in the Shepherd's Crook 254

Epilogue 265

"When thou hast found such a man, and proved the sincerity of his friendship; when he has been faithful . . . to thee, grapple him to thyself with hooks of steel and never let him go."
Charles Spurgeon

Prologue

In the beginning, Brooklyn was alone.

She filled years of school notebooks with three words that were a mystery to her then.

You are loved.

Brooklyn wrote them, but she didn't feel them. As much as she longed to believe the words were true, she always had the general sense that she was impossible to love. Brooklyn didn't know why she felt it then. Or why she sometimes still felt it now.

In the fourth grade, Brooklyn's teacher read books aloud to the class after lunch. She encouraged her students to draw or paint.

You are loved.

Brooklyn wrote—and the three words flowed in blurred sentences across soft printing paper. The repetitive pattern comforted her. The rhythm of writing them helped put her back together after recess.

"Why is your butt so big?"

"You're so ugly; who cuts your hair?"

"Why don't you brush your teeth; your breath stinks!"

"You look like an idiot when you run!"

The other children drew pictures and wrote notes to be passed to friends. Not Brooklyn. On the cusp of puberty and feeling scorched by their assessment, she couldn't help but agree. They were right. Their words hurt, but given the truth that Brooklyn already felt impossible to love, they felt fitting. Their words fit better into the world than she did, and as those three words filled pages of paper, Brooklyn willed them to be true.

You are loved. You are loved. You are loved. You are loved.

The summer between fifth and sixth grade, her mother—a confusion of wonderful and terrible—brought her a plain cardboard box. In it were the bras, worn and outgrown by her three older sisters.

"Here. Wear these." She'd shoved the box into Brooklyn's hands.

Brooklyn directed a questioning gaze at her mother, but it wasn't met with her mom's warm, dimpled smile. Instead, her returned expression was flat and cool and unseeing.

Turning her back, Brooklyn's mom walked out of the room and slammed the door shut behind her. This was against the rules, but the door seemed to grant permission to the exclaimed imperative. Adults made the rules, but they didn't have to obey them. This confused Brooklyn, but she got the point.

Don't ask questions.

She felt caged by the bras–as if she couldn't breathe. They itched and didn't fit right. They bulged under her shirt and made her budding breasts feel unwelcome. The bras made a statement themselves, and Brooklyn felt everyone could hear their exclamations. "Look! Brooklyn's wearing a bra now!"

Terrified as puberty dragged her from childhood, Brooklyn felt violated by her own body. Betrayed, she hated the unstoppable train of growth that hurled down the tracks of her lengthening spine. Alone in her room, she cried too many tears. At least that's what her mom said.

Why weren't children given more time to grieve during adolescence? Couldn't grown-ups see how hard it was? Having no choice but to abandon childhood was traumatic, yet the change came for everyone. Period.

The three words continued to fill pages in Brooklyn's journal.

You are loved. You are loved. You are loved. You are loved.

Even though he was missing the thumb on his right hand, her junior high teacher had elegant handwriting. Brooklyn resented him for it because of what he was doing to the boys in her class. She didn't want her teacher to be associated with anything beautiful. Everything about him made her feel ugly. A predator in the classroom, he called the boys up to the front of the class and felt out their private parts. Brooklyn never forgot the color of shame; it was the red in the boys' cheeks.

She held the trauma like a cold stone in her stomach every day, but the boys just joked about it.

"Watch out for the four-fingered feel-out." They said this to each other while playing air piano with four fingers. Right hand only.

Was making a joke the only way they could carry it? Even her family kidded about it at the dinner table, which made Brooklyn hate herself. She couldn't escape belonging to a system that joked about boys being felt up in front of the class. It wasn't funny, and it added to Brooklyn's loneliness. She knew what her teacher was doing was wrong. *Didn't everyone?* Why didn't anyone say anything? Why didn't *she?*

Her cowardice convicted her. She wanted to be a faithful friend, but when she tried to speak out against him, Four-Fingers' venomous words sliced her. She couldn't help the boys in her class. Her teacher's words were a hand over Brooklyn's mouth to silence her. They were a hand over the mouths of thirty years of girls to silence thirty years of schoolboys unprotected and humiliated by shame.

Living in the oxymoron of a public secret was the sin of Brooklyn's small town. Shhh…her pen rushed across the pages, trying to soothe the ache of loneliness.

You are loved. You are loved. You are loved. You are loved.

As a twelve-year-old girl, Brooklyn had looked out the sliding glass door of her parents' kitchen into the night. Seeing nothing but the reflection of her own face in the window, Brooklyn studied it. The cheekbones, the mouth, the eyes. In looking at her own reflected eyes, she felt she was observing a stranger.

Who are you, girl?

The haunted eyes of her reflection looked back at her, but the young girl had no answer. Nor could she give reason to the felt sense that she never belonged. *Did all twelve-year-olds feel lost like this?* Feeling impossible to love was the dark thread woven into Brooklyn's life. Trying to understand the adults in her world was a mixed bag of deep trauma and loving connection. Brooklyn felt confused about most everything at twelve, but she still wanted answers. She kept asking the reflection of the girl in the window.

Why, little girl?

Brooklyn wondered if all children in the world felt as lonely as she did on nights when she stared at the window glass. Sometimes, she would cry. But she never knew why.

You are loved. You are loved. You are loved. You are loved.

As Brooklyn grew up, she looked for faces like the one reflected in the night glass–ones her heart would know like an old friend. She looked for the scorched expression of the eyes of a searching soul. Ones that would help her make sense of the loneliness and of feeling impossible to love. She looked for the eyes of that twelve-year-old girl in every woman she met.

Brooklyn saw it often in her mother's face as she washed dishes in the sink. Her mom sang songs of worship and made Brooklyn feel safe, but she also spit in Brooklyn's face. She held Brooklyn when nightmares plagued her in her teens, but on Brooklyn's wedding day, her face had been as flat and cold as steel.

"Let's get this over with."

Years passed, and Brooklyn still stared into the night glass looking for answers. A grown woman now with a husband and five children, the deep question kept her writing. The pressure on her fingers holding a pen and the sound of letters falling across paper comforted her. Paper and pen. Her old friends relieved her of melancholy, as did those *words*. After all the years, they still dripped off her pen, offering some relief to the question of her youth. *Who are you?*

An enigma, her mother had been hard—and sometimes cruel—but she had also been kind. Brooklyn grew to know her mother's love. She came to understand it, but not until she married and had children of her own. Not until her marriage almost died. Not until the brokenness of her humanity and her own sin nearly destroyed her. It wasn't until the children started to say—

"I don't want your help."

It was only then Brooklyn had compassion for her mother. It was only then Brooklyn understood the difficult-to-receive message all women longed to hear. It was the message on the pages.

You are loved. You are loved. You are loved. You are loved.

Although it would ultimately be resurrected, when Brooklyn's marriage to William died, she died with it. Trying to hide her tears from her young children, Brooklyn escaped to the basement laundry room. Collapsing into a jumbo-sized laundry basket full of dirty clothes, she pressed her hands into her face so her sadness wouldn't fall.

Brooklyn's mom tiptoed into the basement and whispered, "Oh, honey." Brooklyn could hear the heartbreak in her voice.

"Leave me alone, Mom. Please…just leave me alone." Brooklyn kept her face covered. Rejection and betrayal felt like living things crawling on her skin.

"I'm not going anywhere." Her mother squeezed into the straining laundry basket next to her. Pulling Brooklyn into her arms, she rocked her grown daughter. She held her hard, but the tenderness of the gesture brought a torrent of tears. Brooklyn clung to her mother like a small child. Humiliation rose over her, and she waited for it to shatter her heart into a billion pieces of cutting glass.

Brooklyn could well imagine how ridiculous they looked sitting together amidst the dirty clothes. The metaphor didn't escape her, and she wondered if she would ever feel clean again.

Just when she thought she would be lost, her mother reached for her hand and crushed it violently in her own. Brooklyn's bones crunched together. She yelped as the soft skin on her hands stretched so thin, she thought it would split. Her mother didn't relinquish her grip.

Brooklyn looked at her mom's face. Shocked and hurt, her eyes formed a confused question.

"*Shhhht!*" Her mom hissed. There was a hard edge in her face and eyes as she squeezed even harder. Certain her mother was going to break her hand, Brooklyn held her gaze until the expression of agony turned to surprise. A slow, dawning understanding and a shared, molten grief welded their hands together. All agony was channeled away from Brooklyn's heart to her hand, and it was a pain that made *sense*. Her marriage dying was more than she could process, but the pain in her hand… that was something to understand. It was something she could grasp.

She and her mother locked gazes, their eyes speaking the past and the present. Brooklyn's mouth formed the question she already knew the answer to, but her mother's sharp reply was the same.

"*Shhhht!*"

She pulled Brooklyn forcefully into her arms and held all her trembling weight against her breasts. Brooklyn's mom held. She held her together as Brooklyn's body shook with sobs so violent with anguish, her small home shook on its timbers.

"Mama…"

Brooklyn's mom kept rocking her in the laundry basket until the tears were spent, and Brooklyn was limp in her arms.

"I know, baby. I know…" Her mother's softness returned.

Brooklyn could see the words on the soft printing paper from fourth grade in her mind.

You are loved. You are loved. You are loved. You are loved.

She knew she would never forget this day—this laundry basket day, and the way women bonded together to make sense of a mad, mad world. It was in the holding of both the good and the bad that Brooklyn began to understand.

All mothers were enigmas, and growing up was hard, no matter what your age.

Being a child was wonderful and terrible.

Being a woman was wonderful.

Being a woman was terrible, and for everyone—*growing up was hard.*

***

Writing, Brooklyn now sat at her own kitchen table in the stillness of the night. She thought of all the things she had faced as a woman. The memories, a strange mixture of desperation and joy, flitted like fireflies along the edges of the night glass. Brooklyn saw her face reflected in the sliding door, and the twelve-year-old inside spoke.

Who are you, woman?

Brooklyn smiled at her.

"I'm not who I once was." She spoke aloud to the reflection.

How so, woman? her inner child asked.

"Because I'm loved." Brooklyn thought of her husband, Will, and what the Lord had brought them through. "And because Jesus has shown me how." By His mercy, she and Will had survived unfaithfulness, and God had blessed them with five beautiful children. She noticed her eyes didn't look as haunted. There was a softness in them now—a peace.

Brooklyn reached up to tuck a stray curl behind her ear. She had seen the reflection of her own face expressed in women all around the world:

the exquisite agony of love that was etched in their eyes. Brooklyn longed to be connected to them. She wanted everyday life with them. She wanted to hold them just as her mother had held her in the laundry basket, so they could hold on. Brooklyn was starved for the fellowship of women, and she could see that too, in her reflection.

Jesus walked with His friends. Brooklyn's sigh held a deep longing for women who would just do life with her. She hungered for someone she could trust. But she'd been hurt too many times, and Brooklyn had abandoned hope of having even one true friend.

She sighed again at her reflection and smiled a sad smile. As she thought of Will and the kids, she felt the blessing of her family. She was thankful. *It was okay.*

Brooklyn's hand flew across the pages of her notebook. She wanted her words to reach out in friendship to someone. To anyone. She wrote the same message now that she had written as a questioning twelve-year-old. She wrote it for herself and for other women who might be looking into the night glass. She wrote it for every woman burned to ash because of love. She wrote it for her mama. She wrote it for all the mamas. She wrote it for the little mamas and the single mamas, for women who never could, or would, be mamas. Like the great cloud of witnesses, Brooklyn poured her heart out to them in black ink.

You are loved. You are loved. You are loved. You are loved.

Her pen raced across the page, reaching out to scratch the itch of every woman's heart.

You are loved in the agony of the way you lay down your life. In the ways you follow Jesus all the way to the cross. In the ways you echo His voice as He speaks the Gospel of grace to the wounded. You are loved in this wonderful and terrible life. You are held by grace, and you hold by grace. You are the enduring ones. You are women. You are the strong, and you are loved.

Brooklyn looked at the night glass once more and smiled at the expression she knew so well. The exquisite agony of love etched in her eyes looked back at her, and she spoke aloud to the woman she saw.

"It was always Jesus, you know. It was always Him."

He was the King of friendship. He was the One still holding hope she would find a friend someday. He was the words that continued to fill Brooklyn's notebooks. He was the Word speaking His message of hope to the whole, hurting world...

You are loved. You are loved. You are loved. You are loved.

But in those early days before she met The Mamas...

It was Brooklyn.

Alone.

Chapter 1
Silent Scream

Sometimes "Alone" looked like tears and nights at the window glass. Sometimes, it was desperate moments like these. Moments that made her feel like driftwood on the waves of the sea—tossed and out of control.

Brooklyn tried to stay calm as panic formed itself in beads of sweat on her upper lip. She had to still the rising adrenaline. Adrenaline was not her friend, and she took a deep, cleansing breath. No use. All the pores in her body opened and dumped water down her back.

To her horror, Brooklyn was smack in the middle of a defecation emergency.

"Oh, God. Oh, Jesus. Oh, God. Oh, Jesus."

Pushing her cart at the grocery store, she tried to calm herself. Brooklyn had never recovered from a fourth-degree tear delivering her firstborn. This meant she had never been the same "down there." It also meant she had to get to the bathroom immediately upon sensing "the need."

It wasn't ladylike to discuss it, but many women knew what it meant to carry baby wipes in the diaper bag for more than just the baby. They knew that packing an extra pair of undies, and, in dire cases, an extra pair of *pants,* was more important than lipstick or deodorant. Incomparably so.

Brooklyn squeezed her buttocks together, which made hurrying to the restroom most difficult. She breathed out prayers.

"Oh, God. Oh, Jesus."

Her infant's car seat swung on her arm and bumped on her thigh as she held the two-year-old's hand. The four-year-old, thankfully at this moment, was compliant. Brooklyn had never been so grateful that he kept a hand on the infant seat just as she taught him. He obeyed her "calm" request.

"Mama has to go potty. Stay close to me." Brooklyn breathed the command to her kids, trying not to exert any pressure—"down there."

Please, God, don't let there be a line. Brooklyn begged, tugging the kids forward.

"Can I get a book today, Mama?" Jake asked, oblivious to the crisis. He was only four, but he already loved to read.

"I'll get you whatever you want if we make it to the bathroom on time." Brooklyn practiced her birthing breaths. Desperate for relief and fearing she wouldn't make it, she crashed her cart into the cinderblock wall outside the ladies' room.

"Go!" she barked at the kids. "Go, go, go!"

Mercifully, there was no line in the restroom, and the handicapped bathroom was free. *Oh, I'm so handicapped.* Brooklyn let go of her daughter's hand and started unbuttoning her pants before she was even to the door. *Almost there. Almost there.* Brooklyn shoved four-year-old Jake and two-year-old Sophie through the door and dropped baby Derek's infant carrier on the floor. Throwing her purse at the hook on the wall, she said out loud, "Don't think about germs. Don't think about germs."

Desperation gripped Brooklyn's bowels as she, ashamed of herself, collapsed on the bare seat of the toilet. *Don't think about germs!* Her heart pounded with anxiety as the dread sound of her body waste entered the toilet bowl.

Precious child! Blessed Sophie! Born with a big, beautiful voice, she started singing at the top of her lungs. Her song of mercy covered the sound of Brooklyn's all-consuming humanity. Overwhelmed on so many levels, Brooklyn wanted to kiss her. Too bad her relief was short-lived...

Four. Year. Old. Jake.

So relieved to have made it to the toilet on time, Brooklyn panicked again when she saw the excitement on Jake's face.

Oh, honey, please don't. Please, please, don't. Brooklyn begged him in her thoughts, her eyes pleading with him. It was hopeless.

"Ewww. Mama, you *stink!* Are you going poopy?" His voice echoed in the bathroom, and Sophie chose that moment to stop singing.

"Shhh, son. Yes. I'm going poopy." Brooklyn whispered back, but she could feel the tightness in her chest as she tried to control her voice.

"Can I see?" Jake didn't wait for an answer but pushed around the narrow passage to her backside.

"Son, please don't. It's crowded and—"

"Wow! Good job, Mama! That's a big one, and it smells bad!" Jake looked like he would split with pride, and his voice consumed the space with bragging. "Mama, it smells really bad."

Brooklyn saw feet in the stall next to her. She heard a snort of laughter from someone losing their battle with politeness. She saw feet outside her door. There must be a line gathering.

Oh, Lord, kill me now. What am I doing here with three kids in a public bathroom? Brooklyn's reasons for not trusting her children into the care of others crowded into the stall with them. She sighed.

Brooklyn didn't know what made her remember her husband, William, at that moment, but she thought of the first time he changed a cloth diaper. As first-time parents, they both wanted to use cloth diapers to save money. Brooklyn told Will he had to rinse the poop out in the toilet, and he had looked at her like she was insane. Instead, he threw the cloth diaper into the garbage can.

"I'm not putting my hands anywhere near the toilet! *Or* the poop!" He washed his hands, drove to the store, and came home with a huge bag of disposable diapers. A tidy man, Will never got over his phobia, and changing diapers was still traumatic for him. He was utterly grossed out by human excrement.

But his son? Not so much.

"Sissy! Come and look at Mama's poopy. It's enormous!" Jake wasn't using his inside voice, and he called to his sister as if she was in another room. Another state. Another country.

"It stinks really bad!"

"Wait—Soph—No—" Brooklyn tried to grab her daughter, but the toddler was too fast.

Sophie squeezed along the other side of the toilet, and Brooklyn, now on the verge of tears, sat helplessly hemmed in by her two oldest children. The baby started to cry, and Brooklyn's milk let down. Once again, stress opened all the pores in her body, and Brooklyn was drenched in sweat anew.

"*Pew!*" Sophie, at least, was grounded in reality. "That's gross!"

Curse her loud voice! Brooklyn gave her daughter a dirty look, which she would have seen if she hadn't been consumed by the giant view of her mother's "back porch." Not to mention the "enormous" poop that was apparently floating in the toilet and that, according to Jake, smelled "real bad."

"Ew! That's 'isgusting, Mama!"

Trying to escape Brooklyn's bare bottom, the toilet, and the awful stench, Sophie lost her balance and fell. Her hands went to the floor and then—right to her mouth when she stood up.

Sophie was an addicted thumb sucker.

Brooklyn couldn't even look at her. *Don't think about germs!* She closed her eyes in agony. "Jakey, get out of there, honey. Please. Give Mama some privacy." Brooklyn sighed in defeat. (For there was still the wiping.)

"Yeah, Jake, give Mama her pibacy!" This had been one of Sophie's first words growing up in a small house. Her booming voice echoed, and Brooklyn heard laughter outside the stall door. Jake obeyed his little sister and after one last, loud praise, left the smelly scene.

Brooklyn finished her, "good job," flushed the toilet, and stood, trying to composer herself. Relieved to have her pants buttoned, she slung her purse over her shoulder and the baby's car seat over her arm.

"Come on, Jakey. Hold on to Derek's car seat." Brooklyn grabbed Sophie's filthy hand, and—taking a deep breath, unlatched the lock to face them.

The line of women in the bathroom was now out to the door. Several stalls stood open, but none of the women moved to go inside. Why would they miss the entertainment?

Straightening her shoulders in preparation for smirks and giggles, Brooklyn shrugged at them as if to say, "What can you do?" The agony of being a woman sometimes! How could these women possibly respond?

To her surprise, the entire line erupted in joyful applause.

"Good job, Mama!"

"Wow!"

The women in line laughed, but not out of awkwardness or disgust; they laughed out of unity and out of compassion. Those with children empathized with Brooklyn, and those without sympathized. One of them rushed over and grabbed the baby's car seat.

"Here, let me help, so you can wash everyone's hands!"

The horror in her tone obvious, Brooklyn cried, "Thank you! My daughter fell—then put her thumb in her mouth!"

"I wondered what happened in there. We all heard a silent scream," she said.

Brooklyn shuddered. She couldn't help noticing nobody was going into her stall.

A tall woman with perfect olive skin and long, dark hair said, "My little boy is fascinated with poop right now too. I'm potty training him, and I can't get a moment's privacy. I mean…pibacy." She smiled at Sophie and winked.

The ladies in line chatted and shared their horror stories.

Brooklyn scrubbed Sophie's hands until her little girl cried.

"Thank you," Brooklyn sighed with relief. Taking Derek back from the woman holding his carrier, Brooklyn smiled at all the ladies in the restroom. Nobody seemed in a hurry to leave.

"Thank you, ladies. I really have no words."

"You made our day." The woman patted Brooklyn's arm as she surrendered the car seat. "You really did, you poor girl. You all set to do your shopping now?"

Brooklyn took a deep breath. "After that experience, I think I can do anything!" She walked out of the bathroom to renewed applause and exclamations of, "Good job, Mama!"

**

Brooklyn pushed through the grocery aisles, deep in thought. One wheel on the cart squealed in protest while another refused to work at all. An early reader, Jake sat cross-legged in the front of the cart absorbed in a book while Sophie held on to the edge of Brooklyn's jacket. Derek's infant seat was locked onto the handle of the cart, and Brooklyn admired his perfect little face.

Suddenly, unexpectedly and without warning, the all-too-familiar nausea swept over her. Brooklyn's mouth flooded with saliva, and she focused on her breathing to keep from throwing up. She paused, hardly daring to think. *I'm still nursing, and Derek is only three months old!* Although she'd suspected for a few days, it was still hard to imagine, and after the bathroom fiasco, Brooklyn had almost forgotten why she'd come to the store in the first place.

Brooklyn sighed and smiled. She and Will wanted a big family, but she was nervous about the timing. What would Will think about it? And even though she knew what the result would be, Brooklyn picked up a pregnancy test and tossed it into the cart.

"What's that?" Sophie pointed to the box.

"Something that's going to get your daddy in trouble." Brooklyn smiled sweetly at her daughter, so Sophie smiled back.

"You're so funny, Mama."

Brooklyn snorted. "You think so, huh? Do you think Daddy will think I'm funny?"

"Oh yea, you always make Daddy laugh. Just like those ladies in the bathroom. They thought you were funny too." Sophie picked a booger out of her nose and examined it. "I liked those ladies. They were nice."

And she put her thumb—and the booger…into her mouth.

Chapter 2
Freeze Frame

Over the next few years, Brooklyn and her husband, Will, added Abe and Maylee to their family. Five children. Lonely as it could be sometimes, what an adventure! What a beautiful life!

Brooklyn was changing newborn Maylee on her bed in their small home while Abe, aged three, watched. Without warning, Abe took both of Maylee's legs and lifted them up and over her head.

"Mama, Maylee's penis is broken! Look, she has two butts! We should take her to the doctor!"

"No, son!" Brooklyn burst out laughing. "Maylee is a girl! She doesn't have a penis." She delighted in observing the female anatomy through Abe's eyes. Explaining the difference between boys and girls to him, Brooklyn watched shock register on his face. She wished she could freeze frame his expression.

"I feel sorry for girls. How do they pee outside?"

Abe would have felt this loss severely. He loved peeing outside. Digging a small hole in Brooklyn's empty garden using a plastic sand shovel, Abe was working to fill it. He drank copious amounts of water to reload his bladder.

"Where is my pee going? I fill it up, but it keeps going into the dirt. Maybe there really is such a thing as a hole to China. Maybe my pee is getting on the Chinese people."

What must it be like to be in his mind? Brooklyn wondered. Abe had a keen intellect, and Brooklyn could only guess what was going on in his imagination.

The change of diaper complete once more, Brooklyn took Maylee in her arms and walked to the living room to nurse her. Once she had the baby latched, she pulled Abe up on her lap to read to him.

Derek was in the back yard building a tree fort, and Sophie and Jake were giving him advice. Brooklyn had all the windows open and she could hear the kids talking.

"If you put that piece of plywood across those two branches, you'll have a nice platform, Derek, but the ladder you built is a piece of junk. It'll never hold you." Jake gave constructive help. "If you use the knots in the trunk of the tree, you can get up just fine, and it would be kind of like a secret entrance. Besides, you're a great climber, and it would be way more fun."

Brooklyn listened as their voices drifted through the window. What a good big brother Jake was! How fortunate the kids were to have him!

Derek was too young to be building a tree fort, but he was determined and Brooklyn had given up trying to stop him. Jake was the common sense and council Derek needed, and Brooklyn let the kids build without getting involved.

The rocking chair squeaked. The weight of her two youngest on her lap filled Brooklyn with contentment and warmth. She watched Abe for his sleep cues.

"Hey, Mama? What does 'haddle' mean?" Abe's long, black eyelashes were growing heavy. The time between blinks was lengthening.

"I've never heard that word, Abe. Can you use it in a sentence?" Brooklyn kissed the top of his head.

"You know…'Mary haddle little lamb?'" His eyes closed for a full two seconds.

Brooklyn didn't answer him. She was smiling too hard.

"Mama? What's the most dangerestest job in the world?"

Three seconds.

"And what's the most painfulest way to die?"

Four seconds.

"Mama, do you think I'm handsome, hilarious, and h-adorable?"

Six seconds and Abe was heavy in her arms. He was almost asleep. Brooklyn knew she had to get him to bed in the next few minutes, but she wanted to keep holding him and rocking. If only she could freeze frame this moment!

"Come on, little man," she whispered to Abe.

"No, Mama," he whined. "I'm not tired."

Holding Maylee close to her and putting Abe on his feet, Brooklyn tucked his chubby hand in hers and pulled him to the bedroom. Laying Maylee down in her crib, which was placed in the closet without doors, Brooklyn bent down to pick Abe up in her arms. Holding him and rocking him back and forth as she stood, he grew heavy again with sleep.

"I love you, Abraham. I do. I do. I love you, Abraham. My little boy blue." Brooklyn sang his song before putting him in the other crib in the bedroom. Tucking his teddy bear under his arm, she looked—as she always did, at the three moles under Abe's right ear. They looked like three drops of sweet molasses, and she leaned as far into the crib as she could to kiss them.

"Have a good nap, Abe." Brooklyn moved to the three other beds in the room. Quietly straightening the sheets and blankets, she tidied the crowded space. Derek's toddler bed lay sandwiched between Jake and

Sophie's single beds, and after everything was neat, Brooklyn stood in the door to observe the room.

That's a lot of beds. The Wyers' small home wrapped around Brooklyn, and her feelings were mixed. She and Will were looking for a bigger house. Jake was getting older, and she knew he would need his own space soon. But it was hard to stay mad in a small house. Conflict had to be resolved, and there was a lot of love shared in the tight space. Brooklyn had an affection for their little home, and it gave her deep joy to see all the kids' beds together. Five beds!

Unable to resist, she walked back to Maylee's crib for a last peek at her beautiful, surprise baby girl. She couldn't help remembering that it hadn't been *that* much of a surprise.

***

As a Christian, homeschooling mother, Brooklyn started each school day praying with the kids. For the last two years, Sophie had been kneeling on her face before the Lord praying for a baby sister.

"Please, Jesus, give me a baby sister! I love my brothers so much, but I want a sister."

Sophie's Sunday school teacher had even stopped her after church. "I don't know if you know this, but Sophie has everyone in her class praying for a baby sister. Are you and your husband trying?"

"No," Brooklyn told her. But that night she talked to Will. The two of them had been on the fence about having another baby, but all doubt was removed now for Brooklyn. "William, we're going to have another baby. Sophie's prayers bring me to tears every day, and now she's got the whole church praying!"

She remembered coming together with Will the night Maylee was conceived. Will had prayed Proverbs 5:18-19 out loud. "*Let your fountain be blessed, and rejoice in the wife of your youth, a lovely deer, a graceful doe. Let her breasts fill you at all times with delight; be intoxicated always in her love."*

Brooklyn lay awake deep into the night with her hands over her stomach. Sorrow and joy coursed down her cheeks in tears as she remembered her dead baby. The gift of new life overwhelmed her now, and she thanked God for Sophie's prayers. And for Will's prayer. Brooklyn knew she was pregnant, and she cradled her new baby with her hands over her naval. Praying for hours, Brooklyn finally dropped into sleep with a contented smile on her face.

Maylee had been born nine months later.

Watching Maylee sleep was one of Brooklyn's favorite things. The baby's tiny head was covered in black hair that stuck out in every direction. Her eyelashes fanned out like strokes of black charcoal on her pale cheeks. If only she could freeze frame her tiny form! Sleep gathered on Maylee's red lips, and Brooklyn couldn't get over how beautiful she was—how beautiful her life was!

The Lord had been good. He had rescued Brooklyn's marriage from destruction, and he had set her family on a path of righteousness. Brooklyn was overwhelmed with gratitude for Jesus and for the life he'd given them all. She reached down to stroke Maylee's soft cheek.

"You special girl. May you always know the power of prayer in your life."

Closing the door on her two youngest, Brooklyn walked to the back yard to check on the three oldest. They heard the screen door close and came running.

"Mama! Look what we built! Derek started it, but we helped him finish!" Sophie hugged her. The pressure of her daughter's arms around her waist felt like heaven, and Brooklyn squeezed her in return.

Admiring the work on their fort, Brooklyn checked to make sure it was sound.

"This is amazing, you guys! You've done great work!"

The sun set a halo on Jake's chestnut hair, and the look of pride in Derek's eyes caught Brooklyn's heart. Sophie's chatter caused Brooklyn to blink back tears. Could she freeze frame this moment?

She was just an ordinary woman, afterall.

With ordinary kids.

On an ordinary day.

And that was the glory of it all.

Chapter 3
Runaways

Swishhh, swishhh. Swishhh, swishhh.

The oldest of their five children, Brooklyn's son, Jake, dragged a sleeping bag across the wood floor. Something about the sound dragged on her heart. Her back was to him as she scrubbed carrots in the sink, but she felt something in the sound of the sleeping bag: *Swishhh, swishhh. Swishhh, swishhh.*

Drying her hands, Brooklyn turned to him and looked into his young face. She waited for him to meet her eyes. "What's the trouble, Jake?"

Tears pressed like holy water on the brim of his eyelids. One slid over the edge and made a trail toward his frowning mouth. He brushed it away with the back of his sleeve.

He was ten years old.

"It's too loud here! The kids are always talking! I want an adventure, so I'm running away." The strings on his red hoodie trembled. "I don't like being the oldest! You're always asking me to do stuff. I never have enough time to read. I just…I just wanna go away!"

Guilt struck, leaving the familiar power of shame coursing through Brooklyn's bloodstream. Jake was right, of course.

Brooklyn's husband, William, was a master luthier, a craftsman at making violins, violas, and cellos. He traveled the world teaching, and although it was a profession that provided for his wife and five children, Will was often away from home. While they believed their decision for Brooklyn to stay at home and educate their children was the right one, it didn't come without a cost.

When he wasn't traveling, Will was remodeling the house to add two bedrooms and a bathroom. Presently, the Wyer's had only two bedrooms and one working bathroom to which the door must never be locked. Peeing in the tub was socially acceptable in case of emergency. Desperation and lack of privacy crowded their growing family, and Will worked long hours trying to give them all more room. There were no doors on the bedrooms either, as they had been removed for refinishing. Will traveled at least one week out of the month and sometimes even two or three. When he wasn't traveling, remodeling, or working in his woodshop, he ran their business out of the remaining bedroom in the house.

At best, the Wyer home made the sound of happy bees buzzing in a spring linden tree. At worst, Will would stomp out to the living room while trying to conduct a conference call. Snapping his fingers, his eyes pleaded with Brooklyn. *Quiet, please!* Will's frustration boiled. Brooklyn's boiled over, and the stress was often unbearable for everyone.

Everything about the house was tiny and tight. Like a very pregnant woman, the breaking of her waters loomed. *Her* being the house. *Her* being all of them. Brooklyn imagined the water going out like a tidal wave, and all of them tumbling out the door in a blended concoction of humanity— arms and legs and bodies askew, soaked to the skin and gasping for breath. For life. For room.

Brooklyn, often a single parent, depended on her oldest son. Having long lost his fascination with bowel movements, Jake was now an old hand at changing diapers. He took little ones out of their car seats and helped bring in the groceries. He negotiated arguments. He watched kids in the back yard while Brooklyn was on the phone or in the bathroom. Jake helped Brooklyn all the time. All. The. Time.

"I want to run away, Mama," Jake said again, without tears this time.

The quiet Jake craved was made impossible by sheer numbers and the constant hum of lives being lived in the Wyer's small house. Brooklyn understood her son. His big, brown eyes sorrowed, and he looked down at the floor.

Was he ashamed?

"Oh, son, it's okay." Brooklyn pulled him into her arms and whispered into his ear, "Everyone wants to run away sometimes."

Oh, God! He doesn't get enough! I'm not enough! Brooklyn's insecurity reached its bony hand to squeeze shut the pockets of joy in their home.

But there was the Still Small Voice, that oft present sense that Jesus was speaking, meeting her there in the kitchen. *Hush. This is about him. Focus…on him.*

Jake needed time. He needed space and quiet. Introverted and a lover of books and big ideas, Jake needed a place to dream and plan. He needed more than Brooklyn. He needed a break from the responsibility of being first born and all she asked of him.

Jake's voice was husky and broken. "Can I run away to the back yard? Can I set up my tent back there and be alone? Would it be okay if…Mama, could I just read all day?" Another tear spilled over. Jake was embarrassed to cry in front of her now, but Brooklyn could hardly keep from smiling. *Precious boy. You don't know you're asking an expert on running away.*

"Son, do you see my smile?" Brooklyn tilted his chin up to look at her. "I bet you didn't know one of my favorite things is a good runaway." She searched his eyes and watched surprise replace tears. "How about this? You sit down and make a list of your favorite snacks and drinks. I'll pack you a special lunch and help you set up your tent. I won't let any of the other kids come out, and you can read to your heart's content. All day."

Brooklyn hugged him again. He smelled like her, of books and tears, but he was growing up. Jake's lips were full and red against his olive skin, and she wanted to kiss him.

"When Sarah Mullis gets here, I'll skip running. We'll go to the store together. Just you and me, no other kids."

Sarah wasn't just the babysitter. She was the wise beyond her years babysitter and the kids' best friend. She brought bubble gum and arrived promptly after school, five days a week so Brooklyn could go running. She came for an hour and saved her. She came for an hour and saved them all.

Running had always been a bit of salvation for Brooklyn, but she had been running *away* since she was twelve. She ran from the sick teacher first, then from the traumatic loss of her first love. After that, she ran from the bad-boy boyfriend and then the dead baby. She ran from her mistakes. And more mistakes. She ran from feeling impossible to love.

A teenager unable to process her own life, and with no deep friends to help, Brooklyn ran headlong into rebellion. She knew the consequence of sin was nothing if it wasn't dependable. Its yield for success was zero percent, but Brooklyn had always been bad at math.

Unable to see the sorrow driving her to rebel, her mom was frustrated and hurt by her daughter's choices. "You can have all the rope you want to hang yourself. *Go.* But whatever bed you make is the one you're going to lie in."

Cringing at the memory, Brooklyn took the rope. And ran.

Now, sixty minutes of running gave Brooklyn a space for peace. It held her together. It held her family together. Brooklyn treasured the precious hour of quiet, especially when Will was traveling.

But Jake didn't have that.

Brooklyn finished scrubbing the carrots while Jake made his list. She scrubbed at her running years and the scars they'd left behind. With her back turned to her son, she prayed he would know love. She prayed he would always know she was *for* him, even if he was running. She prayed she could live out the gospel for Jake, even today. She prayed he would know that no matter how far or fast or long or deep his running away took him, he would always find Jesus extending mercy and grace. Friendship and love. Forgiveness and authenticity.

"Here, Mama." Jake handed a sweaty piece of paper to Brooklyn. He was blushing. He'd left nothing off his list, and he looked at Brooklyn with a sideways glance.

Brooklyn's heart beat hard in her chest. The list was long. The budget was short.

Invest. The quiet voice came again as the Holy Spirit's counsel. It brought Brooklyn to tears, but Jake misunderstood them.

"It's okay, Mama. I know that's a lot of stuff we don't usually get, and it's expensive."

"No, son, it's okay. It's just that we don't have any of this at the house. To do running away right, we want to get everything on your list." Brooklyn caressed the top of Jake's brown head, silently blessing him.

Jake nodded, trying to look cool. Delighted surprise twitched around his mouth as he tried to contain a smile. In a family of seven, special requests were neither given nor taken, and he hugged Brooklyn where her waist used to be.

"Thanks, Mama."

When Sarah arrived, Jake and Brooklyn were waiting at the door.

"I'm not running today, Sarah. I'm taking Jake to the store. He's got some big plans for the day, right, son?"

"I'm running away, SarahMullis!" Jake beamed at her. All the kids combined Sarah's first name with her last. None of them could remember why.

"Wow! That sounds awesome!" Sarah rubbed the top of his head, but her eyes locked onto Brooklyn's. She was only sixteen, but she saw it. More importantly, she got it. Sarah saw the exquisite agony of love etched in Brooklyn's eyes, and she extended compassion and understanding instead of judgment.

"Should we tell your mom she's got a different shoe on each foot?"

Jake laughed.

Ecstasy.

Sarah was a hero.

"Mama! Your shoes!"

Brooklyn looked down at her feet and blushed. Her shoes told the story of the desperation she often felt. They told of sleep deprivation, lack of self-care, and loneliness. The shoes—mismatched—were like a neon sign flashing her life in front of a small town. "I'm alone! I'm desperate! And I have no friends!" The Wyer family didn't fit the typical both-parents-working-outside-the-home model. It didn't fit the traditional either, with one parent staying home while the other came home every night after work. Brooklyn ran to the weight of stares expressing a mixture of pity for her and self-righteousness that she and Will had made the wrong choice for their family.

Brooklyn ran like a madwoman, ignoring the breast milk (forgotten nursing pads) that leaked through her t-shirt. She ran to escape the constancy of feeling that she was either too much or not enough. She ran angry, often crying.

The "Blond Bombshell" is what they called her because that's what she looked like—a bombshell that, with just a tap, might explode. Brooklyn was a fixture, and she made the whole town uncomfortable.

Even so, running was a gift. In the quietness of her mind, she prayed and ran. She confessed her sins to God. She reached for Him with all her heart, and He always met her on the road. Brooklyn returned at the end of the hour, replete with joy, and the world set right. Running enabled her to keep loving. It helped her to persevere in the work of raising a family. While her heart still cried out for a friendship she could trust, running gave her gratitude for what she had. It staved off loneliness when Will was gone. After a run, Brooklyn was happy to get home to her little brood, and she knew what a gift she had in SarahMullis.

Sarah looked again at Brooklyn's mismatched shoes and put a hand on her shoulder.

"It's okay, Brook." Her words poured over Brooklyn's insecurity like a blessing. "I've got you. Take Jake on his adventure."

Brooklyn hugged her. "Thanks, Sarah. You're the best." She quickly changed out of her odd running shoes, grabbed her purse, and took her son's hand. "Let's go, Jake!"

At the grocery store, Brooklyn let Jake push the cart and willed herself to slow down. This was not the usual grocery triage. It wasn't even about food.

"We're going aisle by aisle, so we don't miss anything."

Jake could hardly believe Brooklyn's words. He stood tall and chattered the whole time.

"We should get this for me and this for Derek." He held up two bags of chips. "Sophie will want chips too, I guess. Abe likes jawbreakers, so can we get those for him? And Mama, you want chocolate, right? Maylee's too little, but we could get her a stuffed animal or something."

Jake couldn't help himself. He picked something out for each of his siblings and poured items into the cart like water; some of them were even on his list. Finally, standing in front of the drink cooler, Jake slipped his hand into Brooklyn's and pulled her up and down the aisle, agonizing over what to choose.

This is the day the Lord has made. Rejoice and be glad, my daughter. God's Word reached for Brooklyn's heart. Tucking this memory into her mind like Jake's hand, Brooklyn never wanted to forget him or this moment.

His brown head bobbed as he walked beside her, and she treasured him. She admired him. She delighted in him.

After a chatty drive home from the store, Brooklyn packed Jake's runaway lunch. Salami, prosciutto, hard cheese, soft cheese, French bread, flaming hot Cheetos, Reisen's chocolates, and two containers of Sunny D. She wrote him a note—*You are loved*—and slipped it between the pages of *The Dangerous Book for Boys* by Conn and Hal Iggulden. It was Jake's favorite book.

A deep sigh helped calm her breath.

"Okay, all set? Feel ready for this?" Brooklyn tugged the straps on his backpack. "Look at you! You're already such a man!"

He wore shorts and cowboy boots. A pair of binoculars hung from his neck, and one of his thumbs looped around the strap of his backpack. His pockets bulged with bags of marbles, and a flashlight stuck out of the hammer loop in his cargo shorts.

"I put lots of batteries in, just in case." Jake shook his shoulders, and his backpack swung back and forth. The sound of dozens of double A's rolling around in the bottom of his pack made Jake smile. He also held a small notebook in his hand that had "FIELD NOTES" written on the cover. He'd tucked a red pencil inside the wire.

He was the quintessential boy.

"You look like you're ready to conquer the world!" Brooklyn kissed his cheek and let her lips linger too long. Jake shrugged away.

"Have a good time!" Brooklyn knew she was taking a risk in making running away seem glamorous. She hoped she would have this kind of strength when it was really time for him to go. She hoped the rehearsal would make it easier for the live performance of him leaving home for good. Was it selfish of her for wanting to redeem the damage running away had done in *her* life?

Jake stopped at the door. He twirled his foot around; it was a nervous habit Brooklyn had recently noticed. His hand rested on the doorknob.

"Hey, Mama?"

'Don't blow it! Don't blow it! Don't blow it!

Brooklyn felt all the brokenness of her life in that moment. All the running. All the hiding. All the trying to protect herself from getting hurt. But that was her story, not Jake's. Though she wanted to keep him safe, Brooklyn couldn't let her fear take away his thirst for adventure or his need for space.

She turned to him and smiled as honestly as she could.

"You look good and strong, Jake. You were made for this." The future of the world stood with his hand on the doorknob, spinning his foot on the wood floor.

"Yeah, but I was wondering…since you're so good at running away…if maybe, you'd come with me?"

I'll go anywhere with you, my darling. I'll go to my death if that is required. I'll hold your pain when you lose someone you love, and the only rope I'll give you is the one I throw when you're drowning. I'll search for you when you've lost your way. I'll shine the light when you and your hope have floundered. That's the gift left of my running away days, son. I'll stand my ground for you. I'll not leave my post, no matter where you find yourself in this world.

"I'd love to, Jake, but I need to watch the other kids."

"Well…what if they came too?"

"You sure? I could keep them away from you so you can read. You can just be in your tent, and I'll be in the yard with them."

The house was oddly quiet. Silence can be loud, and it hurt Brooklyn's ears.

"It's just…that sounds kind of lonely."

"Do you want me to read aloud in the tent?" Brooklyn kept her voice steady.

"Can everyone bring their snacks?"

"What's read-aloud time without snacks?" A smile. A wink. A growing boy's grin.

"You go tell the kids, and I'll meet you in the tent."

Jake ran to the bedroom, then ran back and hugged Brooklyn hard. His boots made a confident, clomping sound to the door.

"Thank you, Mama! I'm glad you're so good at running away!" Jake burst outside without looking back.

The wonderful and terrible of growing up punched at Brooklyn's heart. Jake's exit was punctuated by an exclamation point in the slamming of the screen door.

Chapter 4
Too Much Mama

Clear the runway, y'all!" Hannie Romano shouted as she ran through the door about to pee her pants. "Clear the runway!"

Her twelve-year-old twins, Eryk and Zac, rushed out of her way. Her daughters, Madison, at ten, and McKenna, at eight, flattened themselves against the wall.

Hannie was unbuttoning her jeans. "Clear the runway!" Closing the bathroom door on the kids, Hannie thought, *Oh yeah, I'm definitely going to be paying for counseling.* She sat down on the toilet, and her dark, red hair fell around her face. She pulled on the edges of her razor cut bob, a habit she'd had for years. An avid runner, Hannie had been awake since five, so she could get some additional miles in. Right now she thought how wonderful it was to have a few minutes alone.

Hannie was watching her sister Heather's infant son for the day. Heather had flown in from Louisiana for a business meeting Hannie had helped network. The sisters rarely saw each other anymore, and Hannie was overjoyed to get some time with her new nephew, Thomas.

This morning, she'd taken baby Thomas and her four kids to the grocery store. Rather than take them all into the bathroom with her, Hannie had "held it" until they got home. Hence, the "clear the runway" emergency, and hence the exhaustion suddenly overwhelming her. The back of the van was still full of groceries, but just as Hannie returned from the bathroom to unlatch the baby's car seat from the car, Thomas started crying.

According to Heather, her baby son was going through a growth spurt, and Hannie had to agree. She could hardly keep up with how much Thomas was eating. She was thankful Heather had pumped plenty of breast milk for him.

"It's okay, Thomas. I'm here. Let's get y'all some milk, hungry boy." Hannie smiled at her sister's handsome son. She loved having a baby in the house! With the infant seat banging against her hip, Hannie broke up a fight between Eryk and Zac as she brought Thomas into the house.

"That's enough, you two! I want you both on the couch reading while I feed the baby. We still need to finish school, and I need to get dinner going. *Please.* Just get along!" Those two were always at each other lately.

Hannie watched the boys on the couch as she fed Thomas, who finished his bottle and drifted to sleep. She marveled at his perfect baby mouth, his long, heavy eyelashes, and hair that swirled like a toupee on top of his head. She watched him suck habitually even though he slept, and she observed the nursing blister on the center of his top lip. *You're keeping your mama busy, aren't you, little man?* Hannie traced Thomas's little face with her fingers. She couldn't get over the miracle of life and how much she loved Heather's boy! She wished they lived closer. She lamented for the hundredth time. *Lord, please send me some friends!*

Hannie's head bobbed with fatigue, and she curled around the baby for a few minutes, cuddling his warm body and admiring his tiny fingers. Five minutes later, Hannie woke with a start. The boys were nowhere to be seen, and she carried Thomas upstairs to his portable crib.

When Hannie got back downstairs, her oldest daughter, Madison, was cleaning up red juice that had spilled all over the kitchen floor. She was trying to mop it up but was smearing it across the tile instead. The white grout turned bright pink, and Hannie stifled a groan. "Okay. Let me help you with that." She grabbed a roll of paper towels and handed it to Madi.

"Sorry, Mama. The pitcher slipped out of my hands." Madison was a helper to the core.

"It's okay, Madi. It happens. Where are the boys? They better not be on Rattlesnake Hill!" Hannie panicked. The hill had earned its name after they'd discovered it was densely populated with rattlesnakes. Zac reported this after a barefoot adventure that still made Hannie's blood run cold. But boys—being boys—her sons couldn't resist the hill. Eryk and Zac were compelled to hunt and kill the poisonous snakes. Mark coached them to be safe, but after discovering a jar of rattlesnake rattles in the boys' room, Hannie didn't want them out of her sight!

"No. They slipped outside to ride their scooters as soon as you fell asleep with Thomas." Madison continued to smear the red juice into the tile grout.

"Those two don't let the grass grow under their feet, do they?" Hannie knew she had only slept for five minutes. After filling a bucket with hot soapy water, she got on her hands and knees to scrub the tile and grout.

Madison came around the table to help and slipped on the suds. Her feet went out from under her, and her head snapped back and struck the tile. Hard.

The sound made Hannie sick, and she scrambled to Madison's side.

"Madison! Are you okay, honey? Lord, have mercy, baby, are you okay?"

"I'm fine." Madison blinked like she didn't know where she was. "I'm fine. Scared, I guess."

"Well, no wonder! Me too!" Still on her hands and knees, Hannie pulled Madison into her arms and held her in the sitting position to make sure she was stable. The pink-stained water seeped into Hannie's light-colored jeans. "Are you sure? Are you sure you're okay? Your head took quite a wallop."

"I'm okay. I don't hurt anywhere." Madison stood.

Hannie also stood and held her daughter around the waist. She was worried Madison might go down again. "Let's get you out of this mess." They walked carefully across the wet tile, both trying not to slip.

"Uh, oh, Mama. Uh oh..." All the blood drained out of Madison's face, and her skin grew white.

"What? What's wro—"

Madison bent over and threw up.

Hannie continued holding her waist, so she wouldn't fall.

"I'm sorry, Mama! I didn't know I was going to puke! I just have a really bad headache!"

"Oh, honey, it's okay. I'm sure you've got a concussion. There's just no way you don't. You hit your head so hard!" Hannie walked Madison to the couch and sat her down. "Stay here a minute and let me get a washcloth, a towel, and a bowl."

Madison was trembling and in shock. "If I can rest for a second, I'll help you clean up the mess. *Why did I spill that juice?*"

"You're not doing anything." Hannie gave Madison a washcloth so she could wipe her face. She put a towel on the couch pillow and helped Madison lay down. Thankfully, there was no puke on her clothes.

"Here's a bowl if you need to throw up again. Just rest for now. I'm right here if you need me." Hannie threw a blanket over Madison, then turned to face the puke mess on the floor. It had splattered up the kitchen walls and cabinets, and the juice wasn't cleaned up yet either.

After much scrubbing, Hannie finally finished cleaning and tossed a mound of washrags into the washer. HEAVY WASH.

Still being careful on the wet tile, Hannie pulled open the refrigerator to see what she could make for dinner. Mark was flying home from Nevada and would be there around six. She was relieved to have Madi settled on the couch. Sighing into the fridge, Hannie heard a sudden scream from the back yard. Everything inside her turned to ice. Like most mothers, she could discern when cries meant *nothing* and when cries meant *something*. That was a scream that meant something. Slamming the refrigerator door, Hannie ran to the back yard, where Zac was lying in a heap on the ground. Eryk was scampering off the trampoline.

"Zac! Zac! What happened?! Zac!" *He broke his neck.* Hannie was sure. *He broke his neck!*

"Eryk! What happened? Oh, Jesus, help me!"

"Mama, we were playing tag. He just ran off the tramp!" Eryk scrambled to the ground next to his brother.

Zac moaned and rolled to his side before sitting up. Holding his elbow out, Hannie burst into tears of relief that he was okay.

"Thank God!" She could see a bulge on the top of Zac's forearm. It was just below his elbow and looked bad. Hannie hugged him until he cried out in pain.

"Mama! You're hurting me!"

"Sorry! I thought you were dead; I can't help it!" She hugged him again, softer this time. Helping him stand, she couldn't stop kissing the top of his head.

Zac started to cry. Then he threw up.

"It's a day for throwing up, isn't it?" Hannie held him close to her side. "Madison threw up just now too!"

"Really? Why did she throw up? What color was it?" Eryk asked the same question every time someone in the family vomited.

"She fell and hit her head."

"How did she do that?" Zac was concerned.

"Zac, honey, can we just focus on you right now? How do you feel? Is it just your arm? Is there anything else that hurts?"

"Nothing else hurts. I think my arm is broken, though."

"You think?" Hannie eyed the bulge, already swollen to twice its size since she'd come upon the scene. "I've got to take you to the ER right now."

"Oh, good!" Zac loved adventure or "venture" as he still called it, even at the age of twelve.

Hannie's youngest daughter, McKenna, was eight. She walked across the yard, and her face paled at the sight of Zac's arm. Born missing her right leg below the knee, McKenna had been fitted with a prosthetic. The missing limb didn't slow Hannie's daughter down, but any medical crisis scared McKenna. Having had many surgeries, it was one thing she just couldn't stand.

"McKenna, I need to take Zac to the hospital. I'll get him strapped in the van, but would you go get baby Thomas for me? Would you put him in his infant seat and bring him to the van?"

Zac was more uncomfortable now and started crying in earnest. "Mom! My arm hurts!"

"Eryk," Hannie turned to Zac's twin. "You guys can watch a movie while I'm gone. Keep an eye on Madison, too, because I'm sure she has a concussion."

"How did she get a concussion?"

"She can tell you all about it."

McKenna scooped Thomas out of his little bed, cuddling him under her chin. She loved babies. After buckling Thomas into his infant seat, she carried him to the van.

Hannie looked at her daughter. "I'll see you back here as soon as I can. I've got my phone; you can call me if you need anything."

Zac was wailing. He sounded like he was dying.

"I've got to go." Hannie gave McKenna a side hug. "Thanks, Kenna."

McKenna's face was still pale. She hated emergencies.

"Everything's fine, honey, don't worry. I'm sure Zac's arm is broken, but he's alright." Hannie took a deep breath and tried to reassure her daughter. "You guys can take the rest of the day off school, but I've got to go!" Leaving the household in Eryk's hands, Hannie strapped the baby's car seat in, and they were off.

After being in the ER with Zac for over four hours, they finally made it home. Hannie thanked God, again, that she'd made the decision to stop drinking after the kids were born. Something strong would've hit the spot about now. She checked on Madison, who seemed to be doing fine.

"The ER was awesome!" Zac wore a bright blue cast. There would be no swimming for him this summer. "The nurses brought me a pop and a sucker! They were so nice! I loved it!" he bragged to Eryk. Zac appreciated gifts.

Hannie checked on Madison. "How do you feel, honey?"

"I'm fine, Mama. Just a headache still." Madi looked pale, and Hannie shuddered as she recalled the sound of her head hitting the tile.

"You really need to be still the next several days, okay? You went down hard." She ran her hands over the smooth, young skin of Madison's cheek, then bent to kiss her.

By now, Hannie was tired, but McKenna, Madison, and Eryk needed interaction and some food. Putting Thomas's infant seat in the middle of the living room, she asked, "Can you guys watch him while I fix lunch? It's two o'clock already! You must be starved!"

McKenna pulled Thomas out of his car seat and cooed at him, getting him to smile. Hannie stopped for a minute and watched her face. She looked so soft and tender with babies. She would be a great mother someday.

Chopping some veggies and throwing them into a pan of olive oil, she added leftover hamburger, tomato sauce, and water. Vegetable soup. "Come on, guys! Time for lunch!"

Zac's friend Broyles had a response to food he didn't like, which had become renowned in the Wyer home. Having come for a sleepover,

Hannie had asked him, "Broyles, I'm making burgers tonight; do you like burgers?"

"They're not my favorite, but I'll eat them anyway." Broyles's infamous response surprised everyone, and the whole family adopted it. Hannie knew she would hear it at lunch, but her kids said it about lots of things. *Putting toys away isn't my favorite, but I'll do it anyway. Pulling weeds isn't my favorite, but I'll do it anyway. Taking out the trash isn't my favorite, but I'll do it anyway.*

Hannie ladled out the soup. Setting bowls and glasses on the table, she shouted, "Wash hands!" As the kids sat down to eat, she smiled to hear the boys say in unison, "Vegie soup? It's not my favorite, but I'll eat it anyway."

After the kids ate, Hannie got out a puzzle for them so she could clean up the kitchen. "Not my favorite, but I'll do it anyway," she said aloud, smiling wryly as she rummaged in the fridge to see what to make for dinner. It was too late to take something out of the freezer, and she'd just used everything they had for lunch.

"Looks like pasta again." She closed the fridge and resigned herself. So much for planning a special dinner for Mark. Glancing at the clock and feeling the familiar, chronic pain in her back, Hannie decided she had time for a bath. Running hot water and pouring in bubbles, she checked in on the baby (sleeping again) and let the kids know where she would be.

Hannie sighed in relief as she submerged in hot water and bubbles that smelled like grapefruit. "Thank You, Jesus." She said aloud and was just closing her eyes as the heat soaked into aching muscles

"Mom, I need you!" Eryk cried, pounding on the door.

Hannie pulled the plug in the drain and grabbed her robe. Tightening the sash, she opened the door. Heavy tears drained from Eryk's eyes, mixing with blood dripping down his face from a blood-soaked towel.

"Mama." His expression was blank with shock. His olive skin was pale, and his eyes were wide with fear.

41

"Eryk! What happened?"

His voice was calm and quiet. "I was running in the kitchen. I had my socks on and slipped. I smacked my head right on the corner of the counter." What Eryk lacked in the volume of his voice, he made up for in copious amounts of heavy tears.

"Okay, son. Head wounds bleed a lot, so don't be afraid. Can you get yourself back downstairs to the couch? I need to get dressed, but I'll be right there. Keep pressure on it. Try not to get blood everywhere, if you can!"

"Sorry, Mama. I know your back hurts. You don't need to get out of the tub. I can just put some ice on it."

"Well, you might need stitches, so give me just a sec, and I'll be down, okay?" Hannie looked at him, her eyes searching his wound and his heart at the same time. "Can you make it downstairs without help?"

"Yes." Tears splashed on his T-shirt, making snowflake patterns.

The tub drained. Hannie was pulling her "pink" jeans back on when the sound of puking came from the bottom of the stairs. She shook her head and laughed out loud. *You're kidding me, right?*

Thomas woke up crying and hungry again.

Packing Heather's baby downstairs and avoiding the puke on the landing, Hannie handed Thomas to McKenna. "Can you fix Thomas a bottle? Heather's milk is in the fridge."

McKenna smiled at Thomas and bounced him in her arms while Hannie examined Eryk's head wound. "Son, that looks bad." Like McKenna, Hannie hated emergencies, and she could never get over how much a head wound could bleed. "It doesn't look too deep though. Can we try just keeping ice and pressure on it for a while and see what it does?"

Tears still drained from Eryk's eyes. "I'm sorry I threw up, Mom. I didn't even feel it coming. I just felt like my head was going to explode, but it doesn't hurt now. I don't even know why I'm crying." Eryk sounded like a recording of Madison from this morning.

"It's the blood. All that blood is really upsetting." Hannie walked to the freezer and pulled out an ice pack. Wrapping it in a clean towel, she handed it to Eryk. "Lay down and keep this pressed on your forehead. Don't let up on the pressure as long as you can stand it."

Madison was lying on her back on the floor.

"And you, Miss? How is your head feeling?"

"I have a headache, but I don't feel sick anymore."

The kids were all looking at her; they looked scared.

"Okay, everyone. I don't know what's going on today, but nobody's leaving this room until Daddy gets home. Zac, hand me our read-aloud book."

McKenna fed Thomas his bottle. Madison, Eryk, and Zac lay in lumps on the couch and floor. Hannie surveyed them for the first time that day. McKenna was quiet, and Hannie realized she hadn't spoken to her except to ask for help. She looked into her daughter's warm, brown eyes now and smiled. "This has been some day, yes?"

McKenna smiled back. "You think?" She fed Thomas with an experienced hand and looked well beyond her eight years.

What would I do if she weren't so affable? "Looks like you're the last woman standing, Kenna. Maybe we should pray." Hannie smiled at her.

"Good idea." McKenna sighed with relief.

"Jesus, please protect us. Take care of us. Please keep everyone safe for the rest of the day and bring Daddy home soon. Amen."

After cleaning up more puke, Hannie read to the kids for hours. One by one, they dropped off to sleep. She put Thomas to bed and came back downstairs to lay blankets over each of the kids. Putting her hands on her hips, Hannie sighed and whispered aloud, "Please, Lord, send me some friends who can help me." Sitting down in the overstuffed chair, she curled her feet up and lay her head down on its warm, wide arm. She had a pounding headache herself, and she just wanted to rest for a minute.

The next thing Hannie knew, Mark was standing there, gently stroking her leg. She saw his love for her on his face and in the warm light of his eyes. Their fight to save their marriage because of Mark's battle with pornography had brought them closer in many ways. Wiping the drool from her face, Hannie sat up, confused. It was seven o'clock, and everyone was asleep.

Mark put his index finger to his lips and took Hannie by the hand. He pulled her up, slipped his arm around her waist, and guided her around four sleeping bodies and outside to the driveway. Mark led her, without a word, to the back of the van.

"Mark…" she groaned. "Oh, Mark, why do you love me?"

"My Hannie." Mark took her in his arms and rocked her close to him. He stroked his wife's hair and kissed her head.

"Mark…" She leaned into her husband. "I'm sorry. You wouldn't believe the day."

"Shhh…it's okay, Han." The faint scent of puke clung to her.

"I can't believe it. I completely forgot."

Dripping out of the trunk was a mixed stream of thick, red and white goo. It was melted ice cream and blood from the meat Hannie had purchased…

Her grocery run that morning.

Chapter 5
Puke in the LEGOs

Hannie sat on the couch folding baskets of laundry while her twin boys played with LEGOs on the floor. Their heads bent together as they worked with mathematical precision on an agreed-upon project. It was nice to see them playing together. Nearly in their teens now, Eryk and Zac were developing their own unique personalities. Her identical twins had always been different, but now their differences were becoming more pronounced. This often led to shoving and shouting matches. The boys loved each other, Hannie knew, but she grew weary of their wrestling, punching, and trying to win their point. To see them playing with such unity for a change was a blessing.

"We should build a secret wall inside the outside wall." Eryk curved his hand around the outer fortress of the castle they were building.

It was a monstrous renaissance construction that had space fighters and war tanks sitting near the castle's portcullis. Hannie had to laugh. Typical homeschool kids—treating the past, present, and future like moving pieces on a chessboard. And why not? What could be better for their minds and imaginations? What twelve-and-half-year-old boys still played with LEGOs, anyway?

"Cool." Eryk was the quieter of the two. His words were becoming fewer and farther apart as he aged. Still waters run deep.

A slight mustache formed on his upper lip, and the muscles in his arms were developing. She could see them bulging slightly beneath his t-shirt as he supported his weight on the floor. It seemed like just yesterday he was a chubby toddler climbing out of his crib to play when he was supposed to be napping. She still saw hints of the baby boy in the curve of the young man's cheek.

Always close to her boys, Hannie had been surprised when Zac called her into the bathroom last week.

"Mom! Look!!!" He'd pulled his underwear down just below his belly button. "I'm getting hair just like Dad!"

"Oh." Hannie had nothing more to say. She'd blushed and rushed out of the bathroom.

Mark had already had "the talk" with the boys, and Hannie knew these changes were coming. But still...she'd been in denial, a denial that crumpled upon seeing the dark pubic hair peeking above Zac's underwear.

"Oh," had been the only word she could squeak out. It did nothing to dampen Eryk's pride, though. "Wait 'til Dad sees! Hey, Zac! Come and look at this!"

Zac had come and demonstrated that he, too, was showing signs of manhood.

It was a weird thing, this moving into manhood. Yet here they were playing with LEGOs and making plans like they did when they were six or seven. She studied their faces, watching them intently. Hannie wanted to freeze time.

At forty-two, Hannie Cohen was on the skinny side of lean. She had no curves to speak of, was flat-chested, boyishly built, and carried almost no body fat on her thin frame. A long-distance runner since high school, Hannie was a born athlete. She wore her naturally dark, red hair in a sharp bob, which she pulled on for comfort and when nervous. Atypical of redheads, Hannie's skin was dark olive, and her eyes were a deep, forest green. She'd heard her beauty described as both unusual and stunning.

But she couldn't have cared less.

Hannie never wore makeup, and she didn't care about shopping or clothes. She was a relaxed tomboy, proud of her home state of Louisiana. She spoke in a deep drawl that became more pronounced when she was excited by any emotion. Moving to Montana had been difficult for Hannie, but that's where her husband found his dream job.

Mark operated a small lumber company outside of Billings. He harvested dead trees off forest service land and milled them for many of the local builders. Mark had a good reputation. He was hard working, and everyone liked him. He was attentive to Hannie, loved his kids, and was intentional about being a husband and father. But after their move almost three years ago now, Hannie was still finding it hard to make friends—real friends. She didn't trust easily. She was still reeling from the recent discovery of Mark's issue with pornography, and trust was harder than ever.

"Lord, please send me a few friends I can trust." Isolated and lonely, Hannie prayed for girlfriends who had integrity and hungered for Christ. Growing up in the church, she knew just how dangerous Christian women could be. She'd watched them gossip her mother almost to death when Hannie had been in her teens. *Job's friends,* Hannie thought for the millionth time. She prayed again, "Lord, please send me some friends who won't gossip about my family or me."

Hannie folded a basket of t-shirts as the boys continued to snap bricks in place. She'd put the pieces together about Mark's addiction without him telling her. It had been the open page on his laptop. There, her heart fell out of her flat chest and onto the breasts of the woman in the image. Hannie couldn't stop staring at her. When she gasped for air, she realized she'd been holding her breath. Not her Mark!

Eryk and Zac locked block after block together. Hannie smiled. How many allowances had they spent to make that big pile of bricks? Their castle expanded and grew.

That's what was happening in her life. She knew Mark's addiction wasn't her fault, but it put her weakness in the crosshairs. The truth of the part she had played still stung. Her kingdom and her castle were growing too large, and she valued them above all things. She was putting Mark and the kids before Christ. She was building her life—her castle—with Mark as the foundation. She depended on his strength and capability to do so many things that she relied on him for everything.

And that—Hannie realized now—was a problem. She'd made Mark her god. She worshiped him and the life he was making for her and the kids. Their home was so full of warmth and laughter, family devotions, and especially Mark's love. She'd had to face the truth that she'd loved Mark more than Jesus. She put so much pressure on him to perform, and her expectations only grew when Mark met and exceeded them. Now her castle was crumbling. It was coming down like sand. Despair rose in her chest. She'd built a sandcastle. *Oh, God, I'm such an idiot.*

Hannie had been processing for months, and still, she felt unsettled. She kept folding clothes, and her mind fell back in time to that painful night that had changed everything.

She had lain in bed with her back turned to Mark. She knew he was awake. Was he thinking about that beautiful woman on his computer screen? Hannie couldn't stop the tears from flowing into her flannel pillowcase. She was trying to work up the courage to confront Mark about the laptop when she heard him sniffling from his side of the bed. His back, too, was turned.

"Hannie?" Mark sounded far away. "Han, I've got something I need to tell you." His voice was shaking, and Hannie could feel him trembling from her side of the bed.

She braced herself for the words. She clenched her eyes and her jaw.

"Hannie." Mark rolled to her side of the bed and pulled her into his arms. "Hannie, I've been looking at porn on my laptop and phone." Barely able to get the words out because he was sobbing now, Mark held her so hard, Hannie felt her ribs might break.

At first, she just lay there and let him crush her in his embrace. She felt like a dead body. Hard. Stiff. Cold. To hear him say the words meant it was true; her suspicions and the beautiful woman on the computer screen became a reality. Pornography was in her life.

Mark's sobbing sounded strange to her. He'd never cried in front of her before. He'd never shown any sign of weakness. Hannie had thought him the most perfect man in the world, and now she didn't know what to think. Anger pulled her lips into a steel line across her mouth, and her voice cut like a knife in the dark. "How did it start?" She could feel her face contort in rage.

"It started when I was in the military, but after we got engaged, I was nervous about the wedding night. As a virgin, I was afraid I wouldn't know what to do. I wanted to be a good lover, and I was looking at porn to get ideas. After we got married, I thought there was no way it would be a problem anymore. I mean, look at you, Hannie. You're the most beautiful woman I've ever known."

Hannie pushed Mark's arms off her. She shoved him away from her body. "You liar." She spoke with calm. Dead calm.

"I've tried to control it on it on my own, believe me. I've tried hard, Hannie, but it's not working. I'm hooked, and it's making me sick. I'm making myself sick. I've been noticing the bulletin at church. They're starting up a men's group for guys who are addicted to porn. I signed up for that, and it starts next week. Maybe meeting with others who are struggling like me will help me kick this demon out of my life." Mark sobbed, and Hannie could hear him wiping his nose and face with his t-shirt. "You have biblical grounds to leave, Hannie, but I hope you won't. I don't deserve you, and I don't know how you could stay with me after this." Mark grew quiet. "Please say something, Hannie. I'm so sorry. Can you ever forgive me?"

Hannie rolled to the edge of the bed and sat up. It felt like she was moving in slow motion. It felt like she was drowning. It felt like the world was falling. It felt like she was going to throw up. It felt like she would die of pain.

"I saw the laptop. I've known for a while now, and I was just working up the courage to talk to you about it." Bitterness dripped from her voice like poison, like death, like hatred personified. "How thoughtful of you to come to me first."

"Hannie, I'm sorry. I should have told you sooner, but I thought I could handle it on my own. And then…then I was just too ashamed."

"Poor Marky." Hannie shuddered at the wickedness in her voice. *Stop it, Han.* "You know how insecure I am about my body, Mark. How am I ever supposed to trust you? That woman had big breasts and a perfect body. How am I supposed to compete with that? How can I have any confidence when we come together? Huh?"

Hannie could see by Mark's expression that he was sickened by the thought of what she'd seen–the images he'd tried so hard to hide.

"Answer me, Mark!"

"It's not about you, Hannie. I want you to know that; It's not about you at all. You're so beautiful." Mark was breathing hard. "Every morning when I wake up, I watch you sleep, and I wonder how you ever came to love such a pig of a man."

Hannie had no words, but her mind was reeling. *How can our intimate life escape the impact of this betrayal? How can I ever be with him again?*

"Please, don't leave me, Hannie. You're the best thing in my life." Mark reached for Hannie's hand.

She pulled away and grabbed her pillow. "I'm sleeping on the couch. I can't stand to be in the same bed as you right now. I'm such an idiot. I'm such a ridiculous, flat-chested idiot." Her lifelong struggle with body image exploded like a bomb. Her heart shattered with the shrapnel of betrayal.

"No, Hannie. I'm the idiot."

"Stop talking, Mark. Leave me alone." Hannie stood and walked to the door. She reached for the handle, then turned back to their torn marriage bed where her husband of fifteen years lay crying. "You know that this is going to mark the rest of our marriage, don't you? You know it's going to mark the rest of our lives, right? Your name suits you, *Mark*." She couldn't keep the meanness from her voice.

Hannie absently watched the boys with their LEGOs. She folded another basket of clothes as the rest of that terrible night unfolded in her memory. She'd gone to the couch. She'd lain awake in the dark, her eyes wide with pain. *What am I going to do?*

Hannie had many women confide in her about their husband's addiction to pornography. Her pride had blinded her, and she cringed now at the response she had held out to those women. She felt herself sinking lower. She felt herself becoming hollow. She felt herself grow colder and colder as she remembered their words:

"I have to drink this cup of suffering, even though it's not my choosing."

Hannie recalled their words as she lay staring into the night. She was one of them now, and she knew she'd been given a cup of suffering that she didn't choose. It wasn't even hers to drink, was it?

I took the cup for you.

His words. The voice of the Holy Spirit spoke to her mind and shattered her pride. They made Hannie cry. They silenced her because it was so, so true. She saw an image of Jesus hanging on the cross in her mind, and like Eryk and Zac's LEGO bricks, something clicked into place. She realized the gift God was giving her. If she would take the cup and drink it, he would give her a front-row seat to the cost of His cross. Hannie thought of Him there.

No games, Lord. You weren't playing games, were You? How it must have pained You to breathe while the nails, engraved with the litany of my sin, held You to the cross!

Hannie's mind returned to the present. The laundry must have folded itself. She couldn't remember having done it. She thought about how lonely this process was and how much she longed for safe friends to help her through it. "Lord, please send me some safe friends who can help me. Send me a few good women who love you with their whole hearts." She was whispering this prayer once more as she continued to watch her boys.

Eryk, very quiet these days, suddenly jerked his head up and looked at Hannie with panic in his eyes.

"What's the matter?" Hannie asked.

Covering his mouth with his hands and trying to unfurl his long legs, Eryk projectile vomited all over their creation.

The smell reaching his nostrils like one of his brother's punches, Zac followed his twin and puked as well.

Both boys scrambled up, one running to the toilet and the other running to the kitchen sink. Too late, it seemed, as the carpet and the plastic bricks were left steaming with puke.

Eryk and Zac looked at Hannie with surprise and confusion. They were both too old for this!

"Mom, I'm sorry!" Eryk was pained. "I don't know where that came from!"

Zac, too, apologized. "Mom, as soon as I smelled the puke, I just started barfing. I couldn't stop. I'm so sorry!"

Nobody liked cleaning up puke. Who would?

"It's okay, boys! Go upstairs and clean up. See how you feel after a shower, but best take a bowl with you in case it happens again."

The boys walked quietly to the stairs; there was no jostling now.

"Sorry, bro." Eryk apologized.

"Dude, it's okay. I just hate the smell of puke!"

Hannie pushed the laundry baskets away and got up for her cleaning supplies. Shoving all the blocks into her lingerie bags, she stacked them onto both racks of the dishwasher. Setting it to heavy wash, Hannie scrubbed her hands, then turned to face the living room carpet.

A writer and a photographer, the metaphor did not escape her.

She'd been building her castle.

The puke of porn had destroyed it.

The bricks of trust and forgiveness had to be washed.

Mark and Hannie had to fight for their marriage.

They had to cleanse the soiled fibers that held them together.

As Hannie scrubbed the carpet, she felt overwhelmed by the process of healing. Would it ever really come? Trying not to gag at the smell of puke—of sin—she'd never felt more isolated or alone.

Hannie prayed once more. She prayed aloud and with all her heart.

"Lord, please send me some friends I can trust."

Chapter 6
Autoimmune Disease

Wren could barely lift her head off the pillow. It felt as if someone had pulled the plug on her life force, and all her strength swirled down a dark drain. She wasn't caring well for herself or her family, and she knew something was wrong in her body.

"Wren, you need to get to the doctor." Steve pushed her hair away from her face as she lay in bed at four in the afternoon. Wren could see fear in his face. She could only imagine what he saw when he looked at her. She'd lost her vibrancy; she had no energy, and she was losing her long, beautiful hair. Wren could almost hear the prayer Steve had prayed so often as he sat on the side of the bed holding her hand. *Lord, please send my wife some friends.*

"I don't have the strength, Steve. I'm struggling to care for the kids as it is. I'm so tired all the time, but I can't sleep. I have no appetite, yet look at me! I've gained thirty pounds!" Wren sighed, feeling hopeless. "My hair's falling out, I'm constipated, and I feel completely useless!"

Steve held Wren's hand. "Wren, I'll take you myself. Matthew is going off the rails. He needs you!"

Steve and Wren had three boys. James was six months old; Josiah was seven; and their oldest son, Matthew, was sixteen. Adopted after Wren's best friend was killed on the Indian Reservation, Matthew went to Wren as her friend's will instructed. Though there was only a ten-year difference between Wren and Matthew, Wren gladly took the then seven-year-old. She'd been packing him on her hip since he was born, and the two of them were close.

Wren and Steve had adopted Mattie as soon as they could. Matthew was now almost seventeen. He was warm and kind—wise beyond his years, and he cared for James and Josiah with such tenderness it made Wren cry sometimes.

But Matthew struggled with everything from cutting to crippling anxiety and migraines. He respected Steve—loved Steve—but Wren knew it was the bond they shared Mattie couldn't live without. He depended on Wren. She was his only tie to his mom and to his Native culture. Wren and Mattie were bonded in a way white people would never understand, and Wren understood Mattie's panic over her illness.

"Please, Lord, send my dear wife some friends," Steve prayed aloud, and Wren knew it was as much for him and the boys as her. She watched him struggle to keep the household going when she was so physically unable. "I'll take you to the doctor tomorrow. I can wait in the waiting room with the boys while you see her. You need help, Wren. Something's not right."

The next day, Wren watched her physician scribble notes on the chart. Wren couldn't even scribble a few lines of poetry these days, and she missed writing as much or more than anything else she had given up.

Dr. Moore read her notes aloud to Wren: *"Patient makes herself walk every day, but her hands go numb, and she feels "devastated" with fatigue after the exercise. Thirty pounds overweight. Patient's voice is hoarse. Her brain feels like it's submerged in water. Patient describes everything around her as distant and fuzzy. Chronic constipation. Hair loss."* Dr. Moore glanced up at Wren, "Anything else?" She smiled.

"I feel physically depressed, and that makes me emotionally depressed. I know something's wrong." Wren's voice had gone up a full octave as she spoke. "I've never felt like this."

"Let's get you up on the table, so I can take a look." Dr. Moore had a warm bedside manner, and she was a good listener.

Wren sat on the familiar white paper. It was impossible not to remember her first miscarriage and how the blood had soaked the table at her OB appointment. The white paper would always remind her of that day.

Dr. Moore rubbed her hands, cupped them together, and blew warm air into them. Throwing her long, ebony braid over her shoulder, she stood near the table where Wren sat.

"Let's see what we've got." The doctor's hands went to Wren's throat.

Lurching away from her, Wren yelled, "What?" She grabbed Dr. Moore's hands, pushed them down, and trapped them on the table. "Don't touch my throat!" Holding them with all her strength, she screamed. Tears she couldn't contain coursed down her cheeks. *Don't silence my voice!*

Dr. Moore stopped, and a shadow crossed her skin, darkening its hue.

Wren's face colored with embarrassment. She remembered her mother. She remembered her stepfather.

She released the doctor's hands and wiped away her tears. Helpless, she let the long, agonizing moments of silence hang in the air like floating puzzle pieces. Dr. Moore sat quietly, putting them together.

"I'm so sorry." Her brown eyes were lit by lights of warmth and concern. Seeing.

Knowing.

Dr. Moore touched Wren's hand, and the exquisite agony of love permeated the lines around her eyes. "I should have given you warning. I need to check your thyroid gland. I can see that it's engorged. I'll need to palpitate to see how much."

Wren's mouth went dry, and she swallowed hard, then licked her lips. Dr. Moore squeezed Wren's hand. The compassion in her touch made Wren's face flush as she tried not to cry.

"Do you want to talk about it?" Dr. Moore asked.

"No. It's okay. I'm fine. Go ahead." Wren avoided her doctor's eyes and gripped the edge of the table. She didn't want Dr. Moore to see the memory—how her stepfather had killed her voice. How her own choices had killed her voice. Wren went away in her mind as the doctor pressed on her throat. And pressed and pressed. Wren's face flushed, and a single tear ran down her cheek.

Dr. Moore smiled a sad smile. "Hang in there. Almost done."

Wren stifled a cough and swallowed. She *hated* having her throat touched.

"I'm going to run some tests, but I think you've got hypothyroid disease." Dr. Moore sat and rolled her stool away, hands folded in her lap. "It's an autoimmune condition that attacks your thyroid gland. This explains why you're not able to do things that would normally be easy for you." Another warm smile. "The good news is that medicine can manage it for you. The bad news is, you're going to be taking that medicine for the rest of your life."

"What's an autoimmune disease?" Wren rubbed her hands over her throat, trying to comfort it and comfort herself. The word seemed familiar, but Wren was in a fog.

"To put it simply, it's when your body attacks and damages its own tissues."

"Oh." Wren's underwater brain could hardly grasp the concept. Her doctor seemed to understand.

"We'll talk more about it after we get you some blood work and some relief. You're going to be feeling much better the next time we see each other, I promise. Meanwhile, take a lot of short walks. Drink plenty of water. Eat your veggies. You know, the usual stuff." Dr. Moore scratched out a few more lines on her chart, then looked up.

"Wren…" Dr. Moore took a deep breath. "I want you to consider getting help for what just happened here. I know you're strong, but to have that kind of visceral reaction tells me there's some work to be done."

Wren sighed. "I know. I feel like I've gotten worse after every baby. I always feel like I'm being choked, but I thought I was okay. I guess I'm not. Did I hurt your hands?" Wren wished she could disappear.

Dr. Moore laughed. "I've had much worse things done to me in this office. But please consider it, Wren. I care about you, and once you're feeling better, I want to hear that you're pursuing help, okay?"

"I will. I guess I didn't realize how affected I was."

"You're going to be feeling like a new person, physically, in a few months, and then you'll have the capacity to face it. You're worth it, Wren. Whatever happened has taken enough from you. Don't let it take any more."

"I won't." The words came too easily, and they both knew it. Wren blushed and smiled a shy smile. "I give you my word; how's that?"

"I like the sound of it!" Dr. Moore grabbed Wren into a hug.

***

"Thank you, Lord!" Three months after seeing Dr. Moore, Wren praised God as she cuddled James in her arms.

"Wren, you look amazing!" Steve slipped his arms around Wren's waist. "I can't believe the change!"

"Thanks, Steve. Thanks for making sure I got help. It's hard for me to ask for it." Wren had noticed the marked brightness in her eyes when she'd looked in the mirror this morning, and her cheeks had color in them again.

"I'm glad to have you back." Steve sat close to her, almost scooping her onto his lap. "We missed you. I missed you." He reached for Wren's hand and held it tight.

Feeling her life force flowing through her again, Wren sat with her journal and thought about that day in Dr. Moore's office. She thought about autoimmune disease and living on this side of heaven. She thought about her voice.

Wren remembered too well the night her stepfather had picked her up by the throat, but she knew he wasn't the only thing that silenced her. It was sin. It was the sin committed against her and the sin she committed against others. It was sin in the world, and it was even sin in the Body of Christ. It was sin in the church when it pretended to see no evil.

Sin was the ultimate autoimmune disease.

Wren knew she had to take the medicine of the gospel if she wanted to be free. She had to forgive her stepfather. She had to forgive the hopelessness of life on the Reservation. She had to forgive herself for leaving, for abandoning her tribe. Jesus had forgiven her. He had set her free and given her a new life with Steve and the boys. She had to forgive white people. She had to forgive the Christians who tried to take the Indian out of her people.

Wren was writing poetry again, and she wrote in jagged prose in her journal.

Autoimmune Disease

Autoimmune disease in the family
You know.
When the Body of Christ.
Turns and attacks itself.
Destroying healthy cells and causing—

Damage.

And the worst is when.

The world looks to the Church and says,

"No, thanks."

To all us hypocrites who preach love but can't seem to live it.

Ahhh yes.

Autoimmune Disease.

Destroys our witness.

Right?

All us sinners sitting next to each other in pews that…

Pee ooo! Stink, stink, stink.

How does Jesus not turn away?

From a barnyard full of animals.

And how is it?

That he came into the world amongst them?

Donkeys. Cows. Sheep.

Stubborn. Hapless. Helpless.

Metaphors can be powerful.

But no matter the stench or dysfunction or disease.

Jesus still moves among us.

Calling us out of sin.

Out of stink.

Out of hating our brothers and sisters in Christ, and…

Into forgiveness.

For. Giveness.

Autoimmune Disease within the Body of Christ is destructive.

We can't even live with our own family without His help.

And sometimes…

Oh, God, I wish it weren't so.

But sometimes…

Things don't get worked out.

The medicine doesn't work.

And just as in regular families like mine.

You have to move on and hold hope that it someday will.

Because the beautiful thing about belonging to the family of God is that

If you are Born Again.

If you are *truly* born again.

It *will* get worked out.

It might be on the other side.

When you are home with Him.

In Heaven.

Where thyroid disease will be no more.

And He will abolish all sickness forever.

Where brothers and sisters in Christ fall before the throne of their King

To proclaim the most extraordinary run-on sentence of all time.

"Worthy is the Lamb who was slain, to receive power and wealth and wisdom and might and honor and glory and blessing!" (Revelation 5:12)

And we'll all finally live together in holiness.

In Righteousness and Purity.

And I.

I won't hesitate at all.

To hold the one who broke my voice and say,

"You are forgiven."

And…

"You are loved."

Chapter 7
The Untold

Wren smiled her warm, disarming smile whenever she introduced herself to someone new. "My name is Wren Alice Romano. My initials spell W.A.R., so consider yourself warned." Wren loved her name because of what it meant to her. It seemed to her as if she'd been born into battle, but she was a fighter, and God had kept her safe. He'd kept them both safe.

Wren sat in a gaming chair next to her adopted son, Matthew. She needed to talk to him, but all she could think about was that terrible night ten years ago. Whenever she remembered it, she felt as if it were still happening. The memory of what they'd been through often swept her away from the present.

Tugging on Matthew's seven-year-old hand, with nothing but a black garbage bag stuffed full of their possessions, Wren had pulled them both through the night.

"Come on, Mattie, we have to keep going."

"No, Auntie! No! We have to go back for Mama!"

"Mama's dead, Mattie. Charlie Big Horse killed her, and now he and my stepdad are looking for us. We've got to keep moving!"

Mattie's mother had been Wren's best friend.

Wren's mother had married a white man. She met and married him while completing her master's in poetry at the University of Montana. After he died in a car accident, Wren's mother, Nuna, had buried her husband and taken their seven-year-old daughter home. Home to the Crow Reservation. Home to the closeness of family and where everyone was "auntie," and everyone was "uncle." But also home to dysfunction and abuse. And loneliness and hopelessness and booze.

Wren kept a firm grip on Matthew's hand. "I'm not letting you go back, Mattie. I'm never letting you go back. Your mama knew this night would come. She wanted you with me, and she even made a will." Wren had stuffed the rough paper into her bra. If anything happened to her tonight, she knew it would be found right away. She could only hope it would be found in the right hands.

Jane Little Deer, her best friend, was gone.

Nuna, her mother, was gone too.

Wren shook her head and came into the present with Matthew and some of his friends. Just ten years apart in age, he was seventeen now and wore his hair in a long, native braid.

"Listen, I want to talk to you guys about drugs, alcohol, and suicide." Like her mother, Wren was a poet too, and a voracious reader. She'd researched the suicide statistics in Montana, and it scared her.

Oozing early manhood and strength, the boys listened. They were used to Wren going right to the heart of matters. She'd earned the right, though. Matthew told them what she'd done for him after his mom died.

"I want to know how you're doing." Wren looked like a teenager herself.

Matthew dove in. "I mean…it's hard, Auntie. I'm not going to lie. I think about suicide every day."

Wren watched Mattie look at his friends, and she knew he was gauging their reaction to her line of conversation. It wasn't the norm, but

Matthew had told her how much he appreciated her bringing it up on occasion.

"Just. Every day, you're never enough, you know?"

Jason spoke up. "I just want to get high all the time, so I don't have to feel." He looked her in the eye, and Wren felt the honor of that. "But just so you know, Mrs. Romano, I never get high in your house. I know the rules."

Wren felt small in the moment with her legs curled up in the gaming chair–like a bird in a nest. "What can I do?"

"There's nothing you can do, Mrs. Romano. It's just hard being a kid." Jason pushed his hair out of his face.

"Well, I want you to know how much it would crush me to lose any one of you. Your lives have value. They have eternal value, okay? It's frustrating for me to see you in the glory of your strength, made in the image of God, and struggling to know your position in Him."

"Auntie, please…you know the guys aren't religious." Matthew wasn't embarrassed. He was just stating the facts.

"I'm not religious either!" Wren thought about how much she loved being free in Christ. "I hate religion, but that doesn't mean you guys can't see the glory of God all around you, does it? I hear you talk about being in the mountains after a backpacking trip. I hear you talk about how beautiful women are and how cute children are. You're not so dull as to think God hasn't created them, are you?"

"I believe in God, Mrs. Romano. I'm just not a Jesus freak like you." Tim rolled his eyes, but Matthew gave him a look. Tim apologized. "I'm sorry. I just don't get it."

"Ultimately, I just want you guys to know I care and that I understand you're under a lot of pressure, okay?"

"How can you know, Auntie? You've got Steve and the boys now. And your dad was so white people can't even tell you've got Native blood!"

"Seriously, Matthew? Don't start with me! I lost my dad when I was exactly the same age you were when you lost your mom. And stop acting like I have a new family with Steve. You're my family, Matt."

"Yeah, but we don't look alike at all. You don't even look Indian."

"You little racist you!" Wren laughed at Matthew. "Do your white friends here struggle any less with suicidal thoughts?" Wren's voice was calm and loving, but she wasn't going to let her son take the point. She and Matthew had been down this road so many times; she wanted to shake him for dragging race into it. "I lost my dad, Matt." Wren remembered him—his white starched shirts and the smell of his aftershave. "You lost your mom. We've suffered a lot in this life, but we're not victims. At least, we don't have to be."

Matthew and his friends looked at each other, but nobody said anything.

Wren scraped herself out of the gaming chair and slapped each long-legged teen on the thigh.

"You matter to me. I would be devastated if I lost you. Know that and call me if you need me." She stood now with her tiny hand on her hip. "I'm going to need a promise here."

The boys didn't know what to do.

"Promise me you won't take your life, Jason." Wren pierced him with her gaze. "I won't stand for it."

"Okay, Mrs. Romano. I promise."

"You promise, what?"

"I promise I won't take my own life." Jason held up his hands in surrender.

"Tim? Promise me."

"I promise not to take my life." Tim couldn't look away from her and added, "I won't smoke as much pot, either."

"Look, Matthew." Wren turned to face her son. "I know the struggle is real, but I can't have you giving in to it. You're worth it, Mattie, and I would be lost without you, you know that! You've got to fight! Please…fight!" Wren clenched her jaw so she wouldn't cry.

"Okay, Auntie, relax. I won't take my life, alright?"

Wren rushed him in a hug, then hugged the other boys. "There's always a bend in the road. There's always hope, and there's so much hope in Christ. Mattie knows He saved us! He was there that night!"

Tim and Jason nodded their heads. Matt had told them the story many times.

"Who's hungry?" Wren's hands were suddenly sweaty, and she rubbed them on her jeans.

"Is that a rhetorical question?" Matthew smiled at her, and Wren's heart melted. He looked just like her. He looked just like Jane Little Deer

***

That night, after tucking her seven-year-old, Josiah, into bed, Wren lay on her side nursing baby James. She was sharing with Steve the conversation she'd had earlier with Matthew and his friends. As her husband crawled into bed next to her, he fluffed his pillow and something flipped out of the covers in front of Wren. It was a postcard with a Hershey's kiss taped to the top.

"What's that?" Steve put his arms around his wife and baby. "From The Boy?" Steve loved calling Matthew that. He loved watching the dimple form in the side of his shy smile whenever he said it.

"Mmmmhmmm…" Tears slid down Wren's only distinguishing Native feature, her high cheekbones. "It's a kiss and a promise."

Dear Auntie,

I'm glad you're named Wren Alice Romano. Thanks for going to war for me and the boys.

I promise you,
Matthew

Chapter 8
Beauty Is Beast

Kate crashed through the door and threw her purse and car keys on the kitchen table. "AAGGGH!"

"Whoa!" Her husband, Brian, came rushing toward her. "What's wrong, beautiful?"

"Can you just—not?" Kate was fuming.

"What? What'd I say?" Brian screwed up his face with that expression he only made when he was afraid of her.

"Can you not tell me I'm beautiful for once?" Kate knew it wasn't Brian's fault, but she couldn't stop. "Couldn't you just once tell me I'm smart? That I have some value to you that comes from within? Can you stop telling me I'm pretty all the time? I mean, could you just stop doing that? It doesn't always feel good, alright?"

"Wow! Okay, do you want to tell me what happened today?" Brian was leaning against the wall. His relaxed state infuriated Kate.

"It's nothing, alright. It's just these women at the homeschool co-op I vetted today. It's the most degrading thing! They take one look at me and start backing out of the room. God forbid if I stand up to my full height! I can clear a room full of insecure women in five seconds flat!" Kate snapped her fingers, then grabbed a scrub brush from under the counter and started scouring the sink.

Brian called this, "mad cleaning."

"You know, it wouldn't hurt them to move toward me for once. Instead, I have to work really hard just to get them to realize I'm not a conceited...a conceited...well, you know—a conceited bitch!"

Brian's eyebrows went up. Kate never swore.

"But noooo...I have to put on my warmest smile and my softest voice, and I have to win them, Brian. Every time! And you should see the way they look at me!"

She pulled an elastic hair tie off her wrist and wrapped her long, blond hair into a ponytail, exposing her long, elegant neck. Brian sucked in a breath of air. She sent him a withering look.

"Christian women are really the worst sometimes, you know? I can see them looking at my legs and face, then my skin and hair. I can feel their eyes all over me! And then that hardened look comes over them, and it just puts a pit in my stomach!"

Brian leaned against the wall and watched as she rinsed the scrub brush. After washing her hands, she pulled pots and pans out of the cabinet.

"Would it kill one of them to ask even a single question about me? I can't stand it! Didn't their mums show them "how to do?" It's not fair, Bri. It's so rude, and it hurts my feelings."

Brian stayed quiet. *Smart man,* Kate thought. *Very smart man.*

"I've been so lonely since we moved to Montana. Everyone seems nice on the surface, but nobody invites you IN. Poor Ethan and Margaret. I can't even get a playdate with other mums to help them form friendships!"

"We just need to keep praying for friends, Kate. This move has been hard on you. It's been a complete culture shock, but the Lord can provide friends for you to do life with."

Dumping pots and pans into a sink of scalding water, Kate ignored Brian and continued to rant.

"Do you know women actually grab their husband's arms when I'm around? It's disgusting! What do they think? I'm going to sweep in and steal their man?" Kate slammed a teapot full of water onto the stove and turned it on high. She glanced up at Brian and saw his face turn white. They both knew the significance of the teakettle. How could she, Kate Norris, a supermodel from England and a transplant from New York City, be living like this—in Montana of all places?

"My flesh wants to dress to the nines and rub it in their face. If that's what they're afraid of, why don't I give it to them in spades, huh? You know I kill in lipstick." Kate pulled two cups out of the cabinet and slammed them on the countertop.

"Oh, I know." Brian nodded. "How could I ever forget the first day I met you? There I was, innocently installing trim work in your agent's office. I was just minding my own business when you come sauntering in, all 6'3" of you wearing that bright red lipstick and your big smile. It felt like I'd been struck by lightning! Your accent is what put me over though. Do you remember what you said?"

"I like your tool belt." She smiled at him and giggled. "I don't know what made me say that."

"Yea? Well, I liked it, and I liked your lipstick pretty well too."

Kate remembered how they'd grinned at each other until she couldn't stand it anymore. She'd fled the office as fast as she could, wondering what kind of woman had just spoken with her mouth? Who would dare to look at a handsome carpenter like that and say, "I like your toolbelt?" Kate felt the embarrassment on her cheeks.

But Brian had gotten her number from her agent and called her that night. She remembered it well. He'd said, "Oh...hi there. It's uh–it's Toolbelt, from the office today."

She'd replied, "Yes, hello. I'm Lipstick; it's nice to hear from you." She'd laughed her girly laugh. The one she knew still made Brian melt inside, even after fifteen years of marriage.

"Listen, Kate, can you stop banging around in here for a second?" Brian crossed to Kate's side of the island. "I know how much this hurts your feelings, and you're right, it's not fair. But—it's going to be okay. As a proper Englishwoman, I know you find it undignified to cry, but I just want you to know I'm here for you. You can spare the pots and pans and cry on my shoulder, alright, my girl?" Brian stood close, without touching her.

"You know what though, Brian?" She finally stopped for a second to look at him. "The thing that saves me from being a complete, a complete…well, you know…is that I know Jesus was misunderstood too. People didn't take the time to get to know him either. They didn't ask him questions about his heart, his mission, his gifts, or anything like that. They asked for signs and wonders. They asked to have their needs met. When I think of Jesus, I think he must have been lonely a lot too."

"But there was nothing beautiful in his physical appearance, Kate."

"I know. But he was misunderstood, Bri, and that's how I feel." Kate slumped against the counter. "Why don't women want to get to know me?" She blinked back unspent tears.

"I'm sorry, hon." Brain walked to her back and pulled her close. "This has been a hard move on you, I know, and I know I'm not much comfort. Those gals are missing out, but ultimately, you have to know that your value comes from God. What other people think of you has no bearing on what's true."

"Right." She swayed in Brian's powerful arms. "Right. I know. Sorry, I took that whole thing out on you. I don't really mind when you tell me I'm beautiful. Just—tell me I'm smart occasionally, okay?"

"You're the smartest woman I know, and that's not me blowing smoke. You have more gifts in your little finger than most everyone I know. Your looks are the least of them. But—I don't mind that you're pretty. Even if you're just a little prettier than me." Brian smiled against the back of her neck. She was taller than him.

"Now you've just gone off the deep end. You're in a league by yourself, Brian." Kate turned her head so he could kiss her cheek.

"You just want me for my body." Brian pulled her closer. The teapot boiled on the stove.

Kate leaned into him, and they swayed in the kitchen until she turned off the whistling kettle.

"Yeah…I just want you for your body."

Left to an empty kitchen, two cups stood alone on the counter.

Chapter 9
The Humanity

Womanhood was beauty and pain. It was honor and humiliation. It was isolation and deep comradery. Without other women to help point the way, Kate felt lost and blind. Sometimes she needed more than glasses to see.

Her long legs protruding far beyond the edge of her chair, Kate sat in the ophthalmologist's office with eight-year-old Margaret and ten-year-old Ethan. She needed new glasses. Waiting for her name to be called while skimming a women's fashion magazine, she sipped coffee from a Styrofoam cup. Ethan drummed lightly on his legs in perfect beat to the office elevator music. Maggie sat absently twirling her ponytail, absorbed in a Nancy Drew mystery.

The glorious ordinary of it all, Kate thought when—without warning—a sudden, warm gush flooded between her legs. She closed her eyes and uttered a slight groan. A prayer.

She placed the magazine on the table next to her and stood. Sure enough, blood pooled on the upholstery of the waiting room chair. The woman next to Kate glanced at it, and her face showed horror and understanding at once. "What can I do?" She opened her purse and started digging like a badger.

Kate opened her own bag and pulled out a package of hand wipes, hoping to spare the woman the effort.

"Here!" The woman handed Kate a tissue that looked to have absorbed many, many tears. It was falling apart with grief, and their eyes locked. The tissue shook in the woman's trembling hand.

"It's all I have."

The exquisite agony of love etched in the woman's eyes pooled like the blood on Kate's chair. The two women instinctively reached for each other's hands.

"I'll see what I can do with these." Kate raised the package of wipes, then started dabbing at the stain, trying to absorb the spot.

"I must be going through early menopause." Kate dabbed and talked. "My cycle is so messed up! I just finished three days ago, at least I thought I was finished." She kept dabbing. The hand wipes were filling with blood. "I'm not prepared. I switched purses, and I don't have anything with me." The wipes got most of the stain, but it was clear the chair needed more attention than what Kate could give.

"Why is it so hard to be a woman sometimes?" The woman in the waiting room was small and timid, even the curls on her graying head trembled as she asked again, "What can I do?"

"Nothing, it would seem. It looks like I just need to face the music." Their eyes held, and the woman nodded her head with her lips firmly pressed together. "I'm sure it will be fine."

Kate cringed, sighed, and walked to the counter.

"May I help you?" The receptionist pushed her cute glasses up on her nose.

"Miss, I'm sorry, but I've just started my period and completely soiled your chair." Kate looked over her shoulder at the chair. "I need to go straight home. I'll have to cancel my appointment and reschedule." Cramps gripped Kate's belly now, and she leaned her 6'-3" frame on the counter for support. "I hate to leave you with that…that mess." She felt dirty, like the blood-stained chair.

The receptionist leaned over the counter to look. The sight of the stain sprung her into action, and she stood. She was lean and athletic, like a dancer.

"Oh, honey, don't you worry about a thing." She came around the counter and started dragging the chair to a supply closet. "I'll take care of that right away; you just do what you need to do." She was light on her feet, and her pencil skirt and heels made Kate imagine her twirling the chair like a tango partner.

"Please, apologize to the doctor for me." Kate turned from the ballerina receptionist to her kids.

Ethan's eyes were wide with shock, and he rose to hug her. "Mom, what's wrong? You've got blood all over your pants!"

"Oh no! Really?" Kate tried to look around at her backside. "No, honey, I'm okay." She squeezed Ethan's hand. "I'm not hurt at all, I promise."

"That's impossible! I think we should call Dad!" Ethan was freaked out, and now Margaret was scared too.

"I'm not injured, guys, but I do need to get out of here right now. Mags, would you mind walking right behind me? Try to give me a little cover? I'll explain it in the car."

"Is that your period, Mom?" Ethan's expression was a comedy of horrors. "I know about those, but if this is what that is, I'm so glad I'm not a girl!"

"I hope I never get my period!" Margaret chimed in, looking worried.

Kate recalled giving them a short health lesson about menstruation. It seemed like a long time ago though, and it surprised her they remembered. Maybe they'd just been doing their own research.

As they turned to leave, the trembling woman shouted, "Wait!"

Handing Kate her windbreaker, she said, "You can tie this around your waist." The woman didn't wait for an answer. She threaded the sleeves of her jacket through Kate's arms.

"Oh, no, really that bad?" Kate tried to look around the back again, but she couldn't see anything. "Oh, brother! Can you write down your phone number? I'm so sorry about this, but I'll get it back to you as soon as I can."

"No. Just take it. Please." She cinched the sleeves around Kate's waist, then touched her lightly on the shoulder.

Her touch said, *I'm with you. I understand.*

"Thanks." Kate tried to laugh. "I'll never forget you." She smiled apologetically.

"I don't suppose you will!" The woman's smile pulled the wrinkles around her eyes into lines of solidarity. Kate saw the anguish of love in her big, gray eyes as she shoved feminine supplies into the outside pocket of Kate's purse.

"You said you weren't prepared."

It was too much kindness, and Kate burst into tears. Her eyes darted from the receptionist to the woman in the waiting room. "Thank you, I—"

"Not another word now." The woman touched Kate's arm again, and she wasn't trembling anymore. "Who hasn't been in your shoes? This gives me the chance to repay a kindness shown to me many years ago. I've no doubt you'll repay it in your life someday too." She looked Ethan square in the eye. "You take care of your mama, okay? Be kind. Be respectful."

"Yes, ma'am." Ethan wrapped his arms around Kate's waist again and smiled at the waiting room woman. "I will."

"That goes for you too." The woman smiled at Margaret, and Maggie smiled back.

Squaring her shoulders and taking a deep breath, Kate walked toward the exit as the receptionist called after her.

"No big deal, darlin'! Just one day in a thousand." She raised her long, thin arm and waved like a homecoming queen.

The curly-haired woman held the door. "With you all the way, Mama. You can do this." Her smile felt like a blessing. "Bye, now."

Kate didn't even know her name.

With the woman's windbreaker tied around her waist to hide her blood-stained pants, Kate left the ophthalmologist's office thinking, *Sometimes, you must go to the eye doctor just so you can see.*

The two women's voices rang in Kate's head, and she heard the still small voice of God in her mind.

"You are loved. You are loved. You are loved. You are loved."

Chapter 10
Wheels Off The Bus

I f you're going to homeschool, you've got to be home." Brooklyn never forgot the advice given at a homeschool conference. It didn't mean she didn't struggle with it.

It seemed like Brooklyn was always in the car. She drove the kids to music and sports, to play dates and youth group. But she appreciated the advice. It gave her permission to be at home in a culture that tended to drive the family out of the house. That simple statement brought some sanity. It brought truth from the far-off country Brooklyn liked to call "The Good Old Days."

Brooklyn needed to be in their new, bigger home to teach reading, history, and math, but being home also kept her more present with her kids. As a Christian, her greatest desire was to foster a love for Jesus and God's Word in the hearts of her kids. The whole concept of homeschooling, to Brooklyn, meant spiritual training and peace in the home.

"Shut up, you poop head!" Abe shouted at Derek and slammed the door to their shared bedroom.

Derek opened the door. "Why don't *you* shut up?"

And here we go, thought Brooklyn, helping her now three-year-old Maylee get her shirt turned right-side out. It sounded like a shoe had been thrown against the wall. Those boys were going to break the door off its hinges! She shouted from the living room downstairs, "What's going on up there, boys?"

Will, as a luthier, was traveling to a university in Tennessee where he was teaching the making of cellos. Brooklyn missed him. The boys missed him. It seemed like these flare-ups between Derek and Abe were happening more often than usual. Jake was a teenager now and kept to himself in his room. His two younger brothers drove him crazy.

"First of all, we don't say 'shut up' in this family! You guys know that!" Brooklyn went to the foot of the stairs and yelled up at the boys. "My hands are on my hips!" The words were a warning. The kids all knew what that meant.

"Hands on hips!" She shouted up again and took a sip of her coffee like she was dragging on a cigarette. She could see a black scuff mark on the wall from where she stood. Derek's hiking boot lay on its side on the carpet. It painted a metaphor, and as a writer, Brooklyn didn't miss it. Her nervous system felt scuffed up, and her humanity was flipped on its side today.

Her "uniform" of jeans and a baggy, black CASH t-shirt taunted her on days like this. Sighing over her coffee, Brooklyn remembered the pencil skirts and business suits she'd once worn to her office. She'd had an *office*. She'd worn *heels!* Being an editor to one of the largest publishing companies in the world had been the job of Brooklyn's dreams.

Until God called her and William to Montana. And then—of all things—to homeschooling!

Brooklyn smirked and puffed a small breath from her mouth. *It's kind of a joke, Lord. Do you see what's happening right now in this godly home? Are you observing your godly daughter? Are you aware of what's happening in the dark heart of this godly mother right now? Help me, Lord!*

She felt defeated. "Boys! Get down here! You're late for school!"

I think I might be late for my life, Brooklyn thought bitterly. Where was Will right now? Were the young women at the university fawning over him? Were they sticking notes in his shop box, telling him how handsome he was? How talented?

Get a grip, Brooklyn! She looked at her jeans and saw a stain from last night's spaghetti sauce. Closing her eyes, she breathed another prayer. *Jesus, help me today. Help me now.*

"...fear not, for I am with you; be not dismayed, for I am your God; I will strengthen you, I will help you, I will uphold you with my righteous right hand." Isaiah 41:10

God's Word sprung to Brooklyn's mind. She knew it was not a coincidence.

Derek and Abe, now nine and seven, pounded down the stairs, jostling each other.

"Don't touch me, you jerk!" Derek's voice was hard.

"Stop breathing." Abe's voice was mean.

Brooklyn didn't have the capacity for this right now. She knew it was wrong; what Derek and Abe needed most was consistency in discipline. But she ignored them both.

"Get your schoolwork."

Brooklyn had been up all night with Sophie. For a few days now, Sophie had been running a low-grade fever and feeling unwell. She'd been uncharacteristically quiet, which concerned Brooklyn more than her fever.

"Baby, are you sure you're okay? You just don't seem yourself at all."

"I'm okay, Mama. I just feel tired." Sophie never complained.

In the middle of the night last night, Brooklyn had come out of a dead sleep to the world's universal call for help.

"Mama!"

Running to Sophie's room, Brooklyn found her pre-teen with her feet on her pillow, and the rest of her body crumpled between the wall and the bed. After projectile vomiting, Sophie must have passed out because there was puke all over the wall, bed, carpet, and herself. Sophie was out cold on the floor.

"Sophie! What on earth???"

Brooklyn quickly assessed the situation, stopping only for a moment to marvel that Maylee was still sound asleep in the bed she shared with her sister.

"Sophie, my love, Oh, God, okay." Brooklyn moved to her daughter's side and pulled her body straight, so she was lying flat on the floor. Checking for a pulse, Brooklyn could see Sophie was breathing, but she was burning up with fever. "Sophie, can you hear me, darling?"

Sophie opened her glazed eyes. "I'm sorry, Mama. I didn't make it to the toilet."

"What's the matter, baby? Are you hurt anywhere?"

"No, I just feel sick. I think it was the tuna sandwich I had for lunch yesterday."

"Yeah, but you've been feeling pretty puny for longer than that. Do you have pain anywhere?"

"No, Mama. I've just been tired. I didn't feel sick until tonight."

"Okay, well, can we get you in the shower?" Brooklyn was already supporting Sophie, so she could sit up.

"Yes, please help me get out of these gross pajamas, and Mama, I'm so sorry about all the puke!"

"Don't worry about that, sweetie. I'll take care of it, but let's get you cleaned up and into my bed."

"You always take such good care of me when I'm sick."

Brooklyn pushed the damp hair out of Sophie's face. "That's what mamas do." She couldn't help admiring Sophie's natural beauty, even in her miserable state. Both her girls had little freckles that ran across the bridges of their noses like sprinkles of brown sugar.

"Mom, I hate to ask you this, but do you think you could get in the shower with me? I don't think I can stand on my own."

Concern gripped Brooklyn. Despite spending her early years in a tiny house where modesty was a luxury, Sophie had grown to be a private young woman. They all teased her now because she wanted her "pibacy." Even though the Wyers had moved to a bigger house where there was little chance that would be invaded, Sophie was careful.

"Of course I can shower with you, love." Brooklyn kept her voice light, but red flags were waving in her mind. It was a good thing she got in the shower with Sophie because she fainted twice more. Brooklyn was near tears with worry after she got Sophie, Sophie's bedroom, carpet, and herself cleaned up. She collapsed next to her daughter in her and Will's big bed. But Brooklyn couldn't sleep. She lay awake, watching Sophie and talking quietly to Will on the phone.

"I think you should take her in." Will sounded concerned. "Something's going on."

Brooklyn felt Will's question even though he didn't ask it.

Isn't there someone you would trust to come and sit with the other kids while you take Sophie to the ER?

Brooklyn never felt her lack of friends more.

"I'd like to wait until tomorrow, Will. I'm just watching her tonight. I have the same feeling, but if we can make it through the night, at least she'll get some rest."

"You need to sleep, too, Brook. I know it's hard when your girl is so sick."

"Yeah, I'm okay. I'm glad to be with her, but...Will? I just want to tell you that I'm sorry I get jealous of your job sometimes. It's not right. You're working so hard for all of us, and I know how much you hate traveling."

"I do hate traveling. But I hate cleaning up puke more, so I don't blame you. You've got the harder job, but thanks for being sensitive,

Brooklyn. We both need to cultivate grateful hearts. We've been given so much."

"My sweet William. I love you. Ooop–gotta go. Our girl is stirring. Bye, hon!"

Sophie rolled toward Brooklyn. Her face still looked waxy.

"Hey, my girl. How do you feel?" Brooklyn didn't think she looked right.

"Don't worry, Mama. I'm okay. I feel better after throwing up."

Brooklyn wasn't so sure. Maybe it *was* the sandwich, but still…something didn't feel right. "Go back to sleep. We'll see how things look in the morning, okay, Soph?"

Sophie was asleep before Brooklyn finished her sentence.

The next morning, Brooklyn woke with a kink in her neck from sleeping sitting up in her bed all night. Checking her daughter's temperature and tucking the blankets around her pale face, Brooklyn decided to shower later. She wished she could go back to sleep next to Sophie, but it was a school day, and she needed to get to it.

"Derek, bring me your map work from yesterday. We're already behind." Brooklyn didn't look either boy in the eye. She was in survival mode.

"I don't know where it is. I can't find it!"

Brooklyn gave Derek a dirty look. Terrible at lying, he blushed and looked away from her.

"The dog again?" It wasn't kind, but Brooklyn didn't care. "The dog ate your homework?"

"Yeah, Mom, the dog ate my homework." It was hard for Derek to be mean, but he was getting better at it. He gave it right back to Brooklyn, double the sarcasm.

"Kitchen duty. Now. For telling your brother to shut up as much as for showing up without your assignment." Brooklyn turned him by the shoulders and gave him a gentle push. Was it too early for a glass of wine? Oh right…Brooklyn had stopped drinking when the kids were born for this reason right here.

"But Mooom!"

"No, sir. No whining. Find the assignment after you unload the dishwasher. Maybe some manual labor will jog your memory, unless you'd like a spanking to warm the wax in your ears."

Why did I say that? Geez, Brooklyn, what is your problem? Derek is too old for a spanking.

Stomping off, Derek proceeded to unload plates and cups out of the dishwasher. Tears flowed openly down his face. He banged glass and porcelain with such force Brooklyn waited for something to break.

Abe sat like a stone in the overstuffed chair in the living room.

"I can hear you cleaning the kitchen, son! Thank you!" Nothing like a little passive aggression first thing in the morning.

"Why are you so mean? You never even asked me why I said shut up!"

It made no sense, but all the blood went to the back of Brooklyn's brain, and she went into raging mom mode. Brooklyn just wanted Derek to obey. She just wanted to get through their school day! The pressure of providing a good education for her children overwhelmed her at times.

"You know what? Why don't you just shut up and clean the kitchen!" Her face felt as lit up as a flashing stoplight. But Brooklyn didn't stop. "You know you lied to me about your assignment, so you're on kitchen duty all day."

"But Mooo—"

"I don't want to hear about it, Derek. Just do your job."

"But, Mom, you said we shouldn't say shut up, and you just said it!"

"Shut up, son!" Brooklyn didn't know why this conversation was happening. Like so many of them, she reacted instead of engaging in intelligent, connecting conversation. She wasn't even being logical! She knew she was out of control but knowing that didn't help. The ironic thing was, as the other kids watched her, Brooklyn kept trying to act as if she *did* have everything under control. Again, knowing the obvious did nothing to help stop her. She was on a track, and she was on it full steam.

Derek loaded the dishwasher and washed the counters, tears flowing down his face.

Brooklyn could feel the tug of the Holy Spirit, but she ignored Him. Her heart felt just like the words the boys had used against each other this morning: hard and mean.

Pulling out their Bible lesson for the day, Brooklyn turned to the Gospel of John. She read in a loud voice as Derek swept the floor with a vengeance. What that boy needed was some good Bible to straighten him out. *Again Jesus spoke to them, saying, "I am the light of the world. Whoever follows me will not walk in darkness, but will have the light of life." John 8:12.*

Derek wasn't crying anymore. He was angry.

Brooklyn read again. *Again Jesus spoke to them, saying, "I am the light of the world. Whoever follows me will not walk in darkness, but will have the light of life." John 8:12.*

The Bible is a powerful book, and like a pin to a balloon, it pricked the pride of Brooklyn's heart. The arrow of truth Brooklyn wanted divinely flung into the heart of her son, smacked with full force into hers instead. She could almost hear the thud as the point hit its mark and left her heart to bleed.

"*OOFT!*" The words came aloud as Brooklyn curled around what felt like a physical wound.

"*OOFT,*" she said again.

"What's wrong, Mama?" Maylee came over and put her hands on Brooklyn's face.

"I'm okay, Maylee." Brooklyn brought her toddler's hands to her lips and kissed them.

"I am the light of the world. Whoever follows me will not walk in darkness, but will have the light of life." John 8:12.

Brooklyn's heart sank like a cold stone.

What a jerk she was! She was abusing her authority in order to control Derek, and she was destroying her relationship with him. Brooklyn remembered her junior-high teacher. *How "four-fingered" of me!* Conviction settled on her like a blanket of thorns. How was she following Jesus in this grotesque kind of parenting? Didn't she feel all the light go out of her because she stubbornly refused to walk in the light of life? Hadn't she brought darkness to her own home today?

"I am the light of the world. Whoever follows me will not walk in darkness, but will have the light of life." John 8:12.

I'm sorry, Lord. Thanks for your Word. Repentance washed over Brooklyn.

Sophie was still upstairs sleeping in her bed, but Brooklyn looked at Jake, Abe, and Maylee, who huddled together on the loveseat. The kids looked away from her, ashamed.

Jesus, forgive me. Please help me make this right.

"Guys, I'm sorry." Tears sprang to Brooklyn's eyes. "Will you forgive me?" She had ruined their morning. She alone, not Derek or Abe. Not fatigue. She, Brooklyn Wyer, had ruined it.

The kids nodded, but remained silent and still.

"Hey, Derek, come here, son." Brooklyn's voice was heavy with contempt for her sin.

"I'm sweeping the floor." His face was flushed. He wouldn't look at her.

"Derek…" Brooklyn put the Bible on the couch and went to the kitchen. She pried the broom from Derek's hand. He still wouldn't look at her.

"Come here, son." Brooklyn's voice was soft with contrition.

Derek allowed Brooklyn to steer him by the shoulders to the living room. The other kids watched as she sat Derek down on the couch. She knelt in front of him so they were face to face. Brooklyn took both his hands in hers.

"I'm sorry I told you to shut up, Derek." Brooklyn's voice trembled with regret, and she didn't try to hide her tears from him. "It was wrong of me, son. I did wrong. I hurt you. I overlooked you. I didn't even show you the courtesy of human kindness. Will you forgive me for ignoring your feelings and telling you to shut up?" Sorrow at hurting her son flowed down Brooklyn's cheeks.

Genuine repentance was a gift from God. It couldn't be manufactured, and Brooklyn trembled with it.

"I forgive you, Mama." Derek fell into her arms, and grace nearly broke her heart.

The sweetness of reconciliation was beyond Brooklyn's grasp. Her children taught her more about the Gospel than anything else in life.

Brooklyn hugged Derek hard, then pulled away to look into his face. His beautiful brown eyes still shimmered with tears.

"Are we okay? Can you tell me why you told your brother to shut up and why you lied about your homework assignment?"

Derek glanced over his shoulder at Abe.

"He was copying everything I said! He wouldn't stop!" Derek leaned into Brooklyn's chest. "I was so frustrated with him. I can never get him to do what I ask. I tried to be nice at first, but then I just got mad at him!"

"And then you got in trouble, right?"

"And you didn't even ask me!" Derek's eyes brimmed with tears again.

"Derek, I'm sorry. That was wrong. Will you forgive me?"

"I forgive you, Mama. I'm sorry I lied to you about my assignment. Will you forgive me?"

"I will." Brooklyn wanted to cancel school for the day and take Derek outside. It was snowing. Big, fat flakes drifted to the ground as if made of sugar paper. They melted as they brushed the earth's wide, warm tongue. *Beautiful.*

Derek was Brooklyn's outdoor boy, and nothing made him feel more alive than playing outside. But, *if you're going to homeschool, you need to be at home.* Those words rang in Brooklyn's head.

"Go get your assignment, and let's get on with our day." Brooklyn looked at him with a big smile. "Unless the dog ate it?" She winked at him and laughed, hugging him tight.

"I wish!" Derek laughed too. They didn't have a dog. "My assignment is in my folder. I just didn't want to do it."

Brooklyn hugged him hard, relating to him in so many ways. How many things in her life did she not want to do? How many things did she wish she could leave forgotten in a folder?

"The sooner we get our schooling finished, the sooner you can get outside. The snow's going to be perfect for forts today."

Derek ran to his folder and went to work on his assignment.

Though it was still early in the morning, Brooklyn felt done for the day. The quick spiral from anger to joy, from regret to happiness, left her feeling spent. She needed to get alone with the Lord.

She wished she had a friend to text, "The wheels came off the homeschool bus this morning. Requesting prayer cover."

Instead, she told the kids, "Everyone? Finish up your map work for geography. Meet me in half an hour for read-aloud time." Passing her youngest son, Brooklyn ran her fingers through his cowlick. "Abe, I'm going to talk to the Lord first, then you and I are going to discuss the way you're treating your brother."

Abe didn't argue. He gulped and nodded.

Sophie was still sleeping in Brooklyn's bed, and she looked peaceful for now. Brooklyn retreated to Jake's room and fell to her knees. She buried her forehead in the carpet. "Jesus!"

Her temper was a problem. Last week, she had grown so exasperated at the kids for not picking up their toys, she'd scooped them up and put them all in a garbage bag. Their precious things, the things children held dear, Brooklyn had threatened to throw away. Worse, she screamed at them in rage, frightening them so they went to their rooms and closed their doors to feel safe from her.

To feel safe from her.

"Lord, help me! Please!" Brooklyn cried her heart out to Jesus. "Revive my soul, Lord! Help me be a godly mother! I want to be a godly mother!"

Like the sugared snowflakes falling outside Jake's window, God's grace melted Brooklyn. It changed her heart, and she knew homeschooling was giving her a spiritual education. Repentance and reconciliation were her daily assignments, even when she wanted to hide them in a folder.

Brooklyn's children watched her fall and rise a thousand times. They felt her wounding words and showed her grace as often as she asked for forgiveness. Jake, Sophie, Derek, Abe, and Maylee schooled Brooklyn in the power of the cross every day, and they didn't even know they were doing it!

As she knelt with her face to the ground, an idea dropped into Brooklyn's mind. She would ask the kids to write a book together: *Homeschooling Your Mom*. She had to laugh at herself imagining the words they would pen.

Brooklyn got up from her knees feeling unworthy but trusting Christ to help her parent. Thankfully, the Lord kept helping her grow, and Brooklyn gave Him the desire of her heart once more. "Help me be a godly mother, Lord, and…you know how much friends have hurt me, so it scares me to ask, but Lord, please send me one friend I can trust."

The words left her mouth just as the sound of vomiting came from her room. Brooklyn braced herself for a visit to the ER with all of her kids in tow as Sophie's cry for help pierced her ears.

"Mama!"

Brooklyn had blown it this morning, but that didn't stop the confidence in the sound of Sophie's voice calling for her. She knew Brooklyn would come. She didn't doubt that Brooklyn would hold her, so she could hold on.

It was just as Brooklyn and her mother had been that terrible day in the laundry basket. "Mama..." Brooklyn had cried, and her mother had held her.

Brooklyn raced to Sophie's side while calling downstairs for Jake to get the kids loaded in the van. She knew she was going to the ER now, and she helped Sophie to her feet.

"Mama!" Sophie cried again, covered in vomit. "It feels like someone is stabbing me in the stomach with a knife."

Appendix! I thought so! Brooklyn supported Sophie down the stairs.

Carefully loading Sophie into the van, Brooklyn buckled her seatbelt.

"Mama!" Sophie screamed now.

It was the name all children called when they were in this kind of pain. It was the name Brooklyn had called that terrible day in the laundry room. It was the name exclaimed with joy when celebrating. It was that name—attached to the person—that children called when they achieved something or when they fell in love. It was the name they cried when they failed and when their hearts broke and when they were dying on a battlefield. It remained the universal cry, and it was the name the whole world cried when they needed someone to hold them.

"Mama!"

Chapter 11
Scrub-a-Dub-Dub
Grace in the Tub

Brooklyn had good reason not to trust.

Women.

Christian women.

And she especially didn't trust homeschooling Christian women! There was hardly a day that went by when she didn't remember what it had been like, and yet she prayed anyway.

"Lord, please send me one trusted friend."

After the fiasco of taking all the kids along with Sophie to the ER to have her appendix removed, Brooklyn was more desperate than ever for a friend. The kids had piled into the hospital room, bored and uncomfortable, and waited the entire day for the surgery to take place. Enduring the disdainful glances from the doctor and the nursing staff, Brooklyn was thankful the kids were well behaved. With everyone hungry, Brooklyn could do nothing but keep giving Jake dollar bills for the vending machine. Nobody ate anything that day except for candy.

She offered the prayer again, "Lord, please send me one friend I can trust."

"I'm never having friends again!" Brooklyn's heart had pounded in her chest as she opened the mailbox. Her skin was cold and clammy as dread spread like a disease, like a sheet covering the dead. *Her secret.* Brooklyn made sure to get to the mailbox every day before Will. He could never know.

Brooklyn had taken a credit card for her friend April to use. As a stay-at-home, homeschooling mother of five, Brooklyn made no income of her own. She knew William would never agree to it. Of course he wouldn't. It was insanity! Why would he agree to give money to a woman who treated his wife the way April did?

Though she claimed to be a fellow Christian sister, Will had heard April telling Brooklyn she was fat and ugly. April called Brook an idiot and told her she was making an idol of her kids. Will didn't like April. Brooklyn knew Will didn't like April. She knew he couldn't understand why she continued in the friendship. He told her all the time, "Brooklyn, this isn't friendship. It's abuse."

Brooklyn hung on to the friendship, believing April would change. She was unsure if April's medication was affecting her behavior, and she hated to abandon a friend in need.

Pulling the dreaded envelope out of the mailbox, Brooklyn stared at it. She'd thought she could cut the budget enough and manage it, and for a while, she had. She'd managed. She'd cut everything out she could, and when Will traveled, she and the kids ate rice and beans.

On the last bill, Brooklyn saw that April had put a thousand dollars on the card, and she almost lost her mind.

"What are you doing?" she'd asked April. "That card is only for food and medicine!"

Brooklyn prayed April hadn't spent any more. Maybe she could still manage it somehow.

Slipping her finger under the corner of the flap, she slid it across the glue strip. The bill glided out with as much ease as spending someone else's money. It trembled in Brooklyn's hands as she clutched the mailbox. Her knees buckled, and she fell to the ground.

Ten thousand dollars!

Brooklyn picked up a stone and threw it as hard as she could. "I will never, ever have friends again!" Everything was wobbling on the inside. "Friends are terrible! Friends...friends *suck*!" Brooklyn struggled to stand. Struggled to walk. Burdened by debt.

How had this happened?

Brooklyn hadn't become a Christian until she was thirty. She hadn't known the first thing about biblical marriage, and the roles God designed for a husband and wife. It was a steep learning curve—a good one—but good and steep. She didn't know that going her own way and stepping out from under her husband's leadership and care would lead to this mess. Brooklyn had been stubborn and careless. "I'm so stupid. How could I be so stupid?" she muttered aloud.

April called Brooklyn her best friend, but Brooklyn never felt free. Every time they talked, Brooklyn had to pay her emotional dues first. She had to endure April's verbal abuse and name calling. April fanned the flames of that familiar lie: "You are impossible to love."

Of course she was fat. Of course she was ugly. Of course she was an idiot. The credit card bill taunted her and confirmed April's words.

Brooklyn rose to her feet, holding onto the post where the innocent mailbox stood.

"Shame on you! Mailboxes are for love letters!" She punched the metal box with her fist.

"Ow! I'm such an idiot!"

Brooklyn tried to shake the pain from her hand. Her legs felt like they weighed ten thousand pounds each, and Brooklyn dragged them across the gravel driveway.

"I'm done." She said the words aloud. Her heart lifted for a moment. "I need to get out of this relationship."

Her body ached everywhere, and she felt feverish with fear. Brooklyn went upstairs and ran a hot bubble bath, even though it was the middle of the day. Submerging herself under water, she held her breath until her lungs burned.

I will never trust another woman as long as I live. Brooklyn formed a tight fist under the water.

Shame flowed like an open faucet down her face and across her mouth. April's verbal abuse was no different from her junior high teacher's. They both silenced her. But Brooklyn was an adult now, no longer a helpless twelve-year-old, and she said the words over and over again, "I'm done. I'm done."

As she sat in the suds, despairing, Brooklyn repented for not listening to Will. Tears of regret and sadness rolled down her face, making audible drops into the bath water. She thought she heard that still small voice— the words that had spilled from a fourth grader's pencil onto the soft printing paper of her childhood.

"You are loved. You are loved. You are loved. You are loved."

Never more impossible to believe, it was at that very moment Will came into their bathroom.

He was wearing a heavily starched blue Oxford shirt, khaki pants with an ebony leather belt, and his best leather dress shoes. He'd been in meetings all morning, and Brooklyn wasn't expecting him home yet. *Will...Oh, no...*

"What's wrong, Brook? What's going on?" Will pulled up short at the sight of her, and Brooklyn observed the concern crowding his face. She didn't deserve it. She didn't deserve his care for her.

"Are you hurt?" Will moved closer to the tub.

"No." Her mascara fell like black ink drops. They rippled out—a mini-storm—until the bubbles on the surface of the water absorbed them. Brooklyn couldn't look at him. She couldn't face him.

"Brooklyn, what's wrong."

"I don't want to tell you. I know if I tell you, you'll leave me, and I wouldn't blame you. *I* would leave me if I were you." She still couldn't look at him, but she knew she had to face this, especially when she heard Will draw in a sharp, pained breath.

Early in their marriage, he'd been unfaithful to her, and now–Brooklyn could see him physically brace himself for impact. "Oh, God, Brooklyn, have you been unfaith–?"

"No." Brooklyn shook her head. Drops that clung to her curls shook loose and splattered Will to make tiny, dark spots on his dress shirt. "No, it's not that." Shame made Brooklyn turn her face away from him. "It feels worse than that."

Will knelt beside the tub and reached for her hand. The storms they'd weathered in their early married years made it hard sometimes for them to be vulnerable. He stroked the soft skin on her hand, the one she'd told him her mother nearly broke on that terrible day years ago. He gentled his tone. "Tell me, Brooklyn." His voice reached to encourage her to be brave.

Brooklyn sighed heavily and spoke with her eyes closed. *No turning back.*

"Remember that accident April had last winter?"

Will bristled at the sound of April's name. "Yes."

"Well, after she lost her job, she couldn't afford to pay the hospital, so I told April I would pay her bill. I didn't tell you because I knew you would say no, and even though we couldn't afford it either, I thought I could just make payments for her over time."

"Are you kidding me, Brooklyn? Why would you do something like that without telling me?"

Brooklyn pulled her hand away from Will and held it up, stopping him from saying anything more. "No… it's so much worse than that, Will!" Tears continued to stream down her face. "I signed April and me up for a joint credit card. I wanted her to be able to take care of her bills, and I thought–if I didn't spend anything extra, I would eventually be able to pay it off. You would be none the wiser, and I could have done it if only…"

"Oh, Lord." Will's voice shook. "What did she do?"

Brooklyn remembered the many conversations they'd had about April. She knew Will didn't like her. He'd never liked her.

"She's manipulative and controlling, and I hate how she beats you down whenever you spend time with her. It takes you days to recover, even after a phone call!" Will had tried to talk to Brooklyn about her friendship with April. He'd tried to warn her, but Brooklyn wouldn't hear it. It made her angry when she overheard Will praying that the Lord would drive a wedge between them.

"Why don't you ask the Lord to heal her, instead?" She'd asked, annoyed. Brooklyn was miserable in the friendship, but she didn't want to give up. She and April had been friends longer than she'd known Will.

In the tub, Brooklyn covered her face with her hands. "Will, I'm so sorry. You were right all along, and I should have listened to you. I want out! *I just want out!* I thought if I kept giving April what she wanted, she would eventually get on her feet. I've been miserable keeping a secret from you, and I've been miserable in this friendship for years. I can't believe April would do such a thing, and now–now she's put so much money on the card, I can never repay it. Ever."

"How much, Brooklyn?" Will's voice held an angry edge.

Brooklyn didn't answer him.

"Brook. *How much?* How much money did April spend?" Brooklyn watched rage flit over Will's face, then vanish. He was fighting for control.

96

Brooklyn peeled her hands from her face and looked into Will's eyes. *No turning back.* "Ten thousand dollars."

Will's mouth fell open, and a loud gasp escaped his lips. He turned his head to the side and raked his fingers through his hair. "This has to end, Brook." Will's voice trembled. He was trying to control his anger.

"I don't want to be friends with April anymore, Will. I haven't for a long time, but I don't know how to get free from her. And… how can you ever trust me? Don't you want to leave? I betrayed you!" In all their years of marriage, William had never spoken a harsh word to her, but Brooklyn waited for them anyway. She knew she deserved them, and Will had every right. She closed her eyes again, unable to face what she knew must come.

Brooklyn heard a leather belt sliding through belt loops.

He isn't going to hit me! Will wouldn't do that!

But Brooklyn knew that sound, and her eyes flew open. She watched in confusion as Will lay his belt across the bathroom counter. He bent to untie his shoes, then slipped them off on the floor. Brooklyn was holding her breath. She didn't know what Will was going to do! He was so quiet; she wished he *would* yell at her!

Picking up his shoes and belt, he turned his back on her and took them to the closet. Turning back to Brooklyn, his face was etched in gray shades of sorrow. Without saying a word, and still fully clothed minus his belt and shoes, Will climbed into the bathtub behind her. He pulled Brooklyn to his chest and held her fast. His clothes absorbed water from the tub, and suds clung to the hair on his arms. Burying his face in her neck, he murmured, "My Brook." He couldn't see her tears falling with renewed force. He murmured again. "My Brook. Your generous heart gets you into trouble sometimes, doesn't it?" His arms went tighter around her wet body. "I've been praying for this for a long time. But…are you sure? Are you *really* sure?"

Brooklyn leaned the full weight of her relief into Will. "I'm positive. I've wanted out for a long time, and I'm ashamed it took me so long to come to it, Will. Why aren't you angry at me? Don't you want to leave?"

"Like I said, Brook, your generous heart gets you into trouble sometimes, but I'm not going anywhere. Don't you know that by now? Don't you know I love all of you, all the time?" He rubbed her arms with his hands. "Please don't keep secrets from me, dear wife. I hate to think of anything being between us. We're *one*." Will kissed Brooklyn's neck. "You were right. I would have said no to paying April's medical bills, but only because I don't trust her. She's never been a friend to you. I've been praying for so long..." Will's voice trailed off, and Brooklyn could feel his relief. She was still trying to process his care for her as they sat in the bathtub together—Will fully clothed. They talked until the water grew cold.

Brooklyn had done many dumb things in their marriage, but *this*—this was humiliating for her, and it would put a significant strain on their finances. Will hadn't even raised his voice! It was hard for her when he proved his love like this. Brooklyn was overwhelmed by his kindness; a kindness she knew she didn't deserve.

Later that day, Brooklyn received a check for ten thousand dollars from Will's hand.

"Pay that jailer's card in full and be done." He looked at her with the softest expression on his face. "The debt is paid. Be free, Brooklyn."

"Oh, Will." Two words carried all her heart to him. Three words sprang to her mind as she kissed him.

You are loved. You are loved. You are loved. You are loved.

Chapter 12
The Five Commandments

Brooklyn's commitment never to have friends again blew up that summer in her back yard. Because of April, she was just as determined her kids wouldn't have them either. Friends were dangerous, after all, and it was Brooklyn's duty to protect them.

Her kids were homeschooled though, and she knew they needed social interaction. Lucky for them, Brooklyn was a shrewd mother. She learned how to provide social time without allowing her kids to form close relationships with other children their age. It wasn't that hard. So far, they'd kept to her rules and not had a single close call.

Brooklyn's Five Commandments:

1. All playdates at my house.
2. Keep conversation light and shallow. Don't discuss the things of God.
3. Ninety-minute time limit on playdates to be strictly enforced. Keep white lie tucked into the pocket of blouse. ("Look at the time! I've got to get supper on the table!")
4. No commitments to meet again.
5. Abandon all playdates if hearts are jeopardized. Refer to rule number one.

April's betrayal had left an indelible mark, and seven years clicked by as Brooklyn clung to her commandments. Her kids had no idea how hard she was trying to keep them safe. Maylee, her youngest, was nine years old now, and Jake was almost graduating high school. Brooklyn didn't understand why they didn't appreciate her efforts, but as the parent, Brooklyn endeavored to hold the line. No friends! Not for any of them!

Understanding this and proceeding with the usual caution, Brooklyn invited Kathryn Norris and her kids for a playdate. Brooklyn had met Kate and a few other moms at a homeschool conference. The Norris family filled a need the Wyer family had, which was homeschooled kids of like ages. Kate gladly accepted the invitation. New to Montana from New York City and originally from England, she was trying to find friends for her kids. Not to mention herself.

Brooklyn had it figured out though.

She'd made a science of avoiding friendship, especially friendship with other Christian women. They were terrifying creatures! But Brooklyn knew how to give her kids that harmless interaction while she chatted with Kathryn in the back yard. After the acceptable ninety minutes, Brooklyn would feign the emergency of getting dinner started.

This was how it worked.

Brooklyn ignored Him as the Holy Spirit convicted her of hypocrisy. *"You're afraid of Christian women, Brooklyn? I've not given you a spirit of fear. Why are you doing this? Didn't you ask for a friend?"* She knew it was His voice, but she shook her head in defiance anyway. She had to stay safe. She had to keep everyone safe. She had been succeeding until that hot summer day when Kathryn Norris and her children came to play. If only it weren't for Kathryn Norris.

If only it hadn't been…for *Kate.*

Brooklyn and Kate sat in lawn chairs watching the kids. Brooklyn's chickens pecked about the yard as the children swam in the blow-up play pool. They were having so much fun, Brooklyn started to worry.

Laughter rang across the yard, and the water in the pool bubbled like a jacuzzi. Outwardly, she sipped her iced tea, but Brooklyn could hardly focus. *Those Norris kids are really nice.* She tried to stop thinking it, but as she watched them, Brooklyn could see they were different.

Brooklyn and Kate both had a stick in their hands to fend off encroaching chickens. The "girls" were being rude, pecking and scratching too near them. Fluffing their feathers, it looked as if they were trying to get in on the two women's conversation. They clucked and squawked as if inviting Brooklyn and Kate to share a bit of gossip.

"Brooklyn, have you ever read the book, *The Heavenly Man?*" Kate launched a missile aimed at Brooklyn's fortress of friendlessness, not to mention her second commandment.

"Hmmm? I'm sorry, what did you say?" Her heart went sixty to a hundred.

"Have you ever read the book, *The Heavenly Man? It's* by Brother Yun."

Thinking of the book, cold fear crept up the back of Brooklyn's neck. With all her heart, she longed for one safe Christian friend, but because of April, she'd given up ever having one. Jesus was her friend. Aside from her husband, William, Jesus was the only One who knew Brooklyn and still accepted her. That was the thing about Christians. Once they knew about you…

"Brooklyn?" Kate kept driving the conversation deeper.

Brooklyn felt her desire to be in close fellowship reaching toward Kate. She had to stop it.

"Yes." Brooklyn took a cleansing breath. *You can do this! This is just about books! Books are safe! The second commandment isn't technically being broken.* "I loved that book."

Brooklyn rebuked one of the chickens with her stick. Too close!

"Do you remember reading about how the underground church in China prayed for hours on their knees?" Kate's face took on a faraway expression, one Brooklyn tried to ignore. "I'm so convicted about my prayer life. I can't pray for ten seconds without thinking about the laundry or what to make for dinner."

"Me too. I've actually been asking the Lord to birth a prayer life in me." The words were out, and they were personal. Brooklyn could see the letters, like soldiers, form into the words that made those two sentences. They marched single file out of her mouth. They marched to their death. They marched to *her*s.

"Do you pray often?" Trying to save her fumble, Brooklyn turned the question to Kathryn. The kids were laughing their heads off in the pool. There *was* something special about Kate's kids, and Brooklyn had to admit it. The youngest was nine, the oldest sixteen, but there was an innocence about them that Brooklyn couldn't help but love. They splashed and played and jumped in and out. Most kids would have been embarrassed to play in that silly pool, but the Norrises were happy just to be in the water. Even grateful.

"Not as much as I'd like." Kate took a whack at a chicken, and Brooklyn had to admire her. She had a decent swing, and the little hen went bobbing away.

Baaawk! Baaawk!

"Brooklyn?" Kate, a high-fashion model from England, tilted her perfect face toward Brooklyn. The sun caught her high cheekbones and warmed her big, wide smile. After marrying her husband, Brian, the Norrises had moved to Montana to live a quiet life. But nothing about Kate's appearance said *quiet*. She was tall, blonde, and drop-dead gorgeous. Three strikes and Brooklyn couldn't help flinching. Kate was so pretty, it hurt a little. And then there was the accent...

Brooklyn's name, in an English accent, still hung in the air with a question mark attached to it. She tried to ignore the warmth in Kate's tone as she gulped her tea in panic. It came again.

"Brooklyn?"

Kate's voice was tender and kind, and all the pores on Brooklyn's skin opened. *Oh, for crying out loud, no! Whatever you want to ask, the answer's no!* Brooklyn forced herself to keep from shouting, *Abort mission! Abort mission!*

"Would you ever consider praying with me once a week on our knees?"

Silence. Brooklyn used the awkward pause and her terror in responding to play a quick game of whack-a-chicken.

Baaawk! Baaawk! The hen ran off.

"I mean. We wouldn't even talk about our lives. We would just go straight to prayer and talk to the Lord about them." Kate's voice shook. "You don't have to answer me now. Just...just think about it?" Kate's voice shook again.

Brooklyn realized Kate was self-conscious.

The chickens pecked all around them.

Most of Brooklyn's adult life had been governed by fear. But she *had* heard the tremor in Kathryn's voice, hadn't she? *Was Kate afraid too?*

One chicken squawked at them.

Brooklyn brushed the hen aside with her foot and answered with an ease that surprised her. "I don't need to think about that, Kate."

The words were out, and they were right.

"I would love to."

Brooklyn didn't fear, and she wasn't sure why. Maybe it was because she sensed the Holy Spirit allowing her a way back into friendship. Maybe the Lord was answering her prayer for a trusted friend. Whatever the reason, Brooklyn had an overwhelming peace that praying together with a woman she hardly knew had potential. Putting her fear aside, she felt a small reassurance that a friendship grown on its knees could last.

"What would you think about inviting Hannie Cohen and Wren Romano?" Kate asked.

They'd met Hannie and Wren at the same homeschool conference.

Bawk! Bawk! A chicken found a water snake, and the other hens were chasing her around the field. They were all trying to get a bite of the meaty morsel, and it made for a bizarre scene. Brooklyn wondered if Kate was thinking what she was thinking. *I used to live in New York City.* Even after many years living in Montana, the culture shock was a bit much.

"I think that's a great idea." Brooklyn could only keep saying yes. "Let's meet on Monday." (There goes commandment four!) She paused for a few seconds, then smiled to herself. "Could we meet at your house?" It looked like all the rules were going to be broken in one fell swoop, and the first commandment crumbled like ancient stones.

"That sounds great!" Kate smiled at Brooklyn and reached for her shoulder. "Thanks, Brooklyn. It's been lonely for me here. I've had a hard time making friends, so I really appreciate you being willing. I know it's a strange request. I didn't come with that on my mind, but I couldn't stop thinking about it as we were sitting here."

The chickens lay down in beds of dust, fluffing their feathers to fan the coolness of dirt into their wings.

You've no idea. Brooklyn was just beginning to grasp what she'd said yes to, and she whacked the ground with her stick. Sipping her tea slowly, she let the sun warm her pale skin as she relaxed back into her lawn chair. *Lord, have your way.*

Kate and her kids stayed for two and a half hours that afternoon when suddenly, she exclaimed, "Look at the time! I've got to get home and get supper on the table!"

Brooklyn laughed out loud as her third commandment went down the drain. She was beaten at her own game, and all the rules might as well be broken now. She tried to keep her composure as she invited Kate for another playdate, breaking the fourth command.

"It's supposed to be hot again tomorrow, and the kids have had such a great time together. Why don't you come back again sometime after lunch?"

***

That night, Will held Brooklyn in his arms. Breathing in the scent of her, he was surprised to hear her giggle. "What's so funny?" he asked.

"You're not going to believe this, Will." Brooklyn snuggled closer to his chest. "I think I made a friend today."

Chapter 13
Prayer Day 1

The irony wasn't lost on any of them. Meeting briefly at a homeschool workshop on prayer, Hannie and Wren responded affirmatively to Kate's invitation to pray on their knees. Together with Brooklyn, the four women made small talk in the entryway at Kate's house. Kicking off their shoes, they hung their purses on a coat rack. They silenced their phones and placed them on a wooden bench by the door. They hadn't known each other long, and they were all nervous.

It was prayer day.

Taking little time for conversation, they made their way to Kate's bedroom. Kneeling by the bed, the women were silent. Brooklyn reached for the tissue box.

Kate closed the door.

***

Afterward, there would be coffee and a rapid growing together. There would be stories told in laughter and tears—none of them in order because that was life. That was *their* life, and they felt like something new was being born...

The Mamas.

Chapter 14
MANipulation

The Mamas had been meeting to pray on their knees for over a year now. Their kids were bonded together in friendship, and they played together almost every day. They loved all four women, and it was their children who'd started calling them "The Mamas."

It was time for their men to meet.

"They should be friends, like us! Brian would love meeting your guys, and I think he needs more male friendships." Kate smiled at the Mamas over her cup of coffee.

"Can you imagine our good men together?" Hannie smiled back at Kate. "I have to admit, I've been obsessing over the idea. Our kids are all so great together, and I've learned so much from you Mamas, I just know Mark would do well with more male, Christian fellowship." She sighed, "Besides. I think Mark is lonesome."

"If only Steve could have with your husbands what I have with you!" Wren looked dreamy-eyed. "It's just what he needs! The fellowship of brothers and some accountability would be so good for him!"

"Right?" Brooklyn entered the conversation. "I just listened to a message from Denton Bible Church in Texas. The pastor took a show of hands to see how many people were meeting in a small group. He asked them if it helped them grow, and it was unanimous! Everyone said they didn't really start to grow until they started doing life together. That's been true of me. Through thick and thin, Mamas, you've helped me so much!" Brooklyn still couldn't get over how fast she and her friends had put down roots—deep roots that were helping her heal and grow.

The four women nodded in agreement with their heads bowed over steaming mugs of coffee.

"Forgive me, England, for I have sinned. It's been many months since I had a cup of tea." Kate's expression of guilt was obvious to everyone as she sipped her coffee.

"Poor Kathryn. What would your mother say?" Hannie laughed.

"The Catholic guilt is heavy upon me." Kate snapped back with an air of false martyrdom. "My Mum would be heartbroken if she knew."

"Speaking of being heartbroken," Brooklyn changed the subject. "I have something serious I need to talk to you gals about."

Hannie, with her raw, unassuming beauty, smiled at her friend. "You? Serious? You can't be serious!" She teased Brooklyn, but there was no sarcasm in her voice. The Mamas called it "scar-casm," and avoided it altogether. Hannie spoke with kindness and, of course, the Louisiana accent Brooklyn loved.

They all laughed. "Our resident melancholic." Wren winked at Brooklyn. "What's up, Brooky?"

"I wanted to brace you a little for this one." Brooklyn had been piecing out her life to the Mamas over the past year. They'd been piecing their lives out together.

"I tried to share this with other Christian women after I first became one, but it didn't go well. Now that we've been praying together for over a year, I'm beginning to feel like a fraud." Brooklyn imagined jumping off the bridge into the water near the river where she grew up. Every time she jumped, she thought, *There's no going back.* That's how she felt right now. She had to have this conversation, no matter how much it scared her.

"You see, I had an abortion when I was eighteen." Tears sprung right to her eyes, but she blinked hard to dam them. She couldn't stop there, or she'd be lost to emotion. Her voice wavered, but she continued. "The Lord's been doing such deep work in my heart, and one by one, I've been telling my kids about it." Brooklyn could hardly believe the grace they'd shown her. Their love and acceptance made this conversation with the Mamas doable. "I wasn't planning on telling you for a while, but I told Maylee yesterday, and I realized she might tell Margaret and Madison. I didn't want you to hear it from your girls. I wanted to tell you first, so you could comfort them if Maylee told."

Kathryn's daughter Margaret was named for the esteemed, late Margaret Thatcher. When Brooklyn had learned this, she knew she would love Kate forever. She'd always been a fan of the Iron Lady, but she was an even bigger fan of Kate's daughter, Margaret Norris. Kate's family called their only daughter Maggie, but Brooklyn refused. Young Margaret had all the potential and wits of the UK's late prime minister, and Brooklyn preferred her given name.

Just two years older than her Maylee, Margaret Norris and Madison Cohen were always up for fun. They loved making short films together, and they had just finished *The Hobbit* and *The Chronicles of Narnia*. They made their own costumes and wrote their own lines. Maylee, Margaret, and Madison loved to read, play on the rope swing, and hunt for water snakes. Innocent and pure-hearted beyond their years, the three pre-teen girls stuck together. The Mamas started calling them 3M after the sticky notes they were all addicted to.

Brooklyn adored 3M. She loved all the Mamas' kids! Loving each other's kids had become a mission without even being talked about. They loved no matter what the kids said, did, or even ate! The Mamas adopted an open fridge policy, and since the share was as equal as could be, the four women made simple adjustments to their food budgets. They refused the demeaning practice of nickel and diming each other. The Mamas were worth more than that. Their kids were worth more too, and it gave Brooklyn joy to see the backside of any of the Mamas' kids sticking out of her refrigerator door. It gave her particular delight to hear them whine, "Maaaan, there's nothing good to eat here eeeither!"

The Wyer, Norris, Cohen, and Romano kids were good kids, and they were good together. They fought and loved like siblings. They loved the Mamas, and Brooklyn didn't want Margaret and Madison to be hurt by her testimony. She should have told the Mamas first about the abortion, but she'd been so overwhelmed by Maylee's reaction, it took her the rest of the day to process.

"You mean I have another sister in heaven?" Maylee had been happy! "Mama, I want to give her a gift."

The bookstore was Maylee's favorite place in the whole world, so Brooklyn had taken her there. Maylee picked out a book for her sister and cuddled with it on the car ride home. Her joy was a sure sign she would tell her friends, but Brooklyn hadn't realized her mistake until this morning.

"I should have told you sooner. I'm sorry, Mamas. Will you forgive me?"

The Mamas were quiet until Kate finally broke the spell.

"Brooklyn, Margaret already told me. Maylee called her right away yesterday." Kate's expression was tight, and Brooklyn could see she was struggling with fear. *Did Kathryn have something to say to her?*

Hannie pulled at the edge of her bob haircut, a habit that endeared her to Brooklyn.

"She called Madison too. Madi told me that you and Maylee went to the bookstore to get her sister a gift. Is that really what Maylee wanted to do?"

Maylee's big heart took everyone by surprise sometimes, no one more than Brooklyn.

Wren moved across the room to sit next to her friend. The Mamas were big hand-holders now, and Wren held Brooklyn's in hers. "Brooky, you waited so long to tell us! Maylee told 3M, no surprise there, but she called to tell me too!"

Brooklyn couldn't stop the tears. "What? She did? I'm so sorry. I should have told you first."

"You should have, Brook, but only because we care for you." Kathryn was pragmatic. "Margaret is fine. She thinks you're the bravest woman she knows for telling all your kids. You're forgiven!"

Hannie's southern drawl was warm and kind. "Madison is fine too. Her heart was just broken *for* you, not *because* of you."

"These kids! Their kindness is killing me! They've all shown such amazing grace!" Brooklyn laughed and blew her nose. She was the reigning queen of the tissue box.

Wren put her head on Brooklyn's shoulder, and Brooklyn felt herself sinking into shame. She turned and spoke to the top of her friend's head. "Wren…I don't know how you can forgive me. After losing two of your boys to miscarriage, I don't–I don't know how you can!"

"Please, stop." Wren spoke with a rare, sharp tone and lifted her head. "I love you because Jesus Christ loved *me,* Brooky. You're brave with your life to share the things you've been through. I'm not that brave. All I know is, we've both lost our children. I don't want you carrying a burden such a deeply personal Savior carried to the cross for you. I won't have it; I just won't! Think of Jesus and the price He paid for you to live free!"

Quiet Wren rarely preached to the Mamas. She was an ardent listener and a careful responder. She grasped Brooklyn's hand again. "Do you see this?" She held up both their hands. "I'm not letting go, Brooky! I'm never letting go!"

Stunned into silence, Kate, Brooklyn, Hannie, and Wren herself sat thinking about this Jesus who had paid so dearly to purchase their eternity, their hope, and their freedom. He had ultimately even purchased their friendships, and it was because of Jesus the Mamas had made the decision: I'm not letting go.

There in Kate's living room, the roots of friendship bound up in Christ went deeper. Praying together had done this, and they knew it.

They felt it.

Kathryn cleared her throat. "Brooklyn, I understand why you were afraid to tell us, and now it is I who am afraid to tell you something." Getting up from her chair, Kate came to kneel by Brooklyn's leg. Cupping one of Brook's kneecaps in her hand, she confessed, "I've hated women just like you in my heart. I have despised them, and I have murdered them in my thoughts. You're the first I've known personally that has had an abortion, and suddenly, there's a face to it." Kate didn't cry, but her voice was heavy with sorrow. "I'm sorry, Brooklyn, for the way I've hurt women like you. Will you forgive me?"

"Of course, Kate! Abortion is just the worst. It's the worst!"

"That's not all, Brook. I had to repent to my husband and all my kids last night. After Margaret's speech about you being brave, I felt so small. So cheap. I'm grateful for your courage to share. It's directed the light at my part in propagating the silent shame of abortion, and—I'm sorry."

Brooklyn patted the top of Kate's lovely head as if she were a child. "I forgive you. It's okay." The women held gazes until they both broke into laughter.

"I told you I had something serious to talk about!" The relief in Brooklyn's voice flooded the living room with light, and the women resumed chatting about their men.

"Well, what are we going to do about our husbands then?" Hannie asked. "Wouldn't they love moments just like this?"

"Look, Mamas. We're not going to do a *thing* about our men." Wren was on a roll today. They could hear that determined tone in her voice. "My Steve can smell manipulation from six counties away. If we try to control our men, it won't work. I know it won't work."

"Wren, can you please stop being right all the time? Even though I have good ideas, if Brian feels I'm trying to control him, he moves to another country, and it's a cold one, believe me."

"Will knows I'm MANipulating him before I do!" Brooklyn smiled at her friends. "Perhaps we should pray and ask the Lord about it?"

"Now there's a good idea." The Mamas laughed. They were fond of their *good ideas*.

"Let's have a potluck dinner at my house." Hannie volunteered. "Bring all the kids, and let's take a chill pill about our men. We can ask the Lord to bring them together and ask Him to help us in our unbelief. Our men are all so independent, the reality is—it's unlikely they'll become friends."

"We better get this thing right, girls, because let's not forget—Jesus is a man!" Wren laughed and said in a booming voice, "The Mamas will now attempt to manipulate the Son of God!"

***

Two weeks later, the kids were downstairs watching a movie at Hannie's house.

Hannie sat upright in the living room with her chin to her chest, a soft snore escaping her mouth. Kate had her long legs stretched over and beyond Hannie's ottoman. Her head was leaned against the back of her chair, and she slept as she looked—like a supermodel. Wren drifted off with her head on Brooklyn's shoulder, reaching up to push back the occasional thread of drool.

But Brooklyn observed in amazement as their men talked in the kitchen. Late into the night and in the early hours of morning, something sacred was born. Brooklyn sighed a deep sigh of contentment, thinking to herself, *It's not just The Mamas now...*

It's our men.

Chapter 15
Beauty Is Fleeting

It was Tuesday morning after prayer.

The Mamas sat in Kate's living room with their legs curled under them. It was snowing outside, so they snuggled under blankets sipping coffee and chatting. Brooklyn set her cup down suddenly and put all her focus on Kate.

"Kate, is there something bothering you?" Brooklyn had seen the unmistakable flicker of pain cross Kathryn's face. The stereotypical stoic from England, Brooklyn knew Kate would never draw attention to her hurt, but she couldn't ignore it. All the Mamas were working at being more transparent with each other. It required courage. "Please tell us?" It required *encouragement*.

"Is it that obvious?" Kate didn't like being the center of attention. None of them did. She took a big gulp of coffee, and made a public confession, "I'm sorry, Mum. The Americans have ruined me on this stuff. I don't much care for tea anymore." Kate imagined her mother's look of disdain.

"Whatever it is, you're wearing it." Brooklyn pointed to her face.

"I thought so too." Wren added, "It looks like you're hurting."

"Oh, well. It's nothing, really." Kate waved her long, elegant arm in the air as if shooing away a fly. "It's just that I had another unpleasant experience visiting a homeschool co-op. That's all."

"Unpleasant, how?" Hannie's olive-green eyes took on a protective glare. "Did y'all get hurt by someone?" Her Louisiana drawl became more pronounced when she was excited, or in this case, angry. Hannie was ready to fight for her friend.

"What happened, Kate?" Wren asked, sipping more coffee.

"I know you'll think I'm vain, but I get so frustrated with women! They take one look at me—my long legs and arms, my body, my skin and smile—and it's over. They take me out of the running for friendship or conversation before even giving me a chance. They don't even try to get to know me, and it hurts my feelings." Kate wouldn't cry in front of them, but the Mamas could see her distress. "I had nothing to do with my looks. The Lord made me this way, but it irritates me that women would allow something so superficial as my appearance to bar me from friendship. I feel excluded when I go into a social gathering with women. In social gatherings with men, I feel inappropriately *included*, if you know what I mean. How can I feel my value if all people see are my looks? My body?" Until you knew the best of her, Kate was what a supermodel from England ought to be: tall, lean, and with cascading, golden hair.

Brooklyn was convicted. She recalled their meeting in the back yard with the chickens. *Tall, thin, and drop-dead gorgeous. Three strikes, Kathryn Norris, and you're out!* She'd thought the same thing about Hannie and Wren when they'd met at a homeschool conference.

Hannie, an exotic beauty, nodded her head in agreement. "I know exactly what you're talking about, Kate! Women are weird around me too, and if I had any of y'alls height and shape, I can well imagine!"

Hannie had dark-olive skin, deep-green eyes, and naturally dark-red hair cut in a bob. Her coloring was striking, and without a stitch of makeup, it was easy to get lost in her perfect features. Hannie was athletic. A runner. She didn't have a curve anywhere, even after delivering four children, but her beauty was natural, raw, and rare.

Wren, too, nodded her head. Average in height and the youngest of the Mamas by ten years, her thick, brown hair fell around her shoulders like a bronzed waterfall. With high cheek bones and dark, almond-shaped eyes, Wren didn't wear makeup either. Her Native features would go unnoticed unless you knew she was part Indian, and everything about her spoke of nature. Of wind. Of the smell of the earth after rain. A runner, like Hannie, Wren had an athletic build, too, but with more curves. "I feel every insecure bone in my body when I'm with women. I have to make a concerted effort to love with the love of Jesus." Wren smiled.

Wren had done just that. When the mamas first met at the homeschool conference workshop on prayer, they'd been placed in a small group together. Wren had smiled at them and moved toward them with the warmth and love of Christ. Her smile brought the light. It brought them all together and helped them get over their insecurity. Wren had taken the dreaded small group experience and made it easy for everyone.

"You're the best, Little Sister." It was the nickname the Mamas had given to Wren. It was their own "Native" name for her, but Wren didn't mind. She had no blood relatives left, and she said the Mamas felt like real sisters to her.

"Your smile is the absolute best." Kate smiled her own broad smile at her beautiful friend.

"Well, I'm convicted." Brooklyn shook her head in disgust and confession. "I'm totally busted." She tried and failed to say it in an English accent.

Hannie and Kate nodded their heads at her. They both had felt her judgment.

Brooklyn uncurled her legs, putting her feet on the floor. "I never gave thought to how my reaction to your beauty might hurt. I wasn't charitable in my judgments to any of you. In fact, when we got put together at the conference, the first thing I thought was, 'Oh no! Not the beautiful people!'" She picked up her coffee and took a sip. "I'm sorry, girls. Truly. I'm so sorry. Please forgive me?" Brooklyn, a "wogger" as she referred to herself whenever she went running with Hannie or Wren, was curly, curvy, and plain. She struggled every day to make peace with her appearance, and she, too, had been judged.

"I forgive you, Brooky." Quick to forgive, Wren smiled over the rim of her cup.

"Brooklyn, y'all are beautiful!" Hannie's protective nature surfaced again. "You have such a beautiful heart; I hate that you don't like the way you look!"

The sin of insecurity.

"Let's do something about this!" Kate was practical to the core. "Let's do a Bible study on what the Lord says about beauty. Let's not keep doing this worldly thing, girls. Let's go higher up!"

"I'd love to be free—totally free—from the world's idea of beauty. Now, wouldn't that be something? I wouldn't have to think about my own or anyone else's." Wren's smile came again.

Just being near Wren built Brooklyn up. "Would you want to study Proverbs 31? All of it, but especially verse 30?" Brooklyn looked at the Mamas. The Lord had been good to her in giving her these women.

"*Charm is deceitful, and beauty is vain, but a woman who fears the LORD is to be praised.*" Hannie quoted the Bible from memory. "Y'all, if the world could get a piece of that, it would save everyone a heap of trouble."

Brooklyn could hardly believe two of her closest friends had such terrific accents.

"Alright then, girls. Come next week with what you've studied for Proverbs 31 verse 30. Let's get clear of this wretched thing getting in the way of so many women becoming close friends." Kate was always

118

teaching, and she especially loved teaching the Bible. It was such a strong gift of hers, she couldn't help it.

To have friends who were grounded in God's Word made them all the safer to Brooklyn. Prayer by prayer. Cup by cup. She was healing from her deep fear of friendship. As she hugged the Mamas going out the door and to her car, she thanked the Lord for her friends.

And for setting her free.

Chapter 16
Prayer Day 2

Brooklyn, Kathryn, Wren, and Hannie stood in the entryway at Kate's house. Kicking off their shoes, they hung their purses on a coat rack they now knew Kate's father had made. They silenced their phones and placed them on the wooden bench by the door.

Taking little time for conversation, they passed along prayer requests their children had made that morning. It was the dads' day to be at home with their kids so everyone knew...

It was prayer day.

Falling to their knees by Kate's bed, Hannie and Wren looked with affection at Brooklyn as she reached for the tissue box.

Kate closed the door.

Afterward, there would be coffee and laughter and more stories out of order. There would be something more and more wonderful that was deepening in their hearts...

The Mamas.

Chapter 17
Smoking in 'The Boys' Room

Brooklyn was heading out the door for a walk when her phone rang. She looked at the number and answered. "Hey, Steve!" Wren's husband never called her, and Brooklyn tried to keep her voice light. "What's up?"

"Listen, Brooklyn, is there any way you can come to the house?" Steve's voice sounded tight. "Matthew ran away, and Wren is... Wren's scaring me, Brook."

"I'll be there in ten minutes. I'm glad you called!" Brooklyn hung up the phone, sprinted up the stairs for something, then jumped in her van. She prayed as she drove.

"Lord, give me wisdom. Please, please, please give me wisdom." Her heart pounded. Wren had been sharing tiny bits of her past with Brooklyn. She knew about the night she and Mattie had escaped the Reservation with their lives.

Steve was in the driveway when Brooklyn pulled up. He opened her door and scooped her into a hug.

"It's like she can't hear me, Brooklyn. She's just sitting in 'The Boys' room staring at the walls. She's been like that since six o'clock this morning."

"What happened? Did Matt leave a note?" Brooklyn was huffing with adrenaline.

"Wren always kisses him in the morning, even though he doesn't wake up. I told her he's too old for that, but she said he doesn't mind. This morning he wasn't there. He left a Hershey's Kiss on his pillow, and that's it." Steve's face was pale with worry.

"Don't these kids know they're all killin' us?" Brooklyn slammed her van door. "Upstairs? In 'The Boys' room?"

It was a term of endearment for all of them, and Matthew liked it too. He was the oldest of all the Mamas' kids and outside their age range for a playmate. Matt was a man now.

Steve's voice shook, "In 'The Boys' room. Thanks, Brooklyn."

Brooklyn cracked open the door to Matthew's room, and there sat Wren. She was on Matt's bed, her back against the wall, knees pulled up to her chest. Wren was tugging at the loose threads on the holes of her jeans with one hand; with the other, she was taking hungry drags of a cigarette.

Brooklyn coughed and waved her hand as she came into the room. It was billowing with smoke, and she'd never seen anyone smoke that hard.

Wren didn't seem to notice her, and in all that tobacco cloud, she looked like a wisp. An apparition. A ghost.

"Wren? Little Sister? It's me…" Brooklyn spoke softly. Was Wren in a trance or something? Noticing a glass of booze on Matthew's nightstand, Brooklyn saw it had fresh ice. Her mouth instinctively watered.

"Okay, Wren." Brooklyn stepped toward her friend and yanked the cigarette from her mouth. "Wren, we're not doing this anymore, remember?"

Knowing her friend wouldn't see her, Brooklyn turned her back toward Wren and took a long drag on the cigarette. Then another. Her eyes rolled slightly back as the comfort of the familiar came alive in her mouth. The warm burn in her lungs felt so good, she wondered why she had to quit. *Why is sin so savory?* She punished the cigarette, and her lust for the old habit, by crushing it out in the ashtray. Then, with a practiced hand, Brooklyn took a stiff swig of the whisky. The light clatter of ice on glass made her shiver with enjoyment.

Brooklyn!

Brooklyn slammed the glass down on the nightstand as if the Holy Spirit had called her name out loud.

"This here is the old man, not the new one, Little Sister." Brooklyn said it more to herself than to Wren. The cigarette and the booze had made her forget all about her friend. Sin was such a trap into selfishness!

Brooklyn suddenly panicked. She and Wren had committed never to drink while being mamas. They didn't know what they would decide after the kids were raised, but they had agreed to hold each other accountable. They would obey Scripture. They wouldn't get drunk. So how long had Wren been drinking?

Turning back to the apparition in the thick cloud of smoke, Brooklyn felt afraid. She couldn't think of anything else to do, so she climbed on the bed and pulled Wren into her arms. *Lord, help me! Help us!*

"It's okay, Wren, I'm here, and I'm not going anywhere. I've got you." Brooklyn said the first words that came to her mind. They must have been the right ones because she could feel Wren's tiny body begin to shake. Her words came in fast, short, run-on sentences.

"Brooky…Mattie left, and he left me a kiss, and I don't know what that means, but I think I do, and I'm scared, and I'm cold."

Brooklyn didn't know what to say, so she just rocked Wren in her arms.

"Remember when I told you how Matthew found his mom after she'd been killed? You remember? Jane Little Deer? Her head was smashed in with a baseball bat by her boyfriend, Charlie. She was my best friend, Brooky, and you just can't know what goes on out there—out there on the Rez. Matt, he was only seven years old then, came running to my

123

house. I was sound asleep on the couch, but he pounded on the door until I woke up. My stepfather woke up too, and he was raging and said Jane had it coming. He picked me up by the throat, Brooky. He told me I was next. He picked Matthew up by the throat, too, and told him he would kill him if he ever tried to leave the Rez."

Wren was trembling in Brooklyn's arms, and her words tumbled out like pearls on a broken chain. For the first time since they'd become friends, Wren didn't try to stop them.

"Jane told me she'd made a will and that she wanted Mattie with me. She knew, Brooky. She knew Charlie was going to kill her." Wren pulled at the thread of her torn jeans as if they were weeds crowding the breath of her soul. "Matt and I ran back to Jane's house to look for the will. That's when Mattie showed me his mom. At first I just saw the bloody bat, but then I saw her in the bathtub and there was so much blood running down the drain, and the whole thing was just disgusting, and Matthew was whimpering, and he wet his pants. Then we both started screaming."

Wren took a deep breath. "I'd been wanting to leave the Reservation for a long time. My stepfather was an animal, and Brooklyn, you have no idea, but I knew he was going to kill me that night. I knew he would kill Matthew too, so we scooped what we could into a garbage bag and left in the dark. We walked in the borrow pit along the highway, and every time a car came, we flattened ourselves to the ground. Mattie was crying, and he wanted to go back for his mom, but I knew she was dead, and there was no way I was going to let him be killed too."

She took a ragged breath this time. "Things turn all of a sudden on the Rez. Everything goes along so slow and lazy and then BOOM! There's a turning, and it's mean and violent and drunk and lonely."

"Wren..." Brooklyn held Wren so she could hold on. She remembered how her mom had held her in the laundry basket on that terrible day. "I've got you, Little Sister. I'm here." Brooklyn had never heard Wren talk so much. She wondered if she would ever stop.

"Matthew has struggled with depression, anxiety, migraines, and suicidal thoughts all his life, Brooklyn. He's felt this weird pull back to the Reservation, back to the scene where he last left Jane. It's haunted him, I know because it's haunted me too. I couldn't help him enough. I never could be enough, don't you see? It's not like the other kids. I wish it wasn't true, but I think Mattie was right. I know you think I'm going to see him again, but I don't think I will, Brooky. I just don't think I ever will." Wren curled into Brooklyn's chest and dissolved into sobs so violent, Brooklyn could barely hold on to her.

"If Matt went back to the Rez...I'm scared I'll never see him again."

Reaching for the whiskey glass, Brooklyn pushed it toward Wren.

"Wren, drink some of this. We're not using alcohol anymore, but this is medicinal, and you've got to sit up. You've got your little boys and Steve to think of, and they're scared too."

Wren took a drink, then abruptly shoved the glass back into Brooklyn's hand. "I need you to hold me accountable, Brooklyn. Alcohol scares me. I'm sorry I poured that glass; I really don't want it." She lifted her shirt and wiped her many tears then blew her nose.

"My mom is dead. My friend Jane Little Deer is dead. And now...my sweet Matthew. I'm so sad. I'm just so sad, Brooky. It happens all the time on the Reservation. The trauma Mattie experienced was luring him back. I felt it. I knew he felt he had to go back. I don't understand it, but it's so hard to lose them all—not just my family, but my heritage. My culture. My songs. My dances. My tribe. I've lost all hope of belonging, don't you see, Brooky? I don't belong with white people, and I don't belong as an Indian."

"You belong." Brooklyn stroked Wren's long, straight hair and wondered what had happened to Wren's mom. Her friend's words sounded hollow. And shallow.

"I knew I'd die on the Reservation, Brooky. There was no hope. No hope at all. I had to take Mattie with me because I knew he would die too."

Brooklyn rocked Wren in her arms again. It was good to hear all her words. Her story.

"My people are all dead now, Brooklyn. I have no people. Steve and the boys—and you and the Mamas—you're my family now."

"Wren, I love being your family." Brooklyn hugged Wren to her side. She couldn't believe that Mattie wouldn't come home. She was sure he would, but she kept silent because she knew she didn't understand. There were a lot of things she didn't understand.

Brooklyn took a deep breath and tried to sit them both upright. Digging in her purse she said, "Don't get mad, but I brought you a gift."

Wren looked at Brooklyn with pain and disbelief. "Please tell me you're kidding. A gift? For such a time as this? What a terrible friend!"

"This is a special gift, see?" Brooklyn ignored Wren's insult and rustled something out of her hand. "Kate gave them to Hannie when she was in a deep pit of depression over Mark's struggle with pornography. Hannie gave them back to Kate after she lost her mom. Kate gave them to me when my dad died. And now... I'm giving them to you, Wren. This is who you are. This is the strength God has given you to get through this. You're not going through it alone. We Mamas are going with you, and we can be pretty wonderful, don't you think?"

Wren brushed at her face like she was trying to shoo a fly away. One of Brooklyn's curly hairs had lodged itself in her eye.

"Wonder Woman bracelets?" Wren sounded confused.

"Let's put them on." Brooklyn didn't wait for an answer but slipped the gold cuffs with the trademark red star onto Wren's tiny wrists.

Wren stared at them, then smiled. "Is it weird that I feel a little better?"

"You're going to be alright, Little Sister, and we Mamas are going to take care of you until you are." The women sat in silence for a long time. Wren turned her wrists over and over, and the gold cuffs caught the sunlight coming through 'The Boy's' window.

"Thanks for coming, Brooklyn. Thanks for being here."

"There's no place I'd rather be right now, Wren. You've honored me with your story, and it's sacred to me." Brooklyn smiled at her friend. "I have to admit, though, I've never seen anyone smoke so hard as you! You're a little scary, Wren!"

Wren laughed through her tears. "Smokin' in 'The Boys' room, right? Wouldn't Mattie laugh at that?"

"He would! I'm serious though, Wren. You impressed me, and I'm not that easy to impress." Brooklyn laughed and squeezed her friend again. "I'm so glad Steve called me!"

***

Wren wore her gold cuffs every day until they found Matthew's body on the Reservation. She wore them every day for a year. And every time she saw them, she was reminded of the Mamas. She was reminded of the strength God had given her. She could keep loving. She could be a wonder woman and keep holding on.

The image of Jesus hanging on the cross came often to Wren's mind in those days. He had endured such agony! Jesus had gone all the way for her, and He'd paid such a price! Wren wondered how she could get through losing her son when she heard the voice of the Holy Spirit in her mind.

"Endure."

If Jesus could endure the cross, Wren could endure the weight of her story and the loss of Jane Little Deer's beautiful son…

Matthew.

Chapter 18
Kneeling Nighty

Hey, Hannie?" Brooklyn sipped her coffee and peeked over the rim of her cup at Hannie's olive-green eyes. Hannie put thick slices of chocolate chip pumpkin bread on a plate between them. She was eating one, but Brooklyn couldn't afford the calories. "Do you and Mark pray together?"

Brooklyn had driven out to Hannie's place that morning to go for a run. Hannie and Mark lived out of town on a lush, forty-acre property with great running trails. She and Brooklyn ran together whenever they could, which wasn't often anymore. Their older kids were in their teens now, and activities were keeping both mamas on the road too much. Even though Hannie was an athlete, a distance runner with almost no body fat, she slowed her pace to run with her friend. Brooklyn mostly just "got along," and her body was everything but zero body fat. She bounced all over the place; there was nothing at all athletic in her lines. But Brooklyn loved running. And she loved running with Hannie.

Brooklyn took another sip. "I mean regularly. Like, do you pray every night before bed or something?" It was still hard for Brooklyn not to stare at Hannie. They'd known each other for years now, but Hannie's smooth, olive skin and green eyes, paired with her dark-red hair always took Brooklyn by surprise. Hannie was gorgeous, and Brooklyn wondered how Mark could stand it.

After Kate had led them through a Bible study on beauty, all the Mamas had settled into their God-given genetics. Hannie was strong but thin. She accepted her body, but still longed sometimes to have bigger breasts and rounder hips. It was a struggle for Hannie to take in enough calories to keep weight on, and she was always eating.

The Cohens operated a small lumber yard for the forest service and Hannie's husband, Mark, was also thin. Often after Madison, McKenna, and their twin boys, Eryk and Zac, were in bed for the night, Hannie and Mark stayed up too late watching movies and eating ice cream out of a gallon bucket.

Brooklyn had the opposite problem. She might have been a runner, but she was round everywhere. Round face, round shoulders, round... everything. Even her hair was round! She wished she were thin, but she and Hannie had agreed to hold each other accountable to honor their bodies. And given that even Kathryn-the-supermodel was prone to insecurity, all the Mamas were trying to let go of the world's opinion of beauty. As they studied what the Bible said about it in Proverbs 31: *"Charm is deceitful, and beauty is vain, but a woman who fears the LORD is to be praised."* The Mamas were committed to defeating any kind of pride in their appearance.

"Do Mark and I pray together?" Hannie smiled at her friend to put her at ease. "No. Can't say as we do." Hannie was from Louisiana, and Brooklyn couldn't get enough of her accent. It reminded Brooklyn of melted chocolate.

"It's somethin' I long for, that's for sure." Hannie pulled the edge of her bob.

"Me too." Brooklyn couldn't hold Hannie's gaze. "It's something I've wanted my whole married life. We just can't seem to get anything consistent going. Every time I bring it up, I feel like I'm manipulating

Will. He's such a good man; I don't want to pressure him. Sometimes, it feels like begging."

"Oh, I know." The olive-green eyes. The warmth. "As soon as I try to force somethin', Mark smells it comin' a mile away."

"The resistance." The steam from her coffee cup fogged Brooklyn's glasses.

"The resistance." Hannie shook her head but smiled. "Bless their hearts." She reached for a second, thick slice of chocolate-chip-pumpkin bread. "Are you sure you won't eat one?"

"Hannie…you know I can't be doing that." Brooklyn laughed. "Believe me, I would if I could. Go ahead! You need the calories!"

Hannie saluted Brooklyn with her treat and ate the whole thing.

"What can we do, Han? It breaks my heart that Will and I don't pray together." Brooklyn thought of Will's work schedule and all the responsibility he was carrying on his shoulders. She felt guilty for wanting more. "It breaks my heart." She couldn't help repeating.

"Oh, mine too."

The way Hannie said "mine" sounded like miiine, and Brooklyn wanted her to say it again.

"Yours too?"

"Mmmm. Hmmm."

Just as good. Brooklyn felt Hannie's accent like a warm hug.

Hannie's eyes twinkled over her cup. "Maybe if we got naked and knelt by the bed?" She and Mark were working hard on their marriage, and Hannie was flirting with him again.

"Hannie!" The women laughed together. "That would be the shortest prayer of all time!"

Hannie picked up a rogue chocolate chip. "I can hear Mark now…"Praise the Lord! Thank You, Jesus, and amen!"

"That's probably the worst idea for prayer ever, Hannie!"

"You're right. Wouldn't work, but it would be fun to try. I'll give this some thought and get back to you."

"You mean, you'll do some research?"

"I just might." Hannie took a third slice of bread and double winked at Brooklyn.

Unbelievable. Brooklyn should be used to Hannie's metabolism by now, but she wasn't. She'd never seen anyone eat so much in her life and that included her teenage boys!

Hannie looked at her watch and stood. "Oh, darlin', I gotta run. I've got a photoshoot downtown today, and I still need to shower."

"Want me to stay with the kids until you're out?"

"Would you mind?"

"I wouldn't miiiind." Brooklyn hugged Hannie around her tiny waist, trying to imitate her delicious accent. "I think I gained two pounds just listening to you today."

"How many times I gotta tell you, I don't have an accent? You're the one with an accent." Hannie's voice was slow and calm.

"Get back to me when the results of your research project come in." Brooklyn smiled at her lovely friend. "If it will help Will and me develop a prayer life together, I'll do it."

"I'll get right on it." Hannie's Louisiana giggle made her sound like a little girl, and Brooklyn couldn't help laughing at her double entendre.

"You're terrible."

"Happily married." Hannie winked again.

"Go take your shower… and make it a cold one!" Brooklyn gathered their cups and the empty plate of sweet bread. "I'll wash these up."

***

Months later, Brooklyn and Hannie were again curled up in the chairs at Hannie's house.

131

"I got you a gift." Hannie handed Brooklyn a beautiful box with a big, red bow.

"Han, what's this about?" It was hard for Brooklyn to receive gifts, but that's something the Mamas were helping her with too.

"Y'all better open it first. You might not like it."

Brooklyn lifted the top from the box and burst out laughing.

"Naked didn't work." Hannie smiled her warm smile at Brooklyn. "Believe me. I did a lot of research." Hannie still couldn't believe how well she and Mark were doing.

"So…a cheetah print negligee? You think *that* might work? Not pink or red?" Brooklyn was bent over laughing. This was a far cry from her thick, flannel pajamas!

"Hey, apparently Adam had a thing for animal skins. If it worked for Eve, I thought it might work for y'all too."

"Hannie, you're killin' me! Thank you…I think!"

"Thank me later, Brooky Boobs."

"What did I ever do without my good, Christian friends?"

"I'm guessing you were bored clean out of your mind." Hannie pulled a laundry basket over to her chair with her foot.

Brooklyn ran her hands across the silky material. "So, the research continues, I guess. When at first you don't succeed, try, try again?" Brooklyn raised a questioning eyebrow at Hannie.

"Something like that." Hannie smiled like she'd eaten a chocolate secret as she and Brooklyn folded t-shirts together. "Let's call that the kneeling nighty." With her Louisiana drawl, *nighty* sounded like *naughty*, and they both laughed.

That night, Brooklyn took the courage from what she was learning in Proverbs 31 and approached Will, who was lying in bed reading a bow hunting magazine.

"Will, can I talk to you about something?" She didn't wait for an answer. "I long to pray with you regularly, but I feel like I'm pressuring you when I ask. I hate that, and I don't want you to feel weird about it." She sat on the edge of the bed with her hands behind her back.

Will put his magazine down on his chest. "I know, Brook. I know you want to pray more together. I just don't think of it, and I'm sorry."

"Well...would this help at all?" Brooklyn held up the cheetah print. "It's my new prayer shawl."

"I don't think so!" Will's wide smile split his face. "But it would be wrong not to try! In fact, it would probably be a sin!" His whole body expressed approval.

"You know I'm not that young anymore, husband. I've got no real business wearing this thing." Brooklyn waved the negligee at him and laughed a little nervously. It probably cost Hannie a thousand dollars a pound.

"If it's business in my bed, Wife, you've got every right."

Thank you, God. Brooklyn loved her husband. "But it's for prayer time." She smiled.

"Oh, right. Already forgot." Will was stripping his pajamas off like they were on fire.

Brooklyn went into the bathroom and slipped the tiny cheetah print over her head. Doing her best to scoot it down around her hips, she practiced courage by praying Proverbs 31 over herself. *"Charm is deceitful, and beauty is vain, but a woman who fears the LORD is to be praised."*

"Ta-da!" Brooklyn stepped out of the bathroom and laughed out loud!

Will was kneeling naked by the bed. "Oh, Mama, let us pray!"

Humor in the marriage bed was a must, and they both laughed. And prayed fast!

The more Will and Brooklyn practiced praying together, the more they took their time. They didn't rush, but enjoyed the intimacy of being with the Lord. They teased each other about the celebration that would come after prayer, and even that was richer. Prayer bonded them. It made the one flesh union more sacred than ever before.

133

After nights like that, Will and Brooklyn woke in a tangle. Smiling, they went downstairs to drink coffee. The ripple effect of last night gave the simpleness of having coffee together a sacredness. Holiness clung to them like a fragrance, and they wore it as an invisible prayer shawl for the rest of the day.

Brooklyn sat down at the table after Will left for work. She wrote a card and walked it down the lane to the mailbox.

Dear Hannie,

Thanks so much for the cheetah print prayer shawl. It didn't really work as expected, but we sure enjoyed it! I'm officially onboard with the research project.

With love,

Brooklyn (and her kneeling Knighty)

P.S.

MEEEEOOOOOWWWW!

Chapter 19
Drowning Day

Brooklyn and Will strolled around a small lake in Wyoming holding hands. Their five kids scattered like a jar of spilled marbles, bouncing around the tree-filled campground playing hide-and-go-seek. Brooklyn could see them from where they walked. She watched Maylee hide behind a small rock. She was a little afraid to be separate from her siblings and called out, "I'm ready! I'm hiding by a rock!" She wanted to be found.

Will watched them and laughed his deep, warm laugh. He squeezed Brooklyn's hand. "This is the best day of our lives, Brooklyn." His smile lines caught the light and his love for his children.

It was a comment they often made to each other to remind themselves of the preciousness of their children. And the blessedness of their life. Somehow, they never felt it more than in that moment. Letting the sun warm and melt their shoulders, they breathed the mountain air and relaxed.

"I didn't know how much I needed this." Will slipped his arm around Brooklyn's waist. "Thanks for packing the car and getting the kids ready."

"They helped a lot. You know how much they love camping." She cuddled under William's arm. He stopped to kiss her.

"Mmmm…I didn't know how much I needed this." He said it again, and his smile teased her. She reached up to touch the lines around his eyes and laughed at him.

"Camping with five kids. Remember?"

"Five kids who know their parents are happily married." William kissed her again.

Everything fell silent around them as they looked into each other's eyes with the openness of lovers. Their expressions were naked and unashamed, and they spoke without words. It was amazing to them that their marriage was still intact and deeper than ever before.

Brooklyn kissed him.

Will said, "I love you, my Brooklyn." His thumbs stroked the nape of her neck.

"I need you, my sweet William." Brooklyn stood on her toes and kissed his beautiful mouth once more.

Startled by a sound, Brooklyn and Will looked up to see Jake and Sophie, the two oldest, sprinting toward them. Breathless with panic, they couldn't speak.

"What's the matter? What's wrong?" Brooklyn's senses fired. She knew that look on Sophie's face, and fear gripped her. "Soph? Jake??? Where's Maylee?"

"She's with Abe, but we can't find Derek." Their faces were pulled tight with fear. "We looked everywhere for him. We told him we gave up and to come out, be he won't." Sophie wrapped her arms around Brooklyn and burst into tears.

"Mama. We can't find him. We really can't find him!" Jake was breathing hard and trying not to cry.

Sophie tightened her grip on Brooklyn's waist, and she sensed her daughter's burgeoning intuition. A current ran between them, and Brooklyn *felt* Sophie's fear. All the pores in her body opened, her maternal instincts fired, but Will was already racing to the top of the campground hill.

From that vantage point, they could see everything at once. There was really no place for Derek to hide. He was wearing a bright green jacket and would be impossible to miss.

When Brooklyn joined him at the top of the hill, she could see Will's face was white. Brooklyn had only seen that twice in their marriage—when Abe was born blue with the umbilical cord wrapped around his neck three times, and when April was mean to her.

"Derek!" Will cupped his hands around his face. "Derek!" His voice carried down the hill and covered the campground. Everyone could hear him.

Turning in circles at the top of the hill, Will called again and again. There was nowhere Derek couldn't be seen. He wasn't hiding. So that meant… an animal had carried him off. Or…*he was at the bottom of the lake.*

Brooklyn's legs gave way, and she heard something screaming. Was it the cry of a mountain lion crowing victory over its prey?

Will peeled her off the ground and crushed her against his chest as if to silence a scream of his own. "Shhh. He's got to be here somewhere. I'll find him. *I'll find him, Brook.*"

The hair-raising scream was hers, and in its sound was the wild animal Brooklyn had always known to be lurking there. She knew in that moment she could kill someone if it meant getting her son back. Her arms filled with an unnatural strength in their desire to hold Derek again. She clung to Will, clawing at the muscles in his shoulders.

"*Where,* Will? *Where* are you going to find him?"

They looked at all the cars in the parking lot, and Will cursed loudly. Maybe someone like that disgusting Four-Fingered-Feel-Out had his son in one of those cars. Brooklyn had told him about her junior high teacher, and Will had since been keenly aware of how predators operated in the world. He was always on alert, and Brooklyn just read his mind.

"Will…what if someone took him?"

"I'll search every car. So help me…" Will sprinted down the hill. "I'll find him Brook!" He shouted as he ran. *Oh, God, help me find my dear boy.* "Help! My son is missing! He's wearing a bright green jacket! He's nine years old and has brown hair. Has anyone seen him?" Will ran through the campground, crying out to everyone he could see.

"We were watching your kids play hide and seek. We didn't see him come by here. We'll help you look for him!" The other campers fanned out around the hill. Surely they would be able to see a kid in a bright green jacket.

"Don't let any car leave this campground. Search every vehicle!"

Cries of, "Derek! Deeerek!" rang out across the water while Brooklyn stood frozen at the top of the hill. As she heard her son's name called over and over, she kept looking down at the lake.

"Derek…" She said it aloud, not more than a whisper.

But where else could he be?

Brooklyn dropped to her knees again, and her body felt cold. She couldn't breathe, and she kept picking up handfuls of little rocks. She squeezed them in her fists until they cut her palms. "God, please don't do this. Please don't do this."

"Derek! Deeerrrreeeek!" Dozens of people were scouring the campground, but Brooklyn knew it was hopeless. She could see the entire area from the top of the hill. An animal had taken him. An evil human. *Or the lake.*

She reached for her phone and called Hannie.

"Hi, Brooklyn. Are y'all settled in at the lake?" Hannie's voice was quiet and calm.

Brooklyn couldn't answer her.

"Brooklyn?" Hannie was intuitive.

No reply.

"Oh no, baby, what's wrong?" Hannie could hear the strangled sound in Brooklyn's throat, and she knew she was trying to speak. Hannie understood this. She understood Brooklyn. "Brooklyn, take a deep breath, darlin'. You need to tell me what's wrong."

Brooklyn obeyed Hannie and squeaked, "Derek is missing." Her throat was so tight, she could barely get the words out.

"Wait...What now?"

"Derek..." Brooklyn's voice sounded strange. Distant. Cold. "...is missing."

"What in the world? Brooklyn, what's going on?" Hannie wasn't prone to panic, but Brooklyn could hear the sudden alarm in her voice.

"Call the Mamas." Brooklyn croaked. "Pray, Han!" She hung up the phone and shoved it in her pocket.

Will came up the hill and grabbed Brooklyn's hand. They walked the perimeter of the small lake in silence. Their legs felt rubbery, and their hearts cried their son's name. *"Derek..."*

"One of the guys in the campground called Search and Rescue. I don't have much hope, Brook." How could he have gone from heaven to hell in such a short span? Will felt like an iceberg. Visibly frozen and fathoms of grief gathering.

Somehow, they were back at the van, and Will was leaning Brooklyn against it, so she wouldn't collapse again. The other kids gathered around her like silent apparitions. Brooklyn wondered if they were real. She reached out to touch them. *Was any of this real?*

Brooklyn reached for her phone and handed it to Will.

"Call my mom, Will. I can't bear it."

"I'll get mine. It's in my coat."

Brooklyn nodded numbly and pulled the kids around her. *So, this is what it's like to lose a child.* She didn't cry. She didn't feel. She just knew her life was over. She remembered someone saying once that to lose a child was to become a member of a club nobody wanted to join. She hated this club! She wanted *out* of this *club!*

The people in the campground stood at a respectful distance, likely wondering how they could help. A sick expression covered their faces.

Will opened the back of the van to get his coat, and a strange sound came out of his mouth.

"Brooklyn."

She heard him, but he sounded weird–not like himself. His voice was unrecognizable, and she felt too frozen to move toward him.

"Brooklyn, come here." He was choking back tears, and this got her moving. Brooklyn pushed her children off her and walked to the back of the van.

Will was on his knees clutching the side of the car. His chest was heaving with gasps of air and tears, and Brooklyn thought he was having a heart attack.

"Will!"

The kids scrambled toward them. "Dad! Daddy!" Tears and panic smothered them. "Daaadd!" They collapsed in a heap around Will.

"No, kids! I'm fine. Just...LOOK!" He lifted a shaky finger to the trunk of the van. There was Derek! Covered in jackets and a picnic blanket. He was sound asleep!

Brooklyn and the kids clung to Will. Together, they all knelt and hugged beside the sleeping Derek.

"Thank You, Jesus!" Sophie cried through her tears.

Little Maylee looked in at her brother. "He must be really tired!"

They all stood stupidly staring at Derek, but Jake finally stood and ran through the campground. "My brother's okay! We found my brother!" Even after everyone knew Derek had been found, Jake kept running around the campground loop.

"Will, grab that boy, or he'll run himself to death." Brooklyn jerked her head toward Jake.

Will walked over to intercept his oldest son and caught him, still running, in his arms. "Jake. It's okay. Derek's okay." Will wept openly. "Derek's okay, son. Everything's okay."

Brooklyn watched as they clung to each other. She could see the deep sweat stains in the armpits of both their t-shirts. *How can everything ever really be okay?* She saw Jake tuck his hand in Will's and knew it would be the last time. She watched tears rain down Will's face and even from where she stood, she could see how tightly they gripped each other's hands.

They all stood together, and Brooklyn gently shook Derek's leg. "Derek! Wake up!"

Will pulled his barely awake son out of the trunk and—though he was too big—lifted Derek into his arms and held him. And rocked him and smelled him and savored him. *Derek.*

"What's going on, Mama?" Staggered with heavy sleep, Derek clung to Will as he swayed him in his arms.

"We couldn't find you! We had everyone looking for you!" Brooklyn felt wobblier than ever.

"Oh. I didn't feel good, and I was tired. I didn't want to ruin the fun for everyone, so I just took a nap."

Brooklyn stood behind Will holding his waist. She looked up at Derek. "Derek. You know your mama loves you, right? You KNOW that, right?" It seemed like such a stupid thing to say. She reached up to touch his cheek.

"I know it, Mama." Derek's voice was still sleepy. His long legs hung awkwardly down Will's torso as Will, still crying, buried his face in Derek's neck, and stroked his head. "My son…My son…"

"No matter what comes, promise me that you'll hold my love for you all your life. No matter what happens, Derek. Promise me?" Brooklyn kept her hand on his cheek.

"I promise, Mama, I promise. Am I in trouble?"

Will put Derek down but continued to hold him to his chest.

"Don't cry, Dad. I'm okay." Derek patted Will gently on the shoulder. "Don't cry, Daddy."

"You know you took years off your mother's life today, Derek? Why did you disappear without letting us know where you were going? We were scared to death!" Will touched Derek's face, traced it as if to carve it into his memory.

Derek's eyes brimmed with tears. "I didn't want to ruin everyone's fun! I had a stomachache, and I wanted to lay down. I'm so sorry!" He looked at his siblings. Everyone was crying. "I'm sorry I ruined your fun!" Derek's face crumpled in confusion.

Will pulled Derek back into his arms and held him close. "What would we be without you, Derek? What would I be without you, son?"

Without speaking a word to Brooklyn and Will, the older kids packed up their camping gear and threw it in a messy ball into the van. Everyone wanted to go home.

"I'm so sorry, everyone," Derek said again. He was fully awake now, and he looked embarrassed.

"I don't care, Derek. I'm just thankful you're safe. I was so scared." Sophie reached lightly around his waist to hug him.

"It's okay, buddy." Jake ruffled Derek's hair. He was still sweaty from running around the campground. He was still sweaty from fear.

One by one, Will took each of his children up in his arms—even Jake. He held them and rocked them and stroked their hair. "I love you. I'm sorry I have to travel so much. You're wonderful. My life would be sad without you."

"Are you okay, Sophie?" Brooklyn hugged her daughter tight. "Abe? Are you alright?" She reached for Abe, but he ducked out of her reach. She'd debrief with him later, after he'd had some time to process.

"Let's go home, everyone." Will's face was still white.

Brooklyn wrapped her arms around Derek before he got into the van. "Boy! You do feel warm. I'm sure you're running a fever."

"I just don't feel very well, Mama, but I'm sorry I scared you."

Brooklyn kissed his warm cheek. It was alive with fever, and she was thankful. "We're alright, son. Thank God, everyone's alright."

"Daddy, can we stop for ice cream?" Maylee blinked up at Will. "The Bible says ice cream makes everything better, and it's good for fevers too!"

Will smiled at her. "Maylee, the Bible doesn't say that, but it doesn't mean it's not true."

The Wyer family drove out and around the lake. Brooklyn's eyes locked onto the water, an aqua grave she felt certain held her son only moments ago.

"Thank You, Jesus." The water filled her vision. "Thank You."

Brooklyn's phone buzzed, and she knew it was the Mamas.

"What once was lost has now been found." She texted. "More later."

"Will…" Brooklyn turned to her husband, but he shook his head.

"Not yet, Brook. *Please.* I'm not… not ready yet." His voice cracked, and he reached over to squeeze her knee.

"It's okay. I was just going to say I feel a hundred years old. I was just going to say I love you, and you're a good father."

The van was quiet as they drove. Sophie held fast to her brother's hand as he dropped quietly—and in the presence of those who loved him—back into sleep.

Chapter 20
Pool Day

Brooklyn tried to avoid the public pool, especially on weekends. But the weather was hot, and the kids' pleading could not be ignored. She called the Mamas, and they all agreed. It was pool day.

They gathered at the gate with their usual paraphernalia: baskets of terry cloth towels, cans of sunscreen, swim goggles, dive toys, and color-coded water bottles. Add the coolers, the umbrellas, and the lawn chairs, and the Mamas looked like they were moving in.

Pool Day.

Kate counted the kids as they went through the turnstile. One, two, three, four, five, six, seven, eight, nine, ten, *eleven*. Wren was home with her new baby, so they were three kids short of their usual number.

Brooklyn turned her cellulite-covered hips to squeeze through the turnstile. "My breasts are hanging so low; I could tie them in a knot *and* in a bow." Smiling at her joke, she smooshed her butt around the bars.

Hannie's face flushed as the turnstile spit Brooklyn out the other side. "Bless the body God gave y'all and keep moving! My arms are on fire carrying all this stuff!" Hannie's Louisiana drawl bounced off the concrete walls. Looking like a billboard for public pool day, her sunglasses slipped down her nose as she lifted her cooler and canvas tote over her head to get through the turnstile.

Hannie had no hips, thighs, or butt to squish up against the humiliating metal gate. She was so thin she had to wear a one-piece because no swim bottoms would stay up on her waist. Kate once suggested she shop in the junior section of the clothing store, but Hannie had planted both fists on her narrow hips and declared, "I'm the mother of four kids. I am *not* shopping in the children's department!"

Eleven kids and three tired Mamas finally made it through the entry gate, the dreaded turnstile, and the locker room to the pool. That journey of 100 feet was enough exercise in itself! They plopped their stuff down near the kiddie pool and slathered sunscreen on all the kids. Brooklyn's ten-year-old, Derek, slipped away three times before she could even squirt some SPF 50 on one arm!

Once the kids were off for the sanctuary of the water, the Mamas popped open their lawn chairs and umbrellas.

"We made it!" Kate wiped her sun-blocked hands on a towel.

"Thank the good Lord." Hannie sprayed a heavy layer of sunscreen on Brooklyn's back and shoulders. "Don't forget your hat this time." On the last pool day, Brooklyn had managed to get sunscreen on her five kids, then forgot to put any on herself. She had blistered her shoulders, horrifying the other Mamas. Her sensitivity to the sun was one reason Brooklyn hated pool day.

"You're too old for this, Brooky. You've got to take better care of yourself." Wren had applied aloe vera leaves and a small rebuke. The sunburn, of course, had been the bigger one, and it rebuked her for days.

The Mamas drove extra miles to this pool because it had a well-trained lifeguard team. They knew this because a few of their kids had already been rescued. *All* the lifeguards knew the Mamas. They even called them "the Mamas." Kate, Hannie, Brooklyn, and Wren tried to win them over with cold drinks and home-baked goodies, but you couldn't mistake the disdain on their faces when the four women and their kids came for pool day. *How could anyone not delight in children?* Brooklyn was saddened when she overheard their snide remarks:

"Oh, Lord, it's The Mamas, everyone. Look sharp. Someone's getting rescued today."

"Yeah, but who? The Mamas or one of their five million kids?" The lifeguards' voices carried across the water, snickering at them. The four women had grown accustomed to this treatment whenever they were together as a group. But it saddened them. How could the world not delight in children?

Patrick, the lead lifeguard and pool manager, motioned to another guard. "We'll need four up high today, instead of the usual two. Keep a close watch. There's a lot of kids here."

Brooklyn sighed. At least all the kids would be carefully watched.

Kate sat down hard in her lawn chair. Huffing, she pulled a fashion magazine out of a tote with her long, thin arm. Her long, blonde hair was pulled back into a long ponytail, and her long legs stretched beyond the end of her lawn chair. Everything about Kate was long and lean. She was their very own supermodel, and the Mamas loved to tease her about it.

"I love this pool," Kate said, as a groan of relief escaped her supermodel mouth. "I can really get some downtime here." She flipped the page of her magazine and munched on a cookie.

"You two and your fast metabolisms make me sick, you know that?" Brooklyn couldn't look at a cookie without gaining a pound.

"Getting Kate's giraffe legs out of that chair is going to be the real problem. We'll be sure to give y'all fair warning when it's time to go." Hannie smiled at Kate, tipped her head back in her chair, and closed her eyes. "Mmm…The sun feels so good on my skin, I could kiss it."

Brooklyn admired Hannie's exotic beauty. She was athletic and strong—a runner, just like Wren. Hannie loved the Lord, and Brooklyn was thankful to have such godly friends. She didn't give a hoot how they looked, even if they were supermodels compared to her.

"The Son feels so good, I could kiss Him." Kate laughed at her play on words.

Brooklyn and Hannie smiled at her sympathetically. "Don't hurt yourself, Supermodel. Just sit and look pretty now." Hannie and Brooklyn laughed. Because of Kate, they were learning to make light of their physical appearance. Studying Proverbs 31 together, the Mamas were trying to live in the truth of what the Bible said was beautiful.

Kate glanced up at the kids jumping into the water, then leaned her head back and focused on her magazine. She sighed again, and deep contentment rested on her perfect cheekbones.

Brooklyn envied that contentment. Having long feared drowning, Brooklyn counted eleven familiar heads in the water until her eyes burned. "Look! There must be a hundred kids here today. The water looks like it's boiling." Pool day stressed Brooklyn out. The Mamas stressed her out too. They weren't on duty here, and it drove Brooklyn crazy. She gave Hannie a *look* as she smeared more sunscreen on her shoulders.

"Would you just relax?" Kate rolled up her magazine and slapped Brooklyn's thigh. "Trust God to take care of the kids, okay? You're making it hard for me to enjoy myself, Brook! Besides, these lifeguards are great!"

"I can't help it. Water scares me!" Brooklyn shivered, remembering that terrible day.

"Brooklyn." Hannie's voice softened. She knew the story and understood why pool day was so hard on her. "Give it to Jesus, honey. Your boy is alright."

Hannie and Kate left Brooklyn to struggle with her memories. There was nothing they could do, so they settled back into the sun, sighing deep sighs of relief. Someone else was on the job, the weather was perfect, and all the kids were happy.

But Brooklyn wasn't.

She scanned the water, counting each child's head and watching for any signs of distress. She saw Derek get out of the pool. The sinews of his back muscles glistened in the sun and served as downspouts. Water poured off his skin and splattered the concrete. Brooklyn knew it took every ounce of self-control for him not to run, and she smiled as he speed-walked to the high dive.

Brooklyn couldn't help remembering Derek as a baby. Like all babies, he'd been born perfect. He had a beautiful head covered with lush, black hair, and his skin was olive with a kiss of pink. Even all the nurses wanted to hold him.

Derek may have been a gorgeous baby, but he had been plagued with colic and thrush. He cried all the time, slept poorly, ate poorly, and had sensory issues he couldn't communicate. Derek developed a habit of twisting and pulling out his hair. When she and William noticed large bald patches on his head, Will had shaved Derek's hair to the scalp.

As her husband traveled hard to keep them all eating, Brooklyn would sometimes stand on the porch outside their home in the freezing wind crying. Derek pounded on the door from the inside of the house, while Brooklyn longed for a cigarette. Dreading going back inside, she knew she couldn't comfort her little boy. He cried when she held him. He cried when she didn't. What was she doing wrong? Guilt haunted her.

Brooklyn didn't have the Mamas then. She felt overwhelmed and alone. She felt inadequate and insecure. She wanted to help Derek, and though she never told Will about it, sometimes she would let Derek pull *her* hair. Trying to comfort him, she would sit with him in the rocking chair and let him pull one strand after another until he drifted to sleep. She willed herself to bear the pain for the peace of her son. As she laid Derek in his crib, Brooklyn gave thanks for his respite from torment and for the momentary quiet in her home. Returning to the rocking chair, she scooped a handful of her hair off the floor and put it in the trash.

Those had been desperate days and desperately lonely. It had taken Derek a long time to grow out of that phase. Brooklyn believed it was the reason he now possessed such unusual compassion for people. He was always the first to notice when someone was hurting or felt left out. What a great kid he'd turned out to be! Still awkward at times, but what a great kid!

Brooklyn watched Derek now, standing at the bottom of the ladder to the high dive waiting his turn. So, today was to be the day. He had told Brooklyn so this morning as he bounced into their fifteen-passenger van.

"Mama, this is it. Today's the day! I'm going off the high dive."

Derek was fearless. Coming into the world with an insatiable love for the outdoors and adventure, Brooklyn had no doubt; today was the day. That boy was going off the high dive.

Lean and athletic at ten years old, he ran up the ladder and walked to the end of the board.

"Mama!" He waved his long, brown arm. "Mama! Are you ready?"

Brooklyn's eyes locked onto his face. She knew what he was saying, and tears sprung to her eyes.

Mama, are you ready?

Brooklyn nodded her head, waved back at him, and thought. *How can I ever be ready, Derek?*

Derek stepped out into the air and dropped from the diving board with his arms tucked to his sides. Entering the water with hardly a splash, all Brooklyn heard was *whuuump!*

Pride and joy spread over her like butter on warm toast. She grinned at him as he surfaced; he was looking for her face. Brooklyn waved and whooped. She knew he couldn't hear her, but she shouted anyway, "Great job, son! Wow! So brave!"

Kate pushed her sunglasses back on her head and shielded her eyes from the sun. Squinting at Brooklyn, she said, "Our boy made it off the high dive?"

"Just look at him!" Brooklyn grinned. She couldn't help it. She wanted the Mamas to watch Derek. They prayed for him and loved him as their own, and she wanted them to share the moment.

As the water churned white with splashing children all around him, the Mamas watched Derek swim to the side of the pool. Too many kids were lined up at the ladder to get out, so he pulled himself up without it. Like the water pouring from his back, his motions were fluid. Arched body, arms pulling, left knee to concrete, right foot to concrete, straighten, and speed-walk back to the high dive.

"He's going again! That boy is going to be so tired today, he won't last ten seconds in the van." Kate watched Derek race to the ladder leading up to the high dive. He wasn't her son, but she loved him like one. Kate told Brooklyn she never worried about her kids when Derek was around. He was a watchdog of righteousness and, even at his age, a lover of the Lord. Kate's children adored him, and he was Ethan's best friend. Also, the kid was hilarious, and you couldn't help but adore him. Often unintentionally inappropriate, he kept the Mamas and their families laughing.

"Kate, are you watching this?" Brooklyn couldn't take her eyes off Derek. He stood now at the end of the board. His brown body looked like a perfect stroke of burnt sienna paint against the blue-saturated sky. They could see his white teeth from the opposite end of the pool, his whole face was drenched in delight. "Hannie? Are you watching?"

"I am." Brooklyn could see the pride rushing to fill Hannie's heart as if Derek were her own son. Because Mark struggled with porn, Hannie was sensitive to men who leered at women, taking what didn't belong to them. She'd told Brooklyn she'd never known a boy Derek's age to possess the qualities of wisdom and compassion in such measure. Hannie had said more than once that Derek had more sensitivity to women than almost any of the grown men she knew.

Of course, there were the times when he acted without taste, but all the Mamas understood Derek now. His favorite conversations were of bodily functions. He had a knack for bringing them up at the most unsuitable times, but the Mamas knew it was unintentional. Their favorite thing about Derek was his humility. It hurt him that he was improper at times, and he welcomed the Mamas to teach him through it. In many ways, he had the wisdom of a grown man.

Hannie brushed away tears as she watched Derek on the high dive. "He's so beautiful, Brooklyn. Look at his confidence. Drink in his innocence. The world's coming for him."

A familiar pain pulled on Brooklyn's heart: the exquisite agony of loving someone. "I won't ever forget this moment." It seemed melodramatic, but it was true. Brooklyn etched the picture of her pure-hearted son onto the chambers of her mind. "But. Wait…Why is he standing there like that? He just dropped right off the first time."

Derek was standing at the end of the board, bouncing, not jumping.

"He doesn't look scared." Hannie was leaning forward in her lawn chair.

"No…" Brooklyn felt panic rising in her throat. *She knew her son.* "No…Oh, no. Oh, no!"

Derek was messing with the string around his swim trunks, and they all knew what was coming.

"What? What's the matt—" Kate saw it too, Derek's propensity to be inappropriate.

The Mamas had agreed to love Derek through this stage because they knew he would outgrow it. The world would make sure of that. "Oh, gosh, Brook, what are you going to do?"

Brooklyn's voice felt like it was pinned to the bottom of the pool, but even if it wasn't, she knew Derek couldn't hear her.

"What *can* I do?" Her whole heart pulled to the far end of the pool and up the ladder to the high dive. "I can't stop him, and you know he's proud of it. What can we do but let him have his moment?" Brooklyn sucked air in through her teeth. "Damn...he's going to learn a hard lesson today." Her whole face contorted into a cringe. "Damn."

"Brook, mind your mouth." Hannie chastised her, but only because it gave her something to say. The Mamas were dying for her. They were dying for her pure-hearted son, who was about to embarrass himself in such a public way.

Derek slipped his trunks down around his ankles.

"Oh, *Lord*." Brooklyn could hardly breathe, and her words came out flat. "He couldn't be modest about it, I suppose. That wouldn't be Derek, would it?" Brooklyn cursed the little house that had taught her kids nudity was not a big deal.

"Lord, have mercy, there he goes!" Brooklyn could hear Hannie take a big breath and hold it.

The Mamas watched in horror as a long, golden arc of urine dropped from the high dive into the pool, making a fountain's splash. Derek grinned like he owned the world and was giving it a gift.

As swimmers realized what was happening, they screamed, "Pee! Pee!" and swam in panic to the edge of the pool. The water frothed with their desperation to get out.

Brooklyn's son stood proudly on his high perch. Laughing with glee and turning from side to side, he targeted his brothers and best friend down below in the pool. A lifeguard blew her whistle over and over at Derek, waving both hands at him in a motion that could only communicate *STOP!*

Derek didn't catch on. He thought she was encouraging him and waved back at her.

His teeth and his bottom were moon-white, his legs and torso as brown as dirt. Nervous laughter boiled up from Brooklyn's belly and out of her mouth. She should have been mortified, but she wasn't. She laughed out loud and couldn't help thinking how healthy he looked. How happy. How perfectly *boy*.

The other mamas at the pool didn't feel that way at all.

"Honestly!"

"Gross!"

"Whose kid is that, anyway?"

"Mom! Did you see that kid pee in the pool?" A little girl clung to her mother's side crying.

Finished with his performance, Derek pulled up his trunks and plunged into the water. *Whuuump*.

The other boys stood lined up around the pool's concrete edge, waiting for Derek to surface. Brooklyn stood, poised to run interference. She thought they would try to dunk Derek, at the very least. She knew their words were going to hurt, but she couldn't do anything about that.

Instead, when Derek came up smiling, the boys clapped for him. "Cool, dude! I've always wanted to do that!"

"What was it like, man?" A freckled face boy in red swim trunks slapped Derek's shoulder in approval.

"My mom would kill me! Are you going to have to leave now?"

The Mamas looked at each other in shock. "Boys are weird. They're just so weird sometimes!" Hannie laughed out loud.

The head lifeguard, a tall, seventeen-year-old boy, stomped over to Brooklyn. He looked down at her and rolled his eyes. "Sorry, Mamas, that's it for today. Out you go!"

"Oh, come on, Patrick, he was just being a boy. You know every kid here has peed in the pool at least once already." Kate stood with Brooklyn, her hands on her hips.

"We just got here! You can't make us leave! For crying out loud, Patrick, I'll talk to him; he's a good kid!" Brooklyn's voice shook with emotion, but she knew Patrick was a good kid too. He was just doing his job.

"Listen, Mamas." Patrick sighed as if the burden of the world rested on his young, bony shoulders. He closed his eyes, then opened them. "You see all those boys down there?" He turned his head toward the deep end of the pool. "Now every single one of them wants to pee off the high dive. Derek's a hero! And look at all the little girls around here clinging to their moms! They're scarred for life! No. I'm afraid I have to make an example of you today. Pack up your stuff. You're going." Seeing the pained expressions on the Mamas' faces, Patrick softened his tone. "Listen, it's nothing personal, Mamas; you know I like Derek. I think he's a great kid." He turned on his heel and walked toward the group of boys standing by the deep end.

Thwick, Thwack. Thwick, Thwack. His flip-flops hit the pool deck with the quintessential sound of summer. To the Mamas, it was the sound of a perfect summer day moving out of their grasp. They stood watching breathless and helpless as Patrick scorned Derek and all the other boys. He pointed Brooklyn's son toward her with an index finger that only meant one thing: go home. The Mamas' collective ten kids followed Derek in silence while everyone at the pool watched.

Derek collapsed into Brooklyn's arms when he reached her. Tears as big as his heart wet his eyelashes, and the fun leaked out of pool day like a beach ball with a wide hole.

"What did I do wrong, Mama?" He leaned into Brooklyn with his full weight, and she had to take a step backward to keep from falling. He was big now. He was growing up. This was going to hurt him, and Brooklyn resented how growing up kept coming for everyone.

Even her. Even now.

Brooklyn swallowed her tears hard and worked to steady her voice. "You can't pee in the pool, Derek. It's one of society's rules."

"Well, society sucks!" Humiliation trembled in her arms, and Brooklyn tightened her grip on him.

"I know you didn't mean harm, son, but we have to play by the rules."

"Everyone pees in the pool! I know nobody tells, but they do."

The Mamas gathered their stuff while everyone else kept staring. Mercifully, a boy at the deep end shouted at Derek, "This is for you, Buddy!" He cannonballed back into the pool, and all the kids, even the girls, followed.

You can't stop kids and water.

"See? The other kids aren't mad."

"It's just one of those things, Derek. You can't ever do that again, do you understand?" Brooklyn put her hand on top of Derek's head. "Not ever."

She remembered her pubescent years and how she resented the unstoppable train running down the tracks of her lengthening spine. "You can't stop it, son. You're growing up. You'll be a man soon, and one day–you'll be having conversations like this with your own boy."

"I don't want to grow up, Mama."

Brooklyn's heart ached. *If only that would always be true. If only he would never grow up and leave home.*

"You sure?" Brooklyn tipped his head back so their eyes met. He was always telling her about the adventures he longed to take when he was older. "What about that long road trip with Ethan to snowboard every mountain in North America? You have to be grown up for that. You have to be grown up for lots of wonderful things. God has plans for you as a man, Derek. Even in His Word, He calls you to stop being a child."

"Yeah. I guess you're right." He rested his warm, wet head on Brooklyn's chest. "*When I became a man, I gave up childish ways.* That's from First Corinthians 13:11."

Brooklyn's son knew his Bible better than she did. That he was applying his knowledge to this moment gave her the greatest joy of her life.

"D?" She made Derek look her in the eye again. "You can't pee in the pool." Brooklyn winked at him and let him see the smile gathering in her eyes. "At least not from the high dive."

"I won't, Mom. I promise."

"I'm proud of you, Derek. You understand me?" Brooklyn cupped his chin in her hand and squeezed it. "I'm proud of you—not embarrassed or ashamed. Right?"

"Thanks, Mama, but I have a question." His eyes had a happy spark in them now.

"Hmmm? What's that, son?"

"Did you see me?"

"I sure did, and so did the Mamas!"

Derek's face split like white lightning. "Wasn't it GREAT? I mean, aside from society's dumb rules and all?"

"Like nothing I've ever seen in my life!" Brooklyn smiled at him and kept the rest to herself.

Derek hugged her hard.

"Come on. We wore out our welcome pretty early today. Patrick says we have to go home."

The Mamas and all the kids were waiting on the other side of the turnstile.

Derek's brothers and friends rushed him like a champion, and his smile lit up the day.

"I'm taking y'all out for ice cream, Derek Wyer." Hannie grabbed him in a tight hug. "That was quite the deal! Quite! The deal!"

"Thanks, Mama Hannie." Derek was already bigger than her, but he snuggled close to Hannie anyway. *Maybe for the last time.*

Derek had been the first one to call Brooklyn's friends Mama. After all the kids caught on, the women had been initially annoyed.

"Can't they just call us Auntie?"

Kate, not knowing Derek yet, had narrowed her eyes at him, suspicious of his motives. What did he want from her, anyway? Why couldn't the kids call her by her name in the good old-fashioned homeschool way? She asked Brooklyn. "I like being called Miss Kate. But 'Mama?' It's so weird!"

It hadn't taken long for the Mamas to adjust, and it wasn't much longer until they held the name dear to their hearts. It was hard not to take a larger role in a child's life when he or she was calling you "Mama." It increased their affection, loyalty, and responsibility, and Brooklyn, Kate, Hannie, and Wren loved the kids fiercely.

Derek pulled away and turned to Kate. "Sorry I got us thrown out so fast, Mama Kate. Are you mad at me?"

Kate fanned her face like she smelled something stinky. "I'm just thankful you didn't poop! You had me worried there for a minute, especially when you dropped your trunks all the way to your toes!"

Derek grabbed her in a hug. "That wasn't very cool, was it? I'm really sorry if I embarrassed you."

Kate took Derek by both his shoulders. "Now listen here. There is nothing you will do. Not ever. There is nothing you will say. Not ever, Derek. That's going to make the Mamas unlove you. You got me, boy?" She shook his shoulders, trying to keep her voice hard and tight. Everyone saw Kate struggling to hold back tears. The kids shuffled their feet and looked away. It was rare when Kate wasn't in command of her emotions, and it scared them. She coughed a little to clear her throat. "Now didn't Hannie say something about buying me ice cream?" Kate dabbed her eyes with her towel as everyone piled into Brooklyn's fifteen passenger van.

Fatigue washed over Brooklyn. *How did I ever do life without these women?* Their love for Derek and the rest of her kids was something she could never get over. *Like the love of Jesus.*

"Can we come back next week, Mama B?" The kids shifted and clamored and talked in the back.

"What? For pool day? Are you kidding me?" Brooklyn looked in the review mirror at the happy children. The healthy children. The *safe* children.

Nope. Nothing's changed, she thought.

I still hate pool day.

Chapter 21
Found

T he bedroom door was closed. Tissue boxes were scattered on the comforter, and used tissues lay strewn on the carpet like crumpled divinity. Brooklyn, Wren, Hannie, and Kate knelt around Kate's bed.

"We're not going to talk about our lives. We're just going to pray about them." Kate had a vision for their prayer time from the beginning, and she'd strictly laid down the ground rules. "What happens around this bed doesn't leave this room."

What had been happening around that bed had been happening for a few years. The Mamas had grown close. So had their husbands. And so had their kids. Matthew was gone now, but the rest of the kids, all thirteen of them, played like siblings downstairs while the adults studied the book of Romans upstairs.

Brooklyn scolded Kate's kids just as her own. "Ethan, I just washed that! So help me, if you put your bare belly on that glass one more time, I'm going to make you and Derek wash all the windows in the house!" Or, "Margaret, if you fall off that rope swing and break your arm again, I'm going to spank you first before I take you to the hospital!"

It was hundreds of things like that, and the Mamas were teaching and "admonishing" all the time.

Like when Abe put his butt through Hannie and Mark's new sheetrock wall while the kids were playing tag in the basement.

And when Eryk and Zac covered Wren's walls with thousands of tiny divots by shooting their air guns at a poster.

Or when the girls borrowed each other's clothes, left wet towels on the lawn after swimming, and slapped the boys when they got out of hand.

There was constant scolding for playing soccer in the house, not chewing with your mouth closed, and saying words like "sucks," and "frickin," and "screwed." The kids laughed their heads off one night after hooking a fart app on their phones to an electric guitar amplifier. The sounds of "small explosions between the legs" being amplified up the stairwell soon had the adults laughing too. Nobody could focus on Romans after that.

Brooklyn couldn't believe how the Lord had gone above and beyond to answer her prayers. The Mamas and their families were tight, and it was prayer day again.

Kneeling around Kathryn's bed, Wren cracked open her Bible. Worn from use, a few loose pages hung off the edge of the binding.

"See what kind of love the Father has given to us, that we should be called children of God; and so we are. The reason why the world does not know us is that it did not know him. Beloved, we are God's children now, and what we will be has not yet appeared; but we know that when he appears we shall be like him, because we shall see him as he is." 1 John 3:1-2.

A holy hush fell over them. The Mamas waited for the Lord to lead their prayers.

"Lord, we welcome you this morning. How good it is to be in your presence! Thank you for calling us to yourself. Thank you for making us your children and thank you that we can come boldly to you, just as a daughter would to her father. Purify our hearts and minds this morning, Lord, that our prayers would be effective in the Kingdom of God."

Kate's blond ponytail fell across her shoulder and touched the bed like the end of a paint brush. The morning sun streamed through the window, casting shadows on her high cheekbones.

"Forgive us for sinning, Jesus. Have mercy on our hearts this morning." Hannie confessed the harsh words she'd spoken to her Kenzie before leaving the house. "Forgive me for losing patience." Reaching for the tissue box, Hannie pulled several and blew her nose.

"Father, please give our children a love for your Word. Please make them men and women of The Book."

This was the continual cry of the Mamas' hearts.

"Give our husbands wisdom to lead our families. Give them integrity in their work and bless and prosper the work of their hands." The collar of Hannie's cardigan sweater trembled on her small frame.

"Please help me to be more creative in loving Will, Lord. Help me manifest that aspect of your power, so he doesn't get bored. Help me to be willing and joyful in the bedroom and show me how to support him in his work." Brooklyn ripped several tissues out of the box. "Give me a pure heart for my husband."

"Me too, Lord." Wren brushed at a stray hair on her face.

"Jesus, pour out the gift of repentance on my heart. On the hearts of our families. On the Church and on our nation. Lord, pour out the gift of repentance on the whole world. We can't even be sorry for our sin without your help!" Hannie sniffed. "We want to see a revival in the land of the living, Jesus. We are asking for a massive return to the cross of Christ!"

Brooklyn knocked on the wooden bench at the end of Kate's bed. The sound, a terrible reminder, brought to mind many of their loved ones and prodigals. "Remember the lost, Lord. Bring them to their senses. Please, Lord; Please. Let them be counted among the saved." She couldn't help it. Brooklyn's voice broke, and she sobbed. "Bring them home, Lord."

All the Mamas knocked on the bench and reached for a tissue. They'd been waiting for years, and these were their most personal prayers.

"Jesus, we stand together against the enemy's schemes." The room rang with amens, and the clink of armor could be heard in their minds. It was time to fight.

"We pray against evil in every realm, Lord! We plead your blood over our homes, our families, our marriages, our churches, our state, our nation, and our world." Wren's always quiet voice spilled with power. "We ask you to guard our children for your Name's sake and for the sake of your Kingdom! We pray that every lie of the enemy would be struck down in Jesus' name!" A blaze of morning light fell across Wren's face, and her Native American features stood out more than usual. High cheekbones. High forehead. Perfect symmetry of features.

"Protect the testimony of our children, Lord! Cause them to live for you, and if necessary, to die for you!" Brooklyn was face down on the carpet. "Fight for them, Jesus! Fight for our families and our marriages!"

"Come against the wicked in this land, Lord. Expose them just as you exposed Satan. Make a public spectacle of them, Jesus, and liberate the innocent by the power of Your Name!" Kate's voice rang like a freedom bell. It tolled liberty and justice.

Hannie was crying so hard, she could hardly get the words out. "Jesus, we come against addictions right now. We pray for the next generation and that they would stop cutting and killing themselves. Lord, have mercy on the youth or our nation, and even those in our homes. We pray against the lies of pornography and insecurity. Lord, set our children and all the children of the world free from the wickedness of sin."

Wren was crying now too.

"Free those caught in sex trafficking."

"Free those being sold as slaves."

"Free those in abusive relationships, Jesus."

"Lord, it is for freedom you have set us free. Come quickly to deliver us from the plans of our enemies."

"Give wisdom to our president, our congress, and our judicial branch, Lord. Give them wisdom that comes from above. Help them to give up selfish ambition and to do what is good and right for our country."

"Make them men and women of honor and integrity."

"Keep our soldiers safe today, Jesus."

"We pray for the peace of Israel."

"Give us your power to be good witnesses today."

"Help us to memorize Scripture."

"Keep us in Your Word, Lord. Keep our feet on the Rock. Deliver us every day from religion and into a deep, abiding relationship with you, Jesus."

"Forgive me for gossiping. Place a guard over my lips."

"Please help me stop swearing."

The Mamas laughed at Brooklyn. She hardly swore at all now, but they remembered when she couldn't get through a whole sentence without at least one expletive.

Struggling with depression, Hannie added, "Comfort the grieving, Lord. Bring health and healing to those suffering from depression and anxiety. Give them tools. Give them medication, if needed. Keep them from shame, and Lord, give them safe friendships to help them navigate the dark waters of mental illness." She dabbed at her eyes, wiping mascara from her lashes. "Thank you for my friends."

Wren reached over and squeezed Hannie's arm.

"Lord, we lift up our missionaries. Bless the feet of those who are bringing the good news of the Gospel to foreign and domestic lands. Let your Word fall on fertile soil. Keep their testimony pure, Lord." Brooklyn prayed for her young daughter. Sophie wanted to be a missionary more than anything on earth.

163

"Strengthen the pastors of our churches, Lord. Guard their marriages and their families. Keep them strong in your Word and let them not turn away from the sufficiency of Scripture. Cause them to preach from your Word, the only thing that will not return void. Hold them fast. Keep them safe." Kate's husband was an elder in their church.

"Comfort those who have lost children today, Father. Thank you that you know just how they feel." Wren had suffered two miscarriages, and she missed Matthew every single day.

The Mamas prayed until the room fell silent once more. They prayed until they were out of words. They fell to their knees every week to gain Christ and to lose themselves. It's the way they were found…

Together.

Chapter 22
To the Brim

*O*n the third day there was a wedding at Cana in Galilee, and the mother of Jesus was there. Jesus also was invited to the wedding with his disciples. When the wine ran out, the mother of Jesus said to him, "They have no wine." And Jesus said to her, "Woman, what does this have to do with me? My hour has not yet come." His mother said to the servants, "Do whatever he tells you."

Now there were six stone water jars there for the Jewish rites of purification, each holding twenty or thirty gallons. Jesus said to the servants, "Fill the jars with water." And they filled them up to the brim. And he said to them, "Now draw some out and take it to the master of the feast." So they took it. When the master of the feast tasted the water now become wine, and did not know where it came from (though the servants who had drawn the water knew), the master of the feast called the bridegroom and said to him, "Everyone serves the good wine first, and when people have drunk freely, then the poor wine. But you have kept the good wine until now." This, the first of his signs, Jesus did at Cana in Galilee, and manifested his glory. And his disciples believed in him." John 2:1-11

The Mamas drove to Red Lodge to do some Christmas shopping. In the car, they talked about Jesus turning water into wine at the wedding in Cana.

"What I want to know is how Mary knew. Jesus had just told her it wasn't his time, right? Then she tells the servants to 'Do whatever he tells you.'" Brooklyn sipped coffee from her go cup.

"I've wondered about that too, but I'm curious about the servants. What must have they been thinking? How many servants were there? I mean, those jars were huge, and brimming with water, they had to weigh a ton!" Hannie dug through her purse for some lip balm.

Wren was thoughtful. "I've thought of that too, Han. Not only did the servants do whatever he told them, but they filled the water jars 'to the brim.' That phrase has always struck me as the call to high obedience."

"Obey Him to the brim." Kate had her hands at ten and two on the wheel of her car. "I like that, Wren."

The friends drove for a time in silence. It was so quiet in the car, they all heard Wren whisper to herself, "I want to obey Jesus like that."

"Me too, Wren," Brooklyn nodded. Her curls bounced on her jacket, and a stray hair floated onto her lap. "I'm pretty good at making excuses when the rubber meets the road. I've made an art form out of justifying why obeying Jesus isn't a good idea, especially when it comes to things like forgiveness and mercy." Brooklyn was thinking of her junior high teacher. She was thinking about the bad boyfriend. "I want forgiveness and mercy for myself, of course, but I don't want to obey Christ by forgiving in return. After all the kindness Jesus has shown me, you wouldn't think that would be hard. I'm the chief of sinners, and that's the truth. I get a little annoyed with the Apostle Paul when he says he is."

"You're not the chief of sinners, Brooklyn. I am." Hannie leaned over the front seat and tapped Brooklyn's shoulder. "You've never been inside my mind."

Kate took a quick glance at her friends. "What do you think would happen in the church if everyone really knew and understood that they were the chief among sinners?" She sighed. "I'm the biggest sinner in the world, and I know that's true. I know it's true of all of us. I don't know how we can—each of us—be the biggest sinner. But we are."

"If everyone really gathered that in, it would make forgiveness and mercy easier because, like Brooklyn said, Jesus has forgiven us so much. It's what drives our love for him, right? I didn't truly understand the Gospel until I grasped that it's all about Christ and His sacrifice for me. He rescued me. He rescued me from such a life…" Wren pulled away from them in her mind as she so often did. She didn't share much about her past—Brooklyn was the one who knew the most about her history—but they all knew she was thinking about her life on the Reservation.

Kate glanced at her in the rearview mirror. "Imagine what a difference it would make in the ways we love each other and the church!"

"It takes understanding what Jesus did and that you're helpless without him to make forgiveness even possible. How can you do it otherwise? How can you ever receive it from others?" Hannie asked.

"And how can you withhold it from others?" Brooklyn felt conviction settle on her again.

The women rode on in silence, thinking about the power of the cross for their own souls, and how it had made such a difference in the ways they were able to love and forgive others.

"Even so. Even knowing all that, I don't obey Jesus to the brim like those servants. And they didn't even know he was the Messiah." Brooklyn sighed heavily. *Why do I love my comfort so?*

"Well, let's do another study!" Kate, the ever-teacher exclaimed. "Let's look more deeply into this story and find out what it means to obey Christ to the brim!"

"I'm thinking it might have something to do with joy." Hannie shrugged her shoulders. "I need more joy in my life."

"Wine symbolizes joy, Hannie, so I'm sure you're right about that." Kate continued, "Can you imagine the servants' joy when they saw the results of their obedience? Nobody else knew! But they sure did!"

As they pulled into town, Hannie exclaimed randomly, "I'm starved!"

"Of course you're starved!" Brooklyn laughed. Hannie had to eat a lot of food to keep weight on, and it was something Brooklyn had learned to delight in.

"Would it be okay if we ate lunch first and shopped afterward?" Hannie zipped up her down parka and put a beanie over her red hair. With no makeup, Hannie looked like a natural in this little mountain town.

Wren turned her face to the sky. Like lazy, paper sheep, the snowflakes drifted down and landed on her long eyelashes.

Kate buttoned her heavy, wool sweater and pulled a red scarf around her neck. The sun glinted off her high cheekbones and her lipstick-red lips made her look like a picture on a postcard.

Brooklyn stood in all her plainness, admiring her beautiful friends without the slightest tinge of jealousy. Thanks to their Bible studies, she was getting free from the world's view of beauty. Her friends were holy, and she thanked God in her mind. *Thank you, Jesus, for these amazing, godly women. Thank you for their help in my life. I'm so grateful.*

The women, bundled in their winter gear, made their way to Bogart's restaurant. Hannie asked for a plate of sour cream enchiladas and a full order of nachos. The waitress raised her eyebrows in question, and all the Mamas laughed.

"I'll have a side of cilantro." Brooklyn smiled, and they laughed again.

The Mamas prayed over their food when it arrived, then Kate raised her water glass. "To the brim, girls! Let's obey Jesus to the brim!"

The Mamas cheered, clinked their glasses, and exclaimed, "To the brim!"

Chapter 23
Prayer Day 3

Brooklyn, Kathryn, Wren, and Hannie stood in the entryway at Kate's house. Kicking off their shoes, they hung their purses on the familiar coat rack. They read text messages—pleas for prayer from friends and family—then silenced their phones and placed them on the wooden bench by the door.

It was prayer day.

Taking little time for conversation, the women moved to Kathryn's bedroom where they fell to their knees in desperation. Brooklyn reached for the tissue box.

Kate closed the door.

Afterward, there would be coffee and more deep calling unto deep. There would be the residue of prayer and the holding of the Father's love for the whole world and for them.

For the Mamas.

Chapter 24
Porn and Poetry

Again?! It was happening *again*???

Hannie felt stupid and ugly and ashamed. "I'm such an idiot," she said aloud to Mark's computer screen. "God! I thought he was getting better!"

Hannie's hope died once more on foreign breasts. Her long fingers trembled on the keyboard of the laptop, and it felt like she'd swallowed an entire block of ice. Tight, cold, hard, sinking. Her life dissolved in the arms of that woman. The one who was more than her. Better than her.

"I'm such an idiot."

The insecurity Hannie had always felt roared to life, and she couldn't hold onto the truth in Proverbs 31. She couldn't hold onto the commitment she'd made to the Mamas to rest in God's definition of beauty.

"You're not enough. You'll never be enough. How can you compete with a woman like that? You're shapeless and skinny. There's nothing womanly about you. Nothing like her. Nothing perfect like her and so not worth it." The destroyer spoke the thoughts into her mind that she'd been fighting her whole adult life.

This just cannot be!

Hannie feared facing Mark. She feared the rising tide within herself because she wanted to do something violent. She wanted to smash the computer screen. She wanted to smash Mark's handsome face. She wanted to smash his heart the way he was smashing hers. Again!

"Oh, God. How can I do this? How can I persevere through this?" Her whispered prayer disappeared with her hope—hope born when she and Mark had first addressed his addiction. Like a mirage. Like a vapor. Poof! Gone.

Hannie sat frozen in front of those bare breasts. The breasts of someone not much older than Madison, and she felt sick. *How could he do this? What a pig!*

How did every woman not feel the way she felt right now?

Ripped off. Violated. Ashamed.

"*The LORD is my shepherd; I shall not want.*" The words from Psalm 23 sprang, unbidden, to her lips. She recalled how the words had come to her last time and how she'd been so upset with Mark, she'd gotten it wrong. ""*The LORD is my shepherd...*" He's all I want," she'd said.

Hannie wanted to slam the laptop shut, but she couldn't. The kids were at Kate's, so she sat and stared. And stared. And stared.

And then Mark came home and saw her. He didn't say anything for a long time but finally managed, "Please close that, Hannie." He put his hand on her shoulder. She shrugged it off.

"Get a chair, Mark." Her voice sounded like it was coming from another room in the house.

"No, Hannie, I'm not going to do that."

"Get a chair and come sit with your wife while we admire the beauty of your lover. One of many, I suppose."

Mark reached over her and slammed the lid. "I don't want you looking at that."

"Why? Is she that precious to you?"

171

Hannie heard, *"I took the cup for you,"* in her mind, and she wanted to scream. *This isn't fair, Lord! I've done the work! I've done my part!* She wasn't putting pressure on Mark to perform for her anymore, and she was careful about nagging him. She'd fixed herself; wasn't that enough? Of course it wasn't, and as Hannie stared at the woman, she thought, *How could it be? Look at me?* Hannie looked down at her flat chest and felt the blow of betrayal afresh. It struck at her person—and to her very soul.

I took the cup for you.

Hannie's world spun.

"The LORD is my shepherd…" He's all I want.

Her mind grasped to understand. It felt like she was thinking backward and forward at once, and somehow, she was able to grasp something important. That "something" hurt more than Mark's addiction, and it cut her.

The Lord wasn't all she wanted. And she was so, "not fixed."

The truth was, all she really wanted was for Mark not to have an addiction to pornography. She may have stopped depending on Mark to be the king of her castle, but the Shepherd King was far from all she wanted.

Hannie groaned. "Oh, God…What am I going to do?" She pulled at the edge of her bob haircut and finally turned to face her husband.

"I'm going to have all the truth, and I'm going to have it now, Mark. If you withhold anything from me in this moment, and if I discover something else, I'm leaving you. I'm not going to put up with your infidelity. Or should I say, infidelities?" Hannie's voice was cold. She didn't want Mark to hear how hurt she was, and it was her old way—anger to hide pain.

She wanted to keep her tears from Mark. She didn't want him to see her cry, but she couldn't help it. Tears poured down her cheeks, and all she could do was shake her head in disgust and disbelief. "I'm such an idiot."

"Okay, Hannie. I'm going to tell you everything, but it's bad. Are you sure?"

Hannie glared at Mark. "Kill me more."

I took the cup for you. The Holy Spirit spoke in her mind, and Hannie's flesh felt like it would literally burst into flames.

She tried again. "Please don't leave anything out. I can't go through this again, Mark. I need full disclosure. What are we really dealing with here?"

"The LORD is my shepherd..." He's all I want.

Hannie felt a shifting in her soul, and she felt it physically in her body. She was turning her hope that Mark would ever be "cured" of his addiction and putting it now on Christ. She knew Mark was never going to be "cured."

Hannie said it over and over in her mind as Mark gave the full disclosure she'd asked for.

"The LORD is my shepherd..." He's all I want.

Right now, Hannie wanted to vomit.

"Who are you, really, Mark Cohen?" She stared at him, repulsed by him.

"I'm a man with an addiction, Han. I'm a man who's been lying to the guys in recovery group. I'm a man who's been unfaithful to his wife, who's put her health in danger, and who's violated his covenant of marriage. I'm a disgusting man. I'm a shameful man, and I'm a broken man." Mark's words tumbled out. "Hard as it may be to believe, I'm a man who loves you and who loves his kids. That's who I am, and now you know it all. There's nothing else."

Hannie didn't ask him to promise. She was too tired. What did his words mean to her now, anyway?

"Don't leave me, Hannie," Mark's voice was heavy with sorrow.

"Why not?" Hannie's voice held no edge, no meanness, and no bitterness. It was dead. She felt dead.

"I'll call Brian Norris right now and confess everything to him. You know he's in the group with us guys even though he's been clean since he was a teenager."

"Yes. Do that." Hannie didn't feel anything, though the tears coursed down her face. "And go live with your brother for a few weeks. I need space from you. I need room to process my pain without trying to rescue you from yours. That's done."

"What else can I do?" Mark faced Hannie. "I'll do anything."

"You need to get tested for STDs." Hannie felt like a puppet in a puppet show, and she wondered who was pulling the strings to make her mouth move. "You need to move out of our bedroom, and you need to take the kids to the Mamas. YOU need to tell the Mamas—not details, but you need to let them know what's going on here. I'm not going to shield you, Mark."

"Okay. I'll do that." Mark rolled up the sleeve on his denim shirt. He did it unconsciously, but Hannie knew this about him…

"You can't outwork this thing, Mark. You can't 'work harder' anymore. You have to let Jesus be strong in your weakness, but you can't do that if you're lying to everyone." Great. Now she was preaching at him.

"*The* LORD *is my shepherd…*" He's all I want.

The words rang again in her mind. *What am I going to do now, Lord?*

He makes me lie down in green pastures.

The third sentence in Psalm 23 was for her. Hannie knew it was the Lord. For the first time since Mark had first confessed his addiction, she realized how tired she was. Hannie had been carrying this burden for a long time, and she'd thought she was winning the battle. She knew that just as Mark wasn't going to be able to "try harder" to defeat pornography, Hannie couldn't "try harder" to be a better wife. She had to stop comparing herself to these other women. She had to stop waiting for the other shoe to drop. She had to rest, and the words of the Good Shepherd brought her a small hope.

He makes me like down in green pastures.

"Get your stuff now, Mark. I'll pack the kids for the Mamas. I need two weeks to rest and figure out what's next. You can tell the kids whatever you want."

"Okay."

Hannie saw the shame in his face, and she knew his heart must be breaking. His hand covered his chest. She suddenly noticed the familiar scars on Mark's hands, the ones he'd gotten fixing her car.

It was the scars that made her start sobbing. Mark was the man who had taken care of their family so well—the man who had kept everything in perfect working order. He was the man who loved the Lord and whom she knew was hurting.

Jesus had scars on his hands too, and Hannie let the power of the cross move her mind, body, and soul.

Mark reached to hold her, but she pulled away.

"I'm sorry, Hannie. Do you know I'm sorry?" He barely whispered the words.

Hannie nodded but said nothing. She wasn't going to try to be his savior anymore. She wasn't going to hold him accountable, and she wasn't going to spy on him. Something big had changed, and she felt grown up in a new way, somehow—a much bigger way. Hannie was going to trust in Christ to help her through this. She knew she had to. She knew she could.

He makes me like down in green pastures.

After Mark and the kids left, Hannie went to her room and picked up her Bible from the nightstand. She flipped to Psalm 23. The familiar statement she'd written in the margin stood out as if the letters were raised.

The LORD is my shepherd; I shall not want. He's all I want.
He makes me lie down in green pastures.
He leads me beside still waters.
He restores my soul.
He leads me in paths of righteousness for his name's sake.
Even though I walk through the valley of the shadow of death, I will fear no evil,
for you are with me; your rod and your staff, they comfort me.

Hannie curled into a fetal ball on her bed. The bed she and Mark had consummated their marriage in. "I'm going to rest, Jesus. I'm going to rest in You. Please show me how."

Hannie fell asleep.

She rested. She woke, ate the food left by the Mamas, and drank water.

She prayed for Mark.

And rested some more.

Hannie clung to the verses in Psalm 23. She'd never felt weaker in her life, but she couldn't deny the experience of Jesus pouring his power and healing into her heart. On the outside, she could barely stand. On the inside, she began to feel more alive than she'd ever been.

As she obeyed the Lord to rest and lie down in green pastures, she stopped doing almost all her normal activities. Knowing this season of rest was going to take some time, she called her church. She couldn't staff the nursery for a while. She stopped hosting Bible study in her home. Mentoring young women was put on hold and visiting the elderly in the nursing home got rescheduled.

Hannie rested. She stopped trying to be good, and for the first time in her life, she just wanted to be *godly*.

The Mamas let themselves into Hannie's house every day. They brought in the mail, straightened the kitchen, and stocked the fridge.

They left notes on Tupperware and jars of smoothies. "Eat all of this, Hannie-girl. Drink all of this."

And she obeyed.

The Mamas left tea, chocolate, and fruit. They brought notes from her kids. Wren left the Wonder Woman cuffs on the counter next to a bouquet of wild roses. She always left a Kiss.

Sometimes, but not always, Hannie wrote a note back, "Please come upstairs and hold my hand."

The Mamas went up and held their friend so that she could hold on.

"It's going to be okay, Hannie. We're going to be here until it is." Brooklyn brushed Hannie's deep red hair.

Hannie thought about Will, Brian, and Steve, as much as she thought about the Mamas. The men had rallied around Mark and were meeting him every day.

"Mark's in good hands, Hannie. We all love him so." Brooklyn choked on her words. Emotion strangled her.

Hannie knew Mark's suffering was untellable, but she waved her hand in the air to cut Brooklyn off. "I can't hear it yet, Brook. Not yet, okay?"

Brooklyn finished brushing Hannie's hair, then bent to kiss her cheek. The words fell from her mouth. "You are loved., Hannie." She squeezed her friend's hand and spoke the ancient truth of God into Hannie's ears.

"You are loved. You are loved. You are loved. You are loved."

Chapter 25
Fragments of Loss

It was Valentine's Day.

And just as she did every year, Brooklyn sat cross-legged on her bedroom floor with a box of tissues in her lap. She held a few ragged pieces of paper in her hands, pages from an old journal. She remembered being young and lost and ashamed. She remembered how alone she felt. Brooklyn held the fraying pages of memory in her trembling hands.

Every year, she read the words aloud and wondered if the baby could hear her. Brooklyn never wanted to forget. She never wanted to let go. While she couldn't change the reality of the consequence of this loss, or the fruit of grief it bore in her life, she could take this day. To remember. To speak of her. To give honor and carry her name to the family waiting downstairs. Brooklyn read the aging words, and her tears fell in heavy drops. They were added to the wrinkled water marks from years of Valentine's days marching like soldiers—on and on, and closer and closer...*To her.*

Fragments

I remember you.

I took a pregnancy test alone in the fieldhouse at school.

I pushed garbage cans against the door so nobody could get in.

Shame doesn't share.

I remember the way I peed on the stick.

And on my shaking hands.

My heart pounded fear. Cold sweat dripped down my back.

Because I knew…

I had you.

And when the test gave me a plus.

I knew I was a minus.

I moved in slow motion.

To put the garbage cans, a lasting metaphor, back against the wall.

To throw the test away.

To vomit fear after it.

And to sit in a dark stall for hours and hours.

Crying and shaking.

Deciding…

Alone.

I remember you.

I was a college work-study student.

Eighteen and broke.

I stole apples on the walk home. Dinner.

I remembered calling the doctor.

He asked how much money I had.

"Five dollars," my reply.

179

He laughed out loud and said I would need two hundred. CASH.

Oh, God. Oh, God. Oh, God.

I put my hands over my stomach.

Over you.

I prayed that I would die.

That God would take us both together.

So that no one would ever know.

That I had you.

That I held you safe in my young womb.

For now.

I remember you.

I remember holding my choice.

Holding my decision.

Deciding to take your life, my daughter.

So nobody would know...

What kind of daughter I had become.

I took a long walk with a safe friend.

Telling.

You must be known somehow.

Because I couldn't afford to throw your life away.

I needed help for that.

"Are you sure, Brooklyn?"

My friend gave me money I know she didn't have either.

And I smeared blood on her hands.

I remember you.

The night before, I laid awake all night.

My hands rested on my flat stomach.

Holding you.

I stared into the *darkness.*

I felt the *darkness.*
I knew what I was going to do.
Would make me forever a child of the *dark.*

What hope for me?
A woman who destroyed everything.
Tears left their warm trail.
And pooled in my ears.
As I cried silently.
At all hope of heaven for me, lost.
Forever...

I remember you.
And the very worst day.
I went to his office.
Another pregnancy test and another plus.
Another minus.
The doctor talked a long time to make sure.
"Brooklyn, are you sure?"
I saw myself talking to him too, but—
I didn't feel connected to that confident woman.
I was scared.
Alone.
I felt lost.

I remember you.
As I stood to shake his hand, he told me to get a gown and lay down.
Get a gown and lay down.
On a table that would bring death today.

And I moved numb.

I obeyed every command.

The nurse watched my face, but I couldn't meet her eyes.

Her voice was hushed.

As I lay back on the crinkly white paper.

A sound I would remember the rest of my life.

We three began it...
Taking you.

I remember you.

I lay exposed.

Naked from my navel.

My bellybutton.

That divoted reminder of the nourishment and safety of my mother's womb.

The doctor inserted a suction tube, and I grew cold.

And dead.

He sucked you away from me, my girl.

He sucked the life out of us.

And I wanted to say,

"Stop!"

"Stop this madness and this cruelty and this crime!"

Stop this *choice.*

Because all I could think about was you.

Holding you.

But I couldn't speak.

My voice was being sucked away too.

Even as the silent plea pounded in my head.

"Stop!"

"Stop!"

The nurse said, "You're doing great, Brooklyn."
The doctor was proud of me.
"Amazing self-control."
I stifled a bitter laugh.
Self-control.

My whole life was spinning wildly.
My ears were pitched keenly to the sound of suction.
Unforgettable sound.
Cramps tore us in two.
Tore you apart.
I cried out, and it felt like the earth shook with shame.
With pain.

But the pain was right.
Just.
Just what I deserved.
And it wasn't enough.
I knew...
It wouldn't ever be enough.
I remember you.
And at last, we were through.
They had you, baby.
And I laid dead and dying and dying.
The doctor said,
"We got it, Brooklyn. Everything looks good."
And I wanted to rip out his tongue.
There, in a rose-colored catch dish.
Floating in blood and water.
Was what was left of you.
And he called you, "It."

I remember you.
I rolled to my side and sobbed.
Baring my whole backside, uncaring.
I shook the whole table of death.
With wailing sobs of grief.
Because I had lost you.
And because I'd lost me too.

The doctor yelled at me.
"What is wrong with you girls?"
"You all come in so sure."
"And you all respond this way."
"Over a stupid ballast of cells."
"That bears no life and..."
"LOOK AT ME! LOOK AT THIS!"

He shoved the rose-pink dish in my face.
So I could see.
The mangled mess I'd made.
And so I could feel.
The full weight of what I'd done.
The death of hope and promise floated there.
And it made me cry harder.

I remember you.
He yelled again. His face contorted in rage looked unhuman.
"Get up! Get dressed! *Get out!*"
"I'm not doing this anymore. You're all the same."
He stormed out of the room with his white coattails flapping.
He slammed them in the door.
Opened again. Slammed again.

Harder.

Louder.

I remember you.

As I laid on that white paper bawling.

The nurse brought me a teddy bear and tucked it into my arms.

Empty arms. Empty life. *Empty soul.*

She traced my face with her fingers and said,

"Take your time, Brooklyn."

I wept my life and yours until I threw up grief.

The floor was splattered with my humanity.

And the nurse was not so patient now.

"Time to get up and go," she said.

Get up and go where? I wondered.

Yes...

Of course...

Get up and go to hell.

I remember you.

Numb and dead, I dressed.

I walked out the door to a beautiful summer.

Where wild pink roses bloomed everywhere.

Pink roses.

The color of your little coffin.

Back there.

One foot in front of the other.

I Walked.

I Drove.

I Left...

Alone.

The days blurred on.
And I embraced what I knew was not true.
Because it was the only way I could breathe.
"Just a ballast of cells."
Cells...
The spark of life.

I remember you.
And I wanted to die too.
I wanted to take the easy way out.
Give me what I deserve!
Maybe that would ease the pain.
"No!"
To live a life of pain.
THAT!
Is what I deserved.
It's the only way I knew how to atone...
For murder.

But my pain atoned for nothing.
I slept every night with my hands over my stomach.
I felt all the loss of you.
And the only comfort I had.
Was staring into the night holding where you once were.
Knowing that I had you once.
That once...
You were mine.
And that once...
You were alive.

I remember you.

And those silent tears again.

Because I was living death every day...

Alone.

Where no church could restore me.

No priest could absolve me.

No person could know me.

No love could hold me.

No light could find me.

No husband could reassure me.

No children could change me.

No life could be returned to me...

No life.

No life!

I was a body of death.

And it hung on me.

I remember you.

I tried to live a moral life.

But it was a joke.

After blowing it like that?

It doesn't matter.

Nothing mattered, really.

When.

You know who you *are*.

And you know what you've *done*.

For me, that meant I hid my life.

From my parents and my siblings.

From my friends.

From my children.

187

Because if they knew who I really was...
They'd take me outside the camp.
And stone me.

I remember you.
And somewhere in my mind, I remembered someone else.
A story.
About a woman caught in adultery.
Me.
A story from the Bible.
About a woman taken by a mob of men.
To be stoned to death for her sin. For her crime.
And...
Wasn't there something in that story about Jesus?
And...
Was it even possible that Jesus looked a bit different?
Than what I had been taught?

Those men picked up stones.
While Jesus stooped to write in the dirt.
And I stood quivering in a strange kind of hope.
Waiting for what was to come.
For what I deserved.
Even though I was sorry.
So sorry.

I remember you.
I lay under my covers of darkness.
Hands holding a belly that would never hold you again.
I said it out loud to black.
I whispered it at first.

188

Then this most desperate grieving sob of the soul.
"Jesus, Son of David, Have mercy on me!"
Over and Over.
"Have mercy on me, Jesus!"
A sinner. The worst of sinners.

Like the woman in the story, I waited for rock to strike flesh.
It was a holy moment somehow.
Finally.
Justice would be done.
And my little daughter's life.
Would mean something. To someone.
And my life. Would mean nothing.
To no one ...
Justice.

I remember you.
The Rock of Salvation struck me hard.
This Jesus.
Spared my life.
This Jesus.
Forgave me.
He cast his arm around me and scattered the mob.
He looked upon me with love.
Compassion.
Go. I paid the penalty for your crime.
He said, *"Go. And sin no more."*
Go. Brooklyn. And live!

I remember you.
I could breathe for the first time in years.
I felt light and whole and free.
The love of Jesus wrapped me in grace
And warmth. And acceptance.
(And you wonder why I love Him?)

But…
But what was this?
This feeling that came over me?
When I was in the Body of Christ.
Among men and women who were champions.
Of life and defending the unborn.
What was it that made me want to crawl?
Under the biggest rock.
Give me my shame grave.
Because when my brothers and sisters in Christ said,
"How could anyone throw the life of a child away?"
I nodded numb.
Silent.
It was true!

And what of friends?
When they miscarried and lost life and love?
And their husbands said,
"Millions of women are killing their unborn babies."
"Why would God take a child my wife and I so wanted?"

I remember you.
I felt it hard, and I was ashamed again.
I knew that in Christ all was forgiven.

That you were with Him.

But the Body cut deep.

And my life cut too.

So, I withdrew into the shadows.

Shhh…

I didn't speak.

The price of sin was that you lay in a silent grave.

My mouth.

When Wren miscarried her son.

I went to my room and curled into a fetal ball.

Like a baby.

I sobbed for them both.

And for me.

And for *us.*

Because Wren didn't deserve to lose her son.

I deserved this pain. This shame.

I could barely reach for the Savior's hand.

"Oh, Jesus."

"This cruel lie that is abortion."

"That it's a solution somehow."

I wished I was dead.

Wren. Incomprehensible. *Wren!*

She took my hand and welcomed me into her grief.

For a little boy.

And she said,

"Tell me about your little girl."

And for the first time in years...

There was a spark in the dark.

That my daughter was known by someone.

That someone wanted to know her.
To know *me,* even so.
Wren said...
"Tell me, Brooky."
And all I could do was cry.

I remember you.
And I sensed your life when I spoke about you.
You were sacred to Wren, to me, and to God.
And suddenly I couldn't stop talking about you.
To everyone, but especially to the family.
Will and the kids cried for you.
And the Mamas cried for you too.
And for the first time since I lost you.
I wasn't alone.
They held my hand and said, "I'm sorry."
They wiped my tears, and we named you.
And we celebrate you now on Valentine's Day.
Because love like that is a miracle.
And grace like that is unfathomable.

I remember you.
And when Shame stalks me still.
And Silence is his weapon.
I place my hands on my belly and hold where you once were.
Knowing I will one day...
One day, my love...
Hold you again.

Brooklyn folded the tear-stained pages of her journal and tucked them into a box. She stood and straightened her blouse. She blew her nose.

Downstairs, she knew there would be balloons and cake. There would be flowers and Will. There would be Jake, Sophie, Derek, Abe, and Maylee.

There would be the Mamas.

There would be life.

Chapter 26
3M

As a writer, Brooklyn couldn't live without Post-it notes. They helped her organize her freelance editing projects, her articles for magazines, interview notes, and random thoughts about characters for her books. Post-its were stuck all over her office walls with little lines of poetry that came as she worked. Yes, she had a computer for all of that, but she was old school, and she liked the feel of paper and pen in her hands.

As she twirled in her office chair, she read all her lines of poetry from the colored squares stuck to her walls. *If only they all fit together. They would make a book in themselves.*

The Post-its reminded Brooklyn of her daughter, Maylee and her friends. The Mamas had started calling their daughters, Margaret, Madison, and Maylee—3M—almost as soon as they met. The girls were tight, and even at a young age, they were intentional about their friendship. They'd even started praying together on their knees!

Maylee announced to Brooklyn when she had only been ten, "Mama, I love my big sister Sophie with all my heart, and you know she's my hero, but Margaret and Madison are like soul sisters."

It was true. The girls had a special relationship, and the Mamas often prayed for them.

Brooklyn was doodling on a Post-it, waiting for inspiration to strike. She remembered how all three girls had surrounded her after they'd found out about her abortion.

"Mama Brooklyn, I'm so sorry about what happened." Margaret wrapped her long, thin arms around Brooklyn's waist. She was going to be as pretty as Kate.

"I didn't know." Madi was more emotional, and she started to cry. "I didn't know." She rushed into Brooklyn's arms.

None of the girls could say the word, and even Brooklyn still struggled.

"Abortion."

"Oh, girls!" Brooklyn was overwhelmed. "Are you okay? Are we okay? I'm so very sorry I made that decision. It was wrong, and I feel it every day. Do you forgive me?"

"We're okay, Mama. We forgive you." Madi's voice was muffled by Brooklyn's blouse.

"Things could get a little rough on you girls, you know. The Lord has set me free from shame, and I'm going to write about abortion in one of my next articles. You might experience some pushback from your homeschool friends." Brooklyn had felt it so often herself. The heavy judgment of unknowing Christians.

"I want you to tell your story, Mama B! If kids don't like us because you're telling the truth about something awful, that's their problem. We're sticking with you." Margaret, named for Margaret Thatcher, was herself, a feisty one.

"You all are truly amazing; do you know that?" Brooklyn pulled the girls into a group hug.

"These girls are the best, Mama." Maylee was so proud of her friends.

I know how you feel.

Brooklyn twirled again in her chair and looked down at a Post-it. There, she had drawn three stick figures of little girls. They held hands and had little colored notes on their dresses that read: "3M! TLA!"

What would they be like as adults? Would their friendship last? Margaret and Madison were well into puberty, and Maylee wasn't far behind. What would they be like as teenagers?

Brooklyn spun her chair again as if it would help her spin a new idea for the article she was working on. Her mind was on all the kids though. The Mamas were in the throes of teenagers now, all of them oozing hormones and emotions and attitudes. Things were changing.

The Mamas were feeling it.

"Does anyone besides me feel like we're exiting the golden years of raising kids?" Brooklyn had asked after prayer one morning.

"There's a shift, for sure." Kate sipped her coffee and made her usual confession. "Forgive me, Mum. Forgive me, England."

"I'm a little worried about all our kids, Mamas. There's so much change happening so fast. What happens if they stop loving each other like they do? And what happens if they start loving each other—you know, *loving* each other?"

"That'll be awfully tight, won't it?" Kate's accent. Brooklyn still couldn't get over it.

"Or…really wonderful. Who wouldn't want y'all for a mother-in-law?" Hannie smiled.

"I think we might be in for some rough weather, gals," Brooklyn warned. "I just want to say that no matter what the storm, I'm in the boat with you." She was thinking about her son Derek and Kate's son, Ethan. They were both still goofy, but they'd matured a lot in the last year. The girls were already taking notice.

"The enemy is upping his game against our kids. You can see that, can't you?" Brooklyn was sensitive to the realm of darkness. "It's like the whole world has gone crazy, and I can't imagine the pressure these kids are under."

Wren was quiet, taking in what her friends were saying. After losing Matthew, her boys were so much younger than the other kids, she didn't have much to say about it. "All I know is that no matter how hard it gets with these kids, to have the privilege to pray for them means everything to me. I don't have that with Mattie anymore. He's gone. I don't think he ever really wandered from the Lord, but even if he had been a rip-roaring rebel, you know…just to have the honor and privilege to pray for him…well, I wouldn't wish it away for anything."

Brooklyn reached for Wren's hand. What more could be said?

"Whatever comes, Mamas, we go through together." Hannie pulled on the edge of her bob. "We keep loving each other's kids and husbands, no matter what."

"No matter what." There was a charge in Wren's voice.

Kate lifted her coffee cup. "And to the brim!"

***

Her thoughts returning to the present, Brooklyn tore off the Post-it note of 3M and stuck it to her wall. "The Lord bless you, girls," she said to the doodle. "And keep you together always."

Inspiration struck her, and Brooklyn was off and writing.

Chapter 27
Prayer Day 4

Brooklyn, Kathryn, Wren, and Hannie stood in the entryway at Kate's house. Kicking off their shoes, they hung their purses on the old coat rack. They read more text messages–pleas for prayer from their kids, their friends and family, and even their community. Then they silenced their phones and placed them on the wooden bench by the door.

It was prayer day.

The women moved to Kathryn's bedroom and fell to their knees. Brooklyn was already reaching for the tissue as Kate closed the door.

Afterward, there would be coffee. And sometimes more stories. And sometimes, only the comfortable quiet that comes from spending an hour with the Savior. It was good to know that He loved them. It was good that He was teaching them how to love.

The Mamas.

Chapter 28
Puberty Works!

It was a good thing puberty worked because Brooklyn's daughter, Maylee, was a hot mess!

Brooklyn tried to comfort her. "Baby, nobody escapes puberty, okay? You only pass through these waters once in your life, so try to enjoy it as much as you can!"

Brooklyn got "the look" and knew her intended encouragement wasn't landing right.

"Look, honey, it doesn't have to be awful. We can make it fun! Let's go shopping and get you a cute bag for feminine supplies." Brooklyn grabbed her keys and shouldered her purse. "In what life does having a new bag not fix a few problems?"

"Mom! I'm not buying tampons or pads!" Maylee's misery squeezed out of her like ripe acne. It wasn't bad, considering, but Brooklyn overheard Maylee call herself "pizza face," and there was nothing Brooklyn could do to comfort her. "I'll die of embarrassment if you make me buy those!"

"You know, I remember my dad going to…"

"I know, Mom," she drawled, rolling her eyes as Brooklyn recounted the tale.

She guessed she'd told the story too many times.

Maylee slipped her thin arms into a jacket. "He went to the warehouse shopping center and pulled cases of pads and tampons onto his shopping truck for you and your sisters."

"And he didn't seem embarrassed at all, so why should you be?" Brooklyn still admired her dad. She wondered what had been going through his mind. What had it been like for him to have five daughters? *What a superhero.*

Brooklyn brushed Maylee's gorgeous hair back from her face, admiring her light-green eyes. "Let's go."

Taking her kids for drives was Brooklyn's favorite place to talk to them about serious things. They referred to the tradition as "car talk." As she and Maylee hopped into the car, Brooklyn broached the sensitive subject again. Maybe within the confines of "car talk" her daughter would be more open to listening.

"Listen, honey, I know you've not started your period yet, but let's get some things out in the open," Brooklyn said, slipping on her sunglasses and putting the car in drive. "You're going to need me, Maylee, and the truth is, even though I'm old, I need you too." Brooklyn glanced out of the corner of her eye to make sure Maylee was listening. The set of her head told Brooklyn she was all ears.

Thank you, Jesus!

"Once you start your period, you need to be careful about keeping your body clean. It can make a real stink if you're not careful." Brooklyn decided not to go into more detail; she could cover that later once Maylee started. "I promise to tell you if you smell, okay? Because if you're not hearing it from your mom, who are you going to hear it from, right?"

Maylee nodded.

Brooklyn continued. "And you can tell me if I stink too, okay? My super sniffer isn't what it used to be." She tried to keep it light, but she knew she wasn't funny.

Maylee shuddered but surprised Brooklyn with a giggle. "Probably from all the poopy diapers you've changed in your life." Maylee had signed up to work in the nursery at church but quit as soon as she found out she had to change diapers. Like her father, Maylee hated messy diapers. It was the reason she wouldn't babysit kids who weren't potty trained. Maybe it was even the reason she didn't really like kids.

"Right?" Brooklyn smiled, thankful Maylee was listening. "The other thing I want you to know is that—as emotional as we can be—we don't get to use our periods as an excuse to sin."

A long silence filled the car, and so did conviction. She thought about all the times she used her period as an excuse to be selfish or to lash out—especially at Will.

"I need your help with this as much as you need mine, May. When you have cramps and you feel awful, it's hard to be kind. It's hard not to make everyone around you suffer. It's especially hard to stay faithful to your work." Brooklyn felt blood rush into her face. *Lord, forgive me.* "You've got to do your best, Maylee. Take your pain and discomfort to the Lord, or to me, or at the very least, to your own room. Remember how much Jesus suffered and know He understands. He was a man, but He made women, and He understands."

Brooklyn reached over and squeezed Maylee's knee. "I fail at this a lot, my girl. I'm not kidding when I say I need your help. Sophie checks me all the time, and I'm giving you permission to call me on it too. It might be the only time in your life you get to send your mom to her room! It's part of the sisterhood you're about to enter. I need my girls. We need each other."

"Is it going to hurt, Mama?"

Brooklyn loved that her kids still called her Mama. "Every woman is different. Some women don't have any pain, and others suffer a great deal. I don't think you're going to have any problems, but if you do, just know I'm here to support you."

Brooklyn pulled into the mall where Maylee picked out a small, feminine backpack. She swung her still-narrow hips through checkout, and the smile on her face was priceless.

"It's so cute! I love it!"

Once back in the car, Maylee looked through all the compartments in her new bag. "I like it a lot, and I think we can get some 'supplies' now, don't you?" Maylee buckled her seatbelt and clutched her new bag as though it was already filled with mini mysteries. She was embracing change.

Two steps forward, one step back—from now until the grave, baby.

"That will be our third stop of the day. The next stop is to get you some cute bras."

"What? Really?" Maylee squealed like a…like a girl and squirmed in her seat. "Oh, Mama, thank you! I don't know if you noticed it or not, but somebody's getting *lumpy* in certain places, if you know what I mean!"

Brooklyn laughed out loud. "As a matter of fact, I have noticed!" In her mind's eye, she saw the box of old, scratchy bras her mother had thrown at her. She felt all the goodness of redemption, and she giggled alongside Maylee.

"Get something soft and pretty. Something comfortable and supportive."

"Mama, thanks!" Maylee leaned over to hug Brooklyn. "I mean it. Thank you so much!"

"It's the least I can do for a little girl becoming a woman right before my eyes."

"Why does it feel scary sometimes?" Maylee picked at the fraying edge of her shorts.

"Your body is changing so fast, May; it's hard to keep up. Sometimes, you'll feel like you're running a fever. Sometimes, you'll feel like a stranger to yourself. You just need to have faith in the process. God designed it, so you can trust it."

Maylee had long, long eyelashes and the most adorable freckles. She was going to be a stunning woman, but Brooklyn was going to miss this little one.

"There are going to be times you feel it's unfair because you don't have a choice in this, my darling. You can only go forward now and not back." Brooklyn brushed Maylee's youthful cheek with the back of her hand. A sob welled in her chest, but she quelled it. Quiet. Brooklyn didn't always understand the Lord's ways. Having something happen to your body that you didn't ask for and you couldn't stop seemed harsh. She remembered puberty. She remembered the nightmares. The result was fine, but oh…the process!

"I feel like an alien is taking over my body, Mama. I just feel strange. Sometimes I like the changes and sometimes, they make me want to cry. It makes me feel crazy." Maylee's long, brown curls rolled over her shoulder like waves of change.

"I remember that feeling. I even felt sick sometimes." Brooklyn pulled into the specialty store that sold bras. She wanted this to be as good an experience for Maylee as possible. She smiled at her daughter and squeezed her knee once more. "What do you say? Should we give the girls some love and support?" She winked, and Maylee smiled back.

"If it will do something to help 'the lumps.'"

Brooklyn laughed and shook her head. "That's my girl. What a good sport!" The familiar tears that came with the agony of love pricked her eyes. "And guess what? Once you start your period, I'll take you to get your ears pierced."

"Yeah! Finally!" Maylee rolled her eyes at Brooklyn as they stepped into the shop. "Are you sure I have to wait? I'm the only girl in the whole wide world who doesn't have pierced ears."

"Really?" Brooklyn poked her finger gently into Maylee's ribs. "The only girl in the whole, wide world, huh?"

Maylee was nervous and excited as they entered the store. The staff gushed over their newest customer and treated Maylee like a princess. She picked out some pretty bras in childish colors, and Brooklyn was glad to see lots of pink and purple going into her basket.

Just a little longer, Lord! Brooklyn blessed the staff under her breath and prayed the day would hold a good memory for her daughter. *My Maylee.*

Chatting without taking a breath, Maylee left the store with a floral print, paper bag hanging off her wrist. She skipped across the parking lot to the car, and Brooklyn watched her. She held her breath as if it could hold time.

Brooklyn tucked the sight of Maylee deep in her memory—these precious, last glimpses…of her little girl.

Chapter 29
Prayer Day 5

Brooklyn, Kathryn, Wren, and Hannie stood in the entryway at Kate's house. Holding onto the wall for balance, they took off their shoes and hung their purses on the coat rack. They read text messages—pleas for prayer from the kids, their family and friends, and their community. The Mamas even got prayer requests now from people around the world.

After silencing their phones, they placed them on the wooden bench by the door.

It was prayer day.

The women moved to Kathryn's bedroom and fell to their knees.

Brooklyn reached for the tissue.

Kate closed the door.

Afterward, there would be coffee. And sometimes more stories. And sometimes, only the comfortable quiet that comes from spending an hour with the Savior.

But sometimes? Sometimes, there was so much heartache and pain and loss and grief that they could only sit in silence and stare. They wiped their eyes and blew their noses and had no words to speak. They felt scared and small, and they didn't know what to do.

The Mamas.

Chapter 30
The Mamas Are Screwed

The Mamas are screwed!" Brooklyn set her coffee cup down too hard. Its contents sloshed over the side and spilled on the table.

"Brooky! Please don't use that word!" Wren rebuked her friend.

The Mamas knew how much Brooklyn struggled with her language, but Kate raised an eyebrow. They'd been praying on their knees for years now. They were all getting wrinkles and going gray.

It was the teenagers.

"It's a terrible word, Brook." Hannie agreed. "But it's an honest one."

"Help me think of another then." Brooklyn blotted the spill with a napkin. "Because I'm about to lose it! I'm walking on eggshells all the time! If I ask the kids to do anything, and I mean aaaanything, it's like they're being burned at the stake!"

Kate, too, thunked down her coffee cup. "Do you know I asked Brian to talk to Margaret last night about her attitude toward me, and he rolled his eyes? My husband rolled his eyes at me!"

"Don't get me started, Kate." Brooklyn's eyes bulged a little. "Will keeps asking me, 'What do you want me to do?' I don't know! I want him to fix it! I want him to *fix* them!" Her cheeks grew warm. Her rosacea had flared up again. She could feel the heat in her skin and recalled the conversation with her dermatologist.

"Isn't there something more you can do?" Brooklyn was self-conscious of her skin.

"I'm sorry, Mrs. Wyer. It's the Luck o' the Irish, as they say." He tried to say it with an Irish accent and blushed. It was terrible. "You're not a drinker, are you?"

"No. I don't drink at all."

"Is there any particular reason, or just because of your skin?"

"I've got three particular reasons and none of them to do with my skin: my heritage, my personal history, and the fact that I have five children." Brooklyn couldn't count the times she'd thanked God for her personal decision not to drink while raising her kids. Homeschooling alone could drive someone to drink. But now? With the teenagers?

Brooklyn sat cross-legged on Kate's couch and pushed her curly hair out of her face with a shaky hand.

"Y'all, we've been doing life together awhile now, but I still thought I was the only one." Hannie, makeup free and gorgeous, screwed up her face. She was physically cringing. "I can't get my teenagers to do their schoolwork or their house chores. You'd think me asking them to walk their dog was like asking them to walk to the electric chair. And Mark! Mr. Wonderful and Helpful? He's not helpful at all, and I'm starting to think he's not so wonderful either!"

"Don't you just want to shout, 'Engage! Engage!'" Kate's English accent seemed to accent their misery.

"I'm so exasperated with everyone; I want to run away!" Brooklyn had to confess this recurring fantasy.

"These teenagers. Seventeen and nature's king! All they can think about is themselves, and I know we didn't raise them that way. Good grief! I'll take the good old days of sleep deprivation and trying to keep everyone fed and alive to this chronic worry. What are they watching?

What are they listening to? Where are they going? Who are they with?" Kate sighed. "Lord, I'm so tired."

"Don't they know we just want them to be safe? Don't they know we have their best interest at heart? Sometimes, I get so depressed I can hardly get out of bed." Hannie pulled the edge of her hair.

Brooklyn's Irish temper flared. "I tell you what. I'd like to give my kids a real piece of my mind! I gave up my career, my body, and my own adventures to give them a shot at their dreams. I gave them the kind of education that taught them to think for themselves. And this attitude of theirs! They treat the Mama who used to be their superhero as if she's now a drooling idiot! Ugh! I can't stand it! The Mamas are screwed, Wren! They just are!"

Kate leaned forward in her chair. "Do you know what Ethan asked Brian last night?" Her tone told them she was still in shock. "He actually said, 'What does Mom do all day, anyway? And what do you do, Dad, because it seems like all you do is talk on the phone!'"

All the Mamas jerked back in their chairs.

"Oh, Kate. Is the boy still alive? What did Brian do?"

"He ignored the comment about him being on the phone all day, but Ethan asked the question at dinner." Kate grabbed her coffee cup and laughed out loud. "Brian picked up Ethan's dinner plate, pushed all the food onto his own, and raved about my cooking the rest of the meal."

"Now that's being Mr. Wonderful, right there, y'all." Hannie lifted her coffee cup in salute to Kate's husband. "Did Ethan get the point?"

"Who knows? All I know is how much he complained about being hungry the entire night!"

"I mean...I do feel for these kids. The culture is rotten, but are we insane for having expectations? Is it a crime? I feel like I can't expect anything from my kids because they're so fragile. I didn't raise my kids to be fragile! I raised them to be helpful and hardworking!" Hannie took a sip of coffee.

"Right? And—don't laugh at me girls—but I thought homeschooling was going to be the answer. The answer! I thought by using all the right curriculum, by doing devotions, by reading and working on projects together, none of this would happen!" Brooklyn couldn't help blushing at her naivety.

"Oh, Brook, I'm so much worse than that!" Kate's eyes were smiling. "I used to believe my teenagers would never treat me the way I saw other teens treating their parents. I used to think, and I used to say, 'Teenagers aren't that hard! What is wrong with all these parents?'"

The Mamas laughed. It helped with the pain.

Brooklyn loved Kate for confessing it. "Me too, Kate. I did the exact same thing. Just like when I told myself my kids' car seats would never have french fries in them. It's the same thing! Only so much worse!" Brooklyn couldn't help laughing. It all seemed so stupid and funny—if only the reality of raising teenagers wasn't so brutal.

"Okay, okay, Mamas. You about done?" Wren took a sip of her coffee and pulled back on the reins. "Take a breath, will you? Your children are amazing. I love them all so much. Just remember, the way you're feeling about your kids is probably the same way Jesus feels about you—only He's nice." She couldn't help joining in their laughter. Wren's kids were younger than the rest of the Mamas kids, but the heavy loss of Matthew clung to all of them. "And don't forget. You have the privilege of praying for them."

The Mamas remembered Matt. They sat in silence, thinking of how he used to fling his long, black braid over his shoulder. They remembered Matt's warm smile, his humor, and the special way he had loved them all so well.

"Shut my mouth, Wren." Brooklyn squeezed her lips together.

"Oh, Mattie…" Stoic Kate dabbed at her eyes.

The Mamas missed Wren's boy.

"You know…you're right, Wren, but I swear sometimes, if it weren't for the Gospel, I'd go out of my cotton-pickin' mind!" Hannie wiped her eyes too. "When I think about the sacrifice Jesus made for me—even while I sit here and complain to y'all about my precious kids and my good man—I can hardly stand myself. But oh…sometimes, sometimes, I just can't take it!" She shuddered in her chair. "Those ungodly, ungrateful, ungracious humans!"

As soon as the words left Hannie's mouth, they knew what Wren would say.

"Exactly." Wren let the word drop.

What could the Mamas do? *Disagree with her?*

"Exactly." They sighed heavily and in unison.

Listening to the clock tick on the wall, they sat in convicting silence. How did Jesus put up with any of them?

When Wren failed to hold back her laughter, it erupted as a loud guffaw. She smiled her bright, Jesus smile at them, and mischief filled her eyes. "But the Mamas *are* screwed!"

They all burst out laughing again, and Wren raised her cup to signal them. It had long been their call to cheerfully obey the Lord, and the Mamas had been saying it now for years..

They lifted their mugs to each other. They lifted their cups to Christ.

"To the brim!"

Chapter 31
Ghost Rider

Brooklyn dropped her keys on the counter and reached into the junk drawer for some Chapstick. Looking at Abe slouched on the couch made her heart sink. She knew he would say no, but she asked him anyway.

"Hey, Abe, I'm heading down to the nursery to pick out some trees. Want to come along?" "Car Talk" had always been her secret weapon, but Abe wanted nothing to do with her these days.

"No." Abe was texting someone. He didn't even look up, and Brooklyn knew what he was thinking. *Here it comes. Mom's going to rag on me for not wanting to go with her.*

"No worries." Brooklyn slung her purse over her shoulder. She was working on letting go. "I'll miss your company, but I understand. Text me if you want anything from town, okay?" She turned for the door, then turned back. "Love you."

Her feet crunched across their gravel driveway. *Lord, please help me let go. Please help me help Abe to know he's loved.* Brooklyn started her car when a sudden movement caught her eye. It was Abe, waving at her from the porch. Hopping toward her on one foot to get his other shoe on; he'd decided to come with her after all. *Does he miss me as much as I miss him?* She wondered. She hoped.

Brooklyn rolled down her window and said as coolly as she could manage, "Do you need something?"

Abe pulled open the door and folded his long frame into the passenger seat. "I changed my mind." He slumped down as if he didn't want anyone to see him. "But I don't want to talk. I just like looking at the trees."

Billings Nursery had the most perfect American elm tree in their yard. Brooklyn went every spring just to admire it. She'd been taking her kids there for years, but now, only Abe wanted to go.

"I don't feel like talking either." Brooklyn lied. "I'm looking for a shade tree for the east side of the house." The gravel crunched beneath her tires as she pulled out of the driveway. The sound stuck in her mind, and as she pulled into the nursery, she heard it again. *That sound reminds me of my relationship with Abe right now. Maybe I should write to the shepherd. I wonder if he could give me some advice on what to do with this boy of mine.*

Brooklyn had a friend who raised sheep on his Wyoming ranch. The old man had become like a father to her and a grandfather to her children. She only called him "Shepherd," and he was a comforting source of wisdom. Brooklyn made up her mind to write to him about Abe.

Abe was smarter than her. He'd been hard to raise and difficult to discipline because he was a master debater. Brooklyn avoided conflict, and though she tried to parent Abe in a godly way, she knew how often she failed him.

"What's your favorite kind of tree?" Brooklyn asked randomly as she and Abe walked down the rows of trees; the old arborist, walking with a limp, led the way.

"I like cedars." Abe had grown to be a man of few words, and it was hard to get him to engage in conversation.

"That was a quick answer! You know trees more than anyone, Abe. Why the cedar?"

"Because of what the Bible says about them in the Book of Ezekiel." Abe's long, lanky body moved with an odd, lumbering grace amongst the young trees.

"I have no idea what Ezekiel says about cedars. Tell me." Brooklyn was surprised to hear Abe mention the Bible. He didn't seem interested in the things of God these days.

"Well, in Ezekiel 31:5 it says, *"So it towered high above all the trees of the field; its boughs grew large and its branches long from abundant water in its shoots."* Abe cleared his throat. His voice was changing, but he continued, "The cedar tree taps deep into water underneath the ground—water that other trees' roots can't reach. That's how it can become 'high above all the trees of the field.' The cedar tree is supposed to symbolize wisdom and strength. Its boughs will grow toward the ground creating a shelter, kind of like the weeping willow. It's said to be a symbol of protection. Also, because they live between three and five hundred years, they're supposed to represent eternity." Abe cleared his throat again. "Actually Mom, I think most of Ezekiel 31 is about cedar trees and their representation of Pharoah and the might of Egypt and all that stuff. You gotta go with the tree that gets an entire chapter in the Bible, right?"

Brooklyn didn't know what to say. Abe's intellect surprised her all the time, even more so now that he was in the throes of puberty. He didn't seem to be interested in anything anymore. And he was so quiet.

"Did I hear you right?" Brooklyn gently sideswiped Abe with her hips. "Quoting from Ezekiel 31! Who are you, my boy?" Brooklyn laughed.

"You've no idea, Mama. There's a lot you don't know about me."

Brooklyn remembered her teen years, and she felt the answer to them in Abe's statement. She remembered the loneliness. She remembered wishing she had someone to talk to about the wash of emotions, not to mention the changes that were happening in her body. Brooklyn remembered. But she also knew the only way out for both of them was through. It was going to be complicated for a while–this teasing apart of their lives. It was the wonderful and terrible thing about growing up, and it was hard for everyone.

"I'm sure you're right about that!" Brooklyn smiled at him. She loved Abe, but she also really *liked* him.

Abe sideswiped her back. Forgetting he was much bigger and stronger than her now, his hips sent her flying to the ground under a mountain ash tree.

Abe's face turned pale.

Brooklyn was laughing as she reached her hand up to him. "Okay, okay, Mr. Cedar. Bigger, stronger, taller. I get it."

Abe pulled her up with ease. "Sorry. I didn't mean to do that so hard." His face flushed with embarrassment.

"Abe! Look at me! I'm fine!"

The arborist turned around and glared at them as Brooklyn dusted the mulch off her jeans. "That'll teach me to mess with you, won't it? You remind me a lot of a cedar tree, you know that?" He was tall and broad-shouldered. He was strong-willed and deep.

Abe smiled. He couldn't hide the delight from his face. "You know I'm still handsome, hilarious, and h-adorable, right?"

"Better than anyone!" Brooklyn laughed, and so did Abe. She realized she hadn't heard him laugh in a long, long time.

The arborist stood with his hand on his hip. "We'll take this one!" Brooklyn and Abe laughed and nudged each other back to the office.

Once inside, Brooklyn stood at the counter waiting to pay. Abe stayed outside, saying he wanted to wait in the car. When Brooklyn handed the cashier her debit card, she looked out the window, stunned. Under the perfect canopy of the elm tree, there were six metal rocking horses–red, orange, yellow, blue, black, and white. They each sat rocking atop a large, black spring. Brooklyn burst into laughter. She could hardly believe what she was seeing!

There was Abe, at 6'-2", running from one horse to the next like an excited boy. His knees protruding way beyond the norm, he rode each one to the point of breaking it, then got off to run for the next. Brooklyn could see he was trying to keep all the miniature horses rocking at once. He ran and ran, his tongue sticking out of his mouth just as it had all those years ago on the rope swing. On the trampoline. And when he, too, had gone off the high dive at the Red Lodge Pool.

Brooklyn laughed but tears streamed down her face. The grumpy arborist followed her eyes and saw it—a boy taking his last stand against adulthood, against what he had no control over and what he couldn't stop. Manhood hurled down his lengthening spine like a bullet train as a dirt devil formed at his feet.

"That's my boy," Brooklyn croaked. "That's my baby boy."

After blowing his nose in an ancient handkerchief, the old arborist brushed at his face with a calloused hand. He quietly pulled a pot of miniature roses from behind the counter.

"These are for you, Mama." He thrust the pot into her hand.

Brooklyn paid him in silence. She wanted to thank him, but she couldn't.

"Go on now," he said in his gruffest voice. "He's walking away." The man pulled the handkerchief from his denim shirt pocket. "They do that." He blew his nose again.

Brooklyn stood outside the arborist's shop and watched Abe's back as he walked toward the car. She stood as he folded his long frame back into the seat. She wanted to say, "Abe, come back! Come back and ride the horses!"

She turned around to look at them, still bouncing on their springs. They rocked as if alive. They rocked as if being ridden by a wild ghost boy.

But when she turned back to the car, all she could see was a young Abe on the threshold of manhood. She knew the crunching sound of tires on gravel would be the defining sound of their relationship for a while.

But for now, she stood watching him, her mind filling with all the funny things he'd said when he was little. She remembered the three moles, like tiny drops of molasses on his right cheek. She remembered his blue eyes and his long eyelashes. She remembered the day he'd gotten the scar on his lip from falling off the porch. Brooklyn remembered his questions and how his head had fit perfectly into the nook of her neck and her shoulder.

You are loved. You are loved. You are loved. You are loved.

The miniature horses rocked, and the memories of Abe rocked. He was a ghost rider now, and the little horses seemed to gallop alongside her memories of a little boy. A little boy who had changed her forever and who was now a young man.

She watched Abe in the car. She turned to the horses once more, hoping for a final glimpse of him, her little son.

But the dust had settled, and the horses were still now. The wild ghost rider had vanished, and her rocking horse boy...

Was gone like the wind.

Chapter 32
Single Saves Them All

Kate was mad-driving, and she knew it. Images of her son floated into her mind. *How can I be so triggered? Aren't I supposed to be the adult in this relationship?* Kate's face flushed with heat. *I should call one of The Mamas.* She knew she should. *But who?* Weren't all of them in the same boat with teens who wouldn't listen to anything? Weren't they also pulling their hair out with kids who couldn't remember to take out the trash, feed the dog, or do their schoolwork?

They say they don't remember to do their chores. Is that really true? Or are they just being lazy and irresponsible?

Kate needed Jill.

Jill had been meeting with the Mamas once a month for many years, and even though she never married or had children, Kate knew she would have perspective. In many ways, Jill was the best Mama of them all. A skilled counselor and a shrewd attorney, she was wise.

Jill…was calm.

Kate screamed at her phone. "Siri! Call Jill!"

"Hey, friend! Good to hear from you!" Jill's voice was warm on the other end.

"He won't listen to anything I say!" Kate shouted angrily into the phone. "Oh, gosh. I'm sorry. Hi, Jills."

Jill had grown used to these calls from the Mamas, the zero-to-a-hundred types. "What've we got today?"

Kate could picture Jill running her pale, elegant hands through her thick, chestnut hair. It was a habit that endeared her to all the Mamas. By default, she was the go-to Mama when the other moms were ready to jump off a cliff. Her nurturing heart and wisdom brought tension down, and the sound of her voice was an instant balm. The Mamas depended on her. Probably too much.

Kate sniffed into the phone. "I'm failing him, Jill. I'm failing!"

"Are you driving right now?" Jill asked.

"Yes! I'm late getting to the grocery store because we fought about him not doing his chores!"

"Kate, pull over. How many times do we need to have the conversation about mad-driving?"

Kate could hear the slight panic in Jill's voice. "Okay, hang on just a sec." Kate already felt a little calmer as she looked for a place to park. Jill's voice did that. Kate knew Jill would have an answer.

"Okay. I'm pulled over now and just shaking! I'm so mad I could kill him!"

"Nope. Not that, Kate. It's homicide, and you'd go straight to jail. Murder is a crime." It seemed like a stupid thing to say, but the reason the Mamas called Jill was because they knew what they often needed was a good, stiff dose of reality. They got so enmeshed in their kids' lives; it was hard for them to see straight sometimes. Especially now that all the kids were in their teens. The kids and their parents were trying to tease apart the knots of childhood, and it was causing everyone stress. The Mamas needed to be reminded that growing up was stressful for their kids too. Growing up was hard for everyone.

"AGH! What am I going to do, Jill???"

"Let's start by taking a few deep breaths to bring blood back into the front part of your brain," Jill instructed.

Kate couldn't count the number of times Jill had walked the Mamas off a ledge. Her maternal instincts were sharp. She knew what to do to help her friends. She helped make them better parents, and the Mamas' kids loved Jill because they knew she sympathized with them. Jill restored humanity to all parties, and she was precious to the Mamas and their families.

"I can't keep doing this!" Kate's voice assaulted Jill's ear. "He's always mad at me! He does the opposite of everything I say!"

"He's seventeen, Kate. Of course, he does the opposite of everything you say! He's testing his limits and moving away from you. You can't keep holding on like this. Set boundaries you can both agree on and give the kid some freedom. Give him some room, Kate. He's an amazing young man."

A pang stung Kate's heart. She knew Jill would have loved a son, even a rebellious one.

"He's going to get hurt, Jills!" Kate thought of Ethan. Handsome and broad-shouldered. Godly and kind. The girls were crawling all over him.

"Yeah?" Jill's logic moved in a sharp, straight line. "That's life! Your kids are going to get hurt!"

"But that...that just sucks!" Kate pounded on the steering wheel, breaking a blood vessel in one of her elegant hands. She hated it. "How can I do this, Jill? Ethan doesn't know how good he is, and he's scaring me!"

"Kate, God is writing his story. It's not yours. You need to stop parenting from the standpoint of fear and trust the process of letting go. Ethan has a good head on his shoulders, okay? He's going to blow it. Accept it! But his story doesn't belong to you. You've given him all he needs, Kate. You've loved him, and you can't project negativity on him like that. It's not fair." Kate knew Jill was right. Ethan really was an extraordinary young man. "Instead of you being the one setting the boundaries with chores, let him do it. Sit down and talk to him as a peer. Give him some room to practice being a man!"

Kate held the phone to her ear, and the silence that filled the car was sacred. She knew Jill was right. "Jills, what would I do without you?" Jill had counseled her and the Mamas out of so many ditches. "What would Ethan do without you?" *What would we all do without you?*

Kate could almost feel Jill's acceptance that she would never bear children roll over her. She hoped being a mama to the other kids, even from a distance, gave Jill some small relief.

"You're okay to drive now?" Kate imagined Jill's long fingers running through her hair again–the habit they all adored. "Just remember that Ethan is stressed out too, Kate. He doesn't want to disappoint you, but he's got to spread his wings. It's the way God set it up. Try to remember that and have compassion, okay? Ethan needs you and is trying to be independent at the same time. Don't you remember how confusing it was to be that age?"

"I do, Jills." Kate shuddered with memories. "Thanks for the perspective. It's such a great help."

"No problem. Now get back on the road and promise me one thing?"

"Anything for you."

"Only love. No homicides. I'm in the middle of a court case, and I don't have time to visit you in jail."

Kate laughed into the phone, and she knew Jill was smiling too.

Kate put on her blinker and pulled back on the road. She took several deep breaths and prayed for Ethan. "Only Love. Love Only."

After picking up groceries, she drove home and unloaded the car. Ethan was still sitting on the couch where Kate had left him.

"Son, you okay? What's wrong, love?" She dropped the bags on the counter and went to the couch. She could see Ethan had been crying. Sitting next to him, Kate squeezed his bony knee.

"Why are girls so weird, Mama?" Ethan's voice had changed. His body had changed too, and the girls were coming out of the woodwork to notice him. "I can't stop thinking about them, and I'm so disgusted with myself sometimes. It makes me sad. It's like all the joy is being sucked out of my soul."

"Oh, my son." Kate kissed him on top of his head. "Some girls will grow out of it, but they do want your attention, Ethan. Not just because you're handsome, but because of your character."

"I can't focus, Mom, and it's driving me crazy. You know, it's not like me!"

Kate laughed, "You should be talking to Dad about this, but keep your eyes on Jesus, Ethan, and He'll see you through it. Beware the girls who are dressing to attract the wrong kind of attention. Beauty is fleeting. Make sure you remain a man of integrity and look for the hidden treasure of a woman's heart."

"I feel so awkward around girls. I feel so…so homeschooled!" Ethan pulled away from Kate and looked into her face. "I don't know how the world is supposed to work, and I don't think being homeschooled is helping!"

"Sweetie, I went all through public school, and I can promise you, nobody knows what they're doing! None of us has this figured out!" She reached for Ethan's hand. "It's the hormones." She looked into Ethan's eyes and smiled at him.

"Hormones are messin' with me, Mama." Ethan smiled back at her. "I hate girls one minute and can't stop looking at their hair the next. It's so annoying!"

"Ooft! You poor man. I remember that feeling—the excitement and terror of looming adulthood!" *Why did growing up have to be so hard?* Kate thought about her brother, and a memory of him made her laugh.

"Hey, Ethan, you know how levelheaded and sweet your Uncle Jim is, and how much you respect him? Well, I went to high school with him, okay? And do you know I watched him drool out the side of his face in front of girls? Actual drool. I'm not even sure he knew it, so don't underestimate the power of hormones!" Kate couldn't help the involuntary shudder as she thought of her teen years. "Thank God we're in it together, Ethan. I'm here for you, and I know you'll make it through."

"Mostly because I have no choice," Ethan grumbled.

"Yep. No choice. But for now, let's forget about girls! I think we should go get pizza and a LEGO set." Kate adored that Ethan still loved building with LEGOs. "But first, let's work together to get the kitchen cleaned up and the groceries put away. Would that be okay with you?"

"Really, Mom? Thanks! And I'm sorry, I didn't do my chores this morning. I was so depressed; I couldn't move off the couch."

"Depression sucks, Ethan." *I can't believe I said that word twice in one day!* "But let's make a good choice and clean the kitchen, then we'll go for LEGOs, yes?" Kate smiled at him. "Thanks for sharing your heart with me. I know you don't have to anymore, but I always appreciate it."

"Thanks for understanding, Mama. I appreciate you."

"Darling." Kate tried to kiss Ethan's cheek, but he pulled away. "You're my life's deepest honor. I'm sorry I was harsh with my words this morning. Will you forgive me?"

"I forgive you, Mom." Ethan stood and hugged her with his long, thin arms. "But why do girls have to be so weird? Why do they have to be so cute? I just want to murder them all!"

Kate laughed out loud.

"Oh, no, son. You can't do that. Homicide is a crime, and you'd go straight to jail."

Chapter 33
When You Love Someone

Brooklyn stood outside Sophie's closed bedroom. With both hands resting on the wood panels, she lay her forehead on the door. Closing her eyes, she whispered three words over and over, "Thank You, Jesus. Thank You, Jesus."

Unaware of her mother's presence, Sophie sang worship songs in her room. Her big, beautiful voice put chills on Brooklyn's skin. The hair on her arms stood up. Goosebumps.

Last night, Brooklyn had come up out of a dead sleep with tears streaming down her face. Sitting straight up in bed, she called, "Sophie! Sophie!" It was the weirdest thing, but it happened every year. Brooklyn woke up in the middle of the night every seventh of October crying and calling, "Sophie! Sophie!"

Brooklyn got out of bed and shakily walked downstairs to make herself a cup of tea. There would be no more sleep for her tonight.

Grabbing the familiar journal off a shelf in her writing studio, Brooklyn sat in a soft armchair under the light of a warm lamp. The pages of the journal fell open by themselves to that spot. Tea stains and tears had smeared some of the ink, making the words look wrinkled and old. The pages read like hell on paper, but Brooklyn read them every year. For ten years in a row now, on every seventh of October, Brooklyn ran her fingers over the words and cried.

"Sophie! Sophie!"

Images of her then thirteen-year-old daughter sprang clearly to Brooklyn's mind. As if she still stood by her hospital bed, Brooklyn watched as Sophie compliantly swallowed a tube that would pump a quart of black-and-green goo out of her stomach. Brooklyn saw the tube taped to her mouth, the feeding port that had been put into her chest, and the IV pumping morphine into her daughter's bloodstream.

Sophie's appendix had ruptured, but after surgery, she didn't get better. She took two more trips to the hospital and was admitted both times. Sophie seemed to decay before Brooklyn's eyes. Her room smelled of death.

Emotionally, Sophie turned her face away from everyone, refusing to look them in the eye, refusing to engage even in small conversation. Physically, she looked like a concentration camp survivor. Spiritually, Sophie told Brooklyn, "God has abandoned me. I'm in hell, Mama."

How could she not feel that way?

Sophie had been stuck many times with needles. As hard-working nurses desperately tried to find a vein so they could start an IV, they failed—and failed again. The call button felt like an endless begging for someone to help her.

When Brooklyn took a break to get coffee from the cafeteria, the alarms on Sophie's monitors went unanswered. When Brooklyn returned, Sophie screamed at her, "Why isn't anyone here? That monitor has been beeping like a demon from hell for half an hour!"

The doctors kept telling Will and Brooklyn not to worry, but they didn't know Sophie!

Sophie was a "grab the bull by the horns" kind of kid. Adventure oozed from her pores, and that girl was always up to something. Sophie had come to know and love Jesus at a young age. She pursued Him with all her heart in Bible study, journaling, prayer, and especially in worship. Sophie was often a catalyst for faith in her family, and the way she loved people was incomparable.

Sophie had never wavered in life, in love, or in faith.

Until now.

Brooklyn and Will watched Sophie fade away.

Her pain was unmanageable, but that Sophie felt abandoned by God stole all her hope. Will and Brooklyn started calling her, "the dead girl in the bed" because there was no light in her eyes. There was only pain and confusion and hurt feelings.

How could God do this to her?

Brooklyn and Will stood with the surgeon and the anesthesiologist in the surgery bay. They explained the need for Sophie's second procedure. Will and Brooklyn tried to listen.

Was this some kind of horror movie?

Will asked a lot of questions.

Brooklyn stood by Sophie's bed holding her hand, but Sophie wouldn't look at her. She wouldn't look at any of them.

Will tried to kiss Sophie's cheek when it was time for them to go. "I love you, baby." But Sophie jerked away from him.

Brooklyn squeezed her hand, but Sophie pulled hers aside. "I love you, my girl."

It was the most impossible thing, but Will and Brooklyn left their daughter behind.

They left her.

They walked out of the surgery bay and stood in the hallway. Will pulled Brooklyn into a panicked embrace. Her glasses smashed into her face, but Brooklyn didn't care. The pain felt good. It felt right. It was something she could understand. It made sense.

"She's going to be okay, Brook. They'll take good care of her! They'll take good care of our girl!" Will was trying to convince himself, and

Brooklyn knew it. Neither of them had much hope that Sophie would ever come back to them.

"Will! Will, don't you see? Haven't you been asking yourself the same question?" Will's chest muffled Brooklyn's voice.

"I know. I know..." Will stopped trying to fix everything and just let the pain take over. He sobbed in Brooklyn's arms.

"We love a God who has allowed this." Brooklyn imagined God sending His Son for her. How had He endured such pain?

"I know." Will was shaking hard. He'd lost his sisters when he'd been a boy. Now he was going to lose another of his best girls. "I know..." It was all he could manage.

"We love a God who owes us no explanation for this. He could take Sophie right now, and there's nothing we can do about it. He holds her life in His hands, and she's always been His to take." Brooklyn stated the obvious. "And, honestly, Will, I can't watch her suffer anymore! It's only been two weeks since her first surgery, but I can't stand to see her suffering!"

"I know." Will wiped his eyes with the sleeve of his long-sleeved t-shirt. "I know."

Brooklyn flipped the journal pages, recalling every detail and Sophie's long recovery from the physical effects of her crisis. Brooklyn remembered with pain the years of depression that followed. She remembered Sophie's long walk back to Christ and to His love.

After being up all night reading, Brooklyn heard Sophie singing worship songs in her room. Standing outside her door listening, Brooklyn whispered three words over and over again, "Thank You, Jesus." Brooklyn wanted to reach through the door and pull Sophie into her arms.

You are loved. You are loved. You are loved. You are loved.

Chapter 34
Weird Uncle

K ate, I've got to do something!"

Kathryn watched as Brian sat on a kitchen chair lacing up his work boots. "Have you seen Sophie Wyer lately? For a girl that nearly died from a ruptured appendix, all of the sudden she's gotten pretty. I watched the boys looking at her at the drive-in movies, and I didn't like it." Brian yanked on his laces so hard, Kate thought they would snap.

"What's the matter, Brian? Sophie's not a boy-crazy girl. She's so grounded in Jesus, I don't know what you're worried about. I don't know why you're concerned. Will's got his daughter's heart. She's not moving away from him or from any of us."

The Mamas and their families had gone to the drive-in movie theater over the weekend, but Kate hadn't noticed anything out of the ordinary.

"I know that Kathryn, and that's why Sophie scares me to death. She doesn't know she's beautiful, and she doesn't know that all men are pigs. It's her goodness that has me worried!" Brian stood and stroked his beard. This was his nervous habit, and Kate wrapped her long arms around his waist.

"You're not her father, Brian."

"I know, but if there's anything we've learned, it's that our own kids don't listen to us. Maybe Soph would listen to me." Brian looked into Kate's eyes. She knew he wasn't asking her permission.

"What do you have in mind?" Kate knew that look. "And you better at least talk to Will about it. He's more civilized than you, Brian Norris." Kate pulled on Brian's lapels, bringing him close to her. "Your wild side can be a little scary sometimes." She smiled and flipped her hair over her shoulder.

"So, what are you saying?" Brian's chest expanded. "You afraid of me, Lipstick?" He smiled the knowing smile of a husband.

Kate flaunted her hair – her prayer shawl as the Mamas had assigned it. Brian pulled it into a ponytail, then tugged her close for a kiss.

Kate smiled at him. "You do scare me a little, Brian."

"Then help me scare these boys away from Sophie. She's completely unaware of how they're looking at her, and they make me sick! They're just like me when I was their age!"

"Your care for Sophie does you credit, Brian." Kate ran her fingers lightly across Brian's strong shoulders. She loved his protector's heart. "Who knows? Maybe you're right and Sophie would hear it from you over Will."

"Stranger things have happened." Brian kissed Kate again.

"Like what?" Kate leaned into him.

"Like a long-legged beauty queen falling in love with a greasy tool like me."

"Hmmm…" Kate reached for Brian's hand. "I haven't seen that tool belt around in a while, have you?"

The next day, Sophie called Kate. "Mama Kate, it's Soph. Is Uncle Brian there? I need to tell you both something. Can you put me on speaker?"

"Hang on, sweetheart. Is everything okay? Is your mom okay?" Kate's thoughts went to Brooklyn. "Bri! Sophie Wyer's on the phone! She's got something to tell us!"

"Mom's fine, I just wanted to let you and Uncle Brian know that I'm dating now."

"Hold on, here's Brian, we're both here on speaker now."

"Hi, Uncle Brian, it's Sophie. I just wanted you and Mama Kate to know that I met a super cool guy. He's pretty cute too, and I'm dating him now."

The kids called the Mamas' husbands "Uncle." They were never "The Papas," and nobody asked why. It was the kids. The kids were why.

"Was he one of the guys at the movie?" Brian met Kate's gaze as she held her cell phone between them. She remembered what he'd told her yesterday when he was lacing his work boots and how distraught he'd been.

"I followed Sophie around all night at the movies, Kate. She didn't know it, but all those guys were checking out her body. And now my own Margaret is old enough to date! What am I supposed to do?"

Kate gave Brian a warning look as Sophie chatted ignorantly on. "Yeah, he was the short guy with the glasses. Isn't he cute, Uncle Brian?"

Kate thought Brian was going to swallow his own tongue! She knew the guy Sophie was talking about had been the worst of them that night. Brian had described him in detail when he told Kate the young man had been devouring Sophie with his eyes. "He's stealing from her, and she doesn't even know it! She's so unaware of her lilting voice and her teasing, feminine laughter." Kate could see Brian in the kitchen in her mind's eye. She didn't think his boot laces would stand a chance as he shared his heart, "Look, Kate, I know it's not something you can understand or relate to, but I remember how far pornography led me away from Christ when I was a teenager. By God's grace, I'm clean now; you know I've been clean for decades. It's been so good for Mark and me to walk together in accountability, but it pains me to watch the behaviors that used to mark the kind of man I was for a season. Their innocence, while beautiful, does our sweet girls no favors when understanding how dangerous men can be. Especially boys their age!

Kathryn tried to soothe Brian with the sound of her voice, even as she continued talking to Sophie on the phone. "What does your dad think about this boy, Soph?"

Sophie answered, "He knows I've wanted a boyfriend for a long time, and I'm past old enough to date. He's been pretty quiet about it, but I think he just wants me to be happy."

Kate knew Will well enough to read between the lines. She watched fire rush into Brian's cheeks and gave him a look that said, "Calm down."

"Sophie, your Uncle Brian didn't have a good feeling about that guy." Kate tried to give Brian an opening. She hoped he would be gentle.

Clearing his throat, Brian choked out, "I'd like to meet him face to face before you're ever alone with him. Is that okay with you, Sophie?"

"Well, okay, Uncle Brian, that's kind of why I'm calling. You always told me you had to meet any boy I wanted to date. So here we are— there's a boy I want to date!" She giggled, and Kate watched Brian roll his eyes in frustration. She put the tip of her index finger into Brian's ribs and pushed hard. *Take it easy, Mister Norris.*

"I didn't even notice him at the movies, but he was following me around all night, I guess. He finally asked me out on a date."

"What do you like about him, Soph?" Brian's voice drilled down.

"I don't really know him, Uncle. I just thought he was kind of cute. A little sarcastic, but he was probably just nervous."

"When are you going out? Is he picking you up?" Kate could sense protectiveness roaring to life in her husband. *He really is scary sometimes!*

"Yea. He's coming tonight. I know it's late notice, but if you want to meet him, you might like to come down." Kate could hear Sophie chewing gum.

"Are you going to let me give you my honest opinion?" Brian asked. "Remember when you asked me to screen your dates?"

Kathryn remembered it too—how it had blessed Brian that Sophie would ask.

"I'm not even her uncle, Kate!" Brian had exclaimed. "But all the Mamas' kids have wormed their way into my heart. I feel every bit like an uncle, maybe even more than one in Sophie's life because she's been so intentional in asking for my counsel. What kid does that? I know I didn't!"

"That's what this is about, Uncle Brian." Sophie's voice was lighthearted on the phone. "Can you come to our house, even with the short notice?"

"I'll be there."

"Isn't he cute though, Uncle Brian?"

"You know what I say about all men, Sophie."

"They're pigs?"

"That's right, honey, so don't get your hopes up." Brian abandoned the conversation, leaving Kate holding the phone.

"Sophie, darling?" Kate recovered from Brian's abrupt departure. "What time should we come down? Right now? I just need to brush my teeth and we'll be there." Kate hung up the phone.

As she was reaching into the drawer for her toothbrush, Brian emerged from their walk-in closet. Kate screamed. "Agh!"

Brian had changed into a pair of cut-off shorts and a "wife-beater" tank top. Strapped across his broad chest was a bandolier of shotgun shells and hanging from his waist was a pistol. He carried an empty shotgun in his hand, and a weathered cowboy hat sat on his head. His white sweat socks showed above his cowboy boots, and the man looked deranged.

Kate screamed again. "Brian, what in the world are you wearing? You can't do that! You'll scare the boy to death!"

"Listen to me, Kathryn. If this guy is the real deal, he won't be the least bit afraid of me. If he's just playing games with our girl Sophie, this'll flush him out in two seconds."

Kate reached for her string of pearls and thought of her life in England and her cups of tea. How could she have known that marrying Brian Norris would be like this? THIS???

"No one's going to hurt that girl." Brian's face was set like a flint.

Kate knew that look. She thought Brian would spit in the house, but he didn't.

"If that boy's worth his salt, he'll know what this is about. Come on, we're taking the bike."

"You can't possibly be serious?" Kate's eyebrows nearly reached her hairline and her English accent became more pronounced. "You'll be pulled over! You can't wear that on the bike!"

"I'll take my chances, Kathryn."

Kate knew it was pointless to argue. She, in her heels and pearls, would sit on the back of "Brian-the-wife-beater's" Harley Davidson so he could go scare the life out of some poor kid.

Minutes later, Kate cringed as Brian revved his Harley in the Wyers' driveway. She put her forehead against Brian's back and gathered her courage. *Oh, Lord, please help us all.* Will was walking toward them.

"Love the outfit. Perfect, and thanks, brother. Wait till you see this guy; he's a total grease pit."

Kate breathed a sigh of relief as Will slapped Brian on the shoulder. At least the guys were on the same page.

"I have seen him! I watched him at the movies last week."

"Sophie won't hear a word from me, Brian. Even at twenty-one, she's all giggles and twirls."

"The poor guy. He just needs the 'What every boy needs to know about becoming a man' speech from crazy Uncle Brian here."

Secondhand Lions was one of the guys' favorite movies. Brian slipped naturally into Uncle Hub's role.

"I've got this, Will, just let me at him!"

The sound of Brian's boots crunching on the gravel driveway sounded like a firing squad to Kate. She couldn't believe the words that came out of Brian's mouth as he and Will walked through the door.

"There's a new sheriff in town, and I'm it!"

The men laughed, but there was strain in it, and Kathryn remembered Brian's words again.

"Young men living by the unrestrained standards of the world are the most dangerous species on the planet. Will, Mark, Steve, and I pray for them often—these unseen and unknown young men who need Christ and His Cross."

Kate rushed ahead of the men through the Wyers' door. Sophie was sitting on the couch with "the boyfriend," and Brooklyn was standing at the kitchen island. Kate rushed to her friend's side and took her hand and squeezed it hard. "Oh, Brook. I have no words for what's about to come through your door."

"What do you me—?"

"WHERE'S THE BOY?" Brian bellowed. *"WHERE'S THE BOY?"*

"The Boy" stood—wide-eyed and suddenly very pale.

Kate watched in horror as Brian took the empty shotgun's barrel and lifted the brim of "the boy's" baseball cap. Kate knew he wanted to look him in the eye. Brian knew all about hiding eyes.

"You taking this pretty girl out tonight, boy?"

Kate was proud of her husband and wanted to hug him. He looked so scary, she squeezed Brooklyn's hand even tighter. She was smiling because this is what it looked like to have a man protect a woman! This is what it looked like when valor stood up for virtue! But it was also really stressful, and Sophie looked like she was going to burst into tears.

Kate couldn't help thinking about Wren's Matthew. Unlike this ill-intentioned young man, already making himself too familiar with Sophie, Matthew had been "The Boy" to the Mamas and their men. For so many years, it had been a term of endearment, but this kid was no Matthew. Wren had told Kate the story of Brooklyn busting her smoking cigarettes like a steam engine in The Boy's room. Kate had never smoked in her life, but she wished she had a cigarette right now! What a wonderful and terrible moment this was!

"Yes, sir, I am." The boy squeaked. The track lights on the ceiling revealed beads of sweat on his cheeks.

"You lay one finger on her—you get her home one minute late, and I will come for you." Brian sounded calm. Kate was relieved at the kindness in his voice, but still, the look in his eye was terrifying and serious.

"This young woman is precious to all of us, and if you do anything to hurt her, I will find you, and I will take you out." Brian smiled at the young man. "Treat her right, and you've got no problems. Treat her wrong, and you're on the wrong side of this crazy cowboy. Do we understand each other?"

"Yes, sir. We do." The boy wouldn't look Brian in the eye.

"Alrighty then. Here's my phone number. You call me anytime you want to talk." He nodded at the boy until the boy nodded back. "Good. I see you're picking up what I'm laying down." Brian shook the boy's hand, gripping it hard. "Sophie? You can go on your date now." Brian never released the boy from his gaze.

Sophie looked confused and uncertain as she stood to hug Brian. "Thanks, Uncle Brian. I think?"

Kate rushed to Sophie's side. "Look at you! This is such a great outfit, and you look amazing!"

"You think so, Mama Kate?" Sophie looked uncharacteristically insecure.

Kathryn took Sophie's arm and twirled her around, admiring the sundress that fit her like a glove. Leaning close to her ear, she whispered, "Uncle Brian is right about this, Sophie. Just wait and see." She squeezed the young woman's shoulder. "You know he loves you so."

***

Kathryn and Brian lay in their bed late, talking about Sophie and the boy. The boy's name was Alex, and he really did call Brian that night. That very night!

"You looked completely insane!" Kate smiled into Brian's chest. She was thinking about her husband's bandolier of bullets, pistol, wife-beater tank top, Harley Davidson, and especially his sweat socks and cowboy boots. "I can't believe Alex actually called you! Tell me exactly what he said!

"He knew I knew, and he told me he took Sophie out for ice cream, then straight home. He said Sophie asked if the abrupt end to their date had anything to do with her weird uncle. Can you believe she called me a weird uncle, Kathryn?"

Kate felt the joy on Brian's skin. She sensed him grinning in the night.

"I had a little hope he'd call me. I've been praying he would have the courage, and Kate, he did! He did!"

"Brian, that was one of the craziest things I've ever seen you do, but I'm so thankful you did it! I can't believe I'm married to you!" Kate giggled like a schoolgirl.

"You girls are all alike, you know that?" He pulled her closer.

"Can't live without me though, can you, Bri?" Kate snuggled against his shoulder.

"That's for sure." Brian sighed long and loud. "Are you...are you ever sorry, Lipstick? I mean, sometimes I wonder. Are you sorry you married such a redneck toolbelt like me?"

"Mmm-hmm…" Kate lifted her head to kiss her husband. "Very…"
And her prayer shawl fell like a holy curtain around his face.

Chapter 35
The Mamas Are Mad

Mark, can you come out here for a second?" Hannie had the mudroom door open, and she shouted so Mark could hear her.

"On my way!"

"I'll be out on the porch!" Hannie could see Eryk in the kitchen, but she was so mad at him, she didn't trust herself to go in the house. She knew this would be humorous at some point, but it was far from that today. "Mark! Are you coming?" Hannie's accent thickened with emotion.

"Han! Just a second, I'm getting my shoes on!"

Anyone would be able to recognize the tone in her voice, but Hannie slammed the door and started pacing on the porch.

"Geez, Hannie, give me a break. What's going on?" Mark pulled on his windbreaker.

"You won't believe what happened! I just got finished praying with The Mamas, and you know what they told me?" Hannie rushed ahead, "They told me that Eryk and Allie were makin' out in the back seat of Kate's suburban on the way up to Bridger Bowl for homeschool ski day!"

"Whoa. What? That's not okay. That's not cool."

"I know, right? But, Mark! They did it in front of all The Mamas' kids–even Wren's littles!" Hannie's tiny frame felt like a compressed spring. "I'm so embarrassed, but I also know Eryk is going to have to break it off with Allie. His heart's going to be broken, and we're all going to be broken-hearted with him. Oh, Mark…what on earth makes a kid do somethin' like this?" Hannie was convicted as soon as the words left her mouth. By God's grace, she'd been a virgin when they married, but she blushed thinking about the things she'd done in the back seat of Mark's Camero when they were dating.

"Come here, Hannie." Mark reached for her hands and pulled them warmly into his chest. "What do you want me to do?"

"I can't talk to him right now, Mark. I know everything will work out, but I just can't believe Eryk would do somethin' like this." She shuddered in his arms. "Please talk to him. I don't even know if he's aware of the damage he's done."

"Hannie, stop." She could feel Mark tense.

"He's not me, okay, Han? Eryk has never been like me." The dangerous cloud of pornography enveloped them both.

"Mark, I didn't mean that. I wasn't even thinking about you. I'm worried about the little kids, and the pain we're all going to have to go through because of this." Hannie wrapped her arms around Mark's waist. "You're a good father and a good husband, and that's why I need you to talk to your son. I'm no good in these situations. I'm too harsh, as you well know. I can be so mean sometimes." Remembered words spoken in anger wilted Hannie's heart, and she whispered her repentance. "I'm sorry I've hurt you so often with my words."

"You're forgiven. I'm sorry I made this about me." He held her loosely, "Why don't you take the rest of the kids out for pizza, and Eryk and I will have a talk, okay?"

"I can't go in there, Mark. I don't trust myself."

Mark laughed at her. "You don't? Really? You always seem to have it so together!"

Hannie loved her husband's laugh, and he was a handsome man, especially when he smiled.

"Don't worry. I'll send Zac and Makenna out to the car. 3M are here too, so I'll tell them you're waiting." Mark kissed her full on the mouth. "I've got this, my wife. Go on! Get out of here, please!" He laughed at her again and winked.

"Babe! Thank you!" Hannie smiled at him and walked to her car.

***

Eryk stood over a boiling pot of water, dropping spaghetti noodles in one by one. He stared into space and sighed. Mark came in from the porch and while Hannie may have filled him in, the look on Eryk's face was so… *strange*. Mark decided in that moment not to think about what Hannie had told him. He just wanted to be there for his son.

"What's going on, Eryk?" He couldn't remember ever seeing Eryk stand so still in all his life. The kid was tall now, athletic, and handsome. And he even had his first girlfriend! *When had he grown up?*

"Huh?" Eryk looked up. His eyes were red from crying. "Oh, hi Dad."

"Hey, son, what's going on?

Eryk let out another weighted sigh. "Dad…The Mamas are mad."

"What? Why is that?" Mark felt like he was hearing it for the first time. He and Hannie were on the road to recovery again, but seeing Hannie mad still scared him. He took the noodles from Eryk and dropped them all into the boiling water.

"You see this water, Dad? It's got nothing on me. I'm in hot water, and not just with my own mama, but with *all* the mamas."

"What happened?" Mark felt sorry for the kid.

239

"I'm so stupid, Dad! You know how it is for us homeschooled kids. It takes a long time for the Mamas to let go, and it takes even more for them to trust us, right?"

"They're not wrong to do that." If Eryk was going to complain about love, he'd lost Mark's sympathy.

"I know, and I'm glad for it, but what I'm trying to tell you is that I totally blew it today." Eryk stared into the boiling water, and Mark leaned closer to listen. "Dad, even though I love Allie, and I think she's the most beautiful woman on earth, I never even thought about kissing her. Kissing has grossed me out my whole life, and I never thought it would be fun."

"Uh-oh. Son, what did you do?" Eryk was nineteen now. Allie was just seventeen. Mark had to let Eryk tell the whole story as if he didn't know what had happened.

"The Mamas FINALLY gave us their permission to go skiing alone, right? So Ethan, Derek, and I took the Norrises' Suburban with all the Mamas' kids up to the mountain. Zac had to work, but even Allie's mom let her go with us. It was going to be such an awesome day!"

It had taken Mark a long time to get all the Mamas' kids straight. Closest in age to his twins, Eryk and Zac, there was Ethan Norris and Derek Wyer. Mark didn't know if it was because they were all close friends, but he thought the boys looked like brothers.

"So, it was you, Ethan, and Derek at the helm, huh?" Mark stirred the spaghetti sauce and slapped Eryk's shoulder with pride. "That's something to be proud of, Eryk! You earned the Mamas' trust. That's a big deal!"

"Daaaad. Listen!" Eryk's eyes filled with tears. "Ethan drove the Suburban to the mountain, and instead of sitting up front with him like I should, Allie and I took the back seat."

Steam boiled from the pot.

"Uh-oh." Mark could feel his face pull into a cringe.

"Allie and I made out the whole way there, Dad! In front of all the Mamas' kids!"

"Oh, no, son..." Mark could guess just how mad the other Mamas were. *Hannie!*

"I had no idea kissing Allie was going to be so great. I really thought it would be gross, but it's not...it's–it's *muy bueno!*" Eryk poked the spaghetti noodles. "It's like my brain stops working whenever Allie's around. I just want to look at her and hold her. I can't think about anything else!"

"What did the Mamas say?"

"Allie's mom doesn't know yet. The other Mamas told Mom this morning at prayer. At least that's what Derek told me. You know how she's working on her temper? Well...I'm afraid this little incident is going to set her back a few years."

Eryk's posture had always been perfect, but he slouched over the boiling noodles. "I made mom mad, Dad. I know I broke her trust. I broke the trust I have with all the Mamas, and worse–I hurt them. How can they ever trust me again? How can I trust myself?"

Eryk lifted the boiling pot off the stove and carried it to the sink. As he dumped the noodles into the colander, the steam blasted him in the face.

"Do you want some spaghetti?" Eryk lifted the noodles onto a plate.

"Sure." Mark took some noodles and poured spaghetti sauce over the top. The two men sat down at the table together.

"Dad, what am I going to do?"

Mark, thinking of all he had gone through to win Hannie's trust again, took a few bites of spaghetti. "You're going to do whatever it takes, Eryk. That's what men do." Stopping to lean back in his chair, he said, "You need to talk to Allie's parents as soon as possible. And you have to apologize to them, and especially to Allie, for not guarding her reputation."

"I know. But what if they make us break up?"

"Do you think they will?" Mark asked.

"Would you? If someone made out with Sophie or Maylee in front of a bunch of kids, would you let him keep dating your daughter?"

Mark was quiet for a while before answering. "I probably wouldn't, but son, let me ask you this…you know Jesus sees it all, right? You've not forgotten that?"

"I know, Dad, but my humanity!" Tears filled Eryk's eyes again. "I love the Mamas, but I also *know* the Mamas. There's no way they're letting me off the hook easy."

"Man!" Mark drew a sharp breath between his teeth. "The Mamas are tough!"

"I'm so embarrassed, Dad, but the worst thing is—you're right—I put Allie's reputation on the line. I guess that makes me just like all the other guys that treat girls like garbage!" Eryk sat over his steaming plate of spaghetti but didn't take a bite. He just stabbed the noodles.

Mark grabbed a toothpick and stuck it in his mouth. "Son, I'm going to let you in on a little secret, okay?" He reached his hand out and rested it on Eryk's shoulder. "When your mom is mad at me, I'm scared to death of her. I can't even imagine all the mamas being mad."

Eryk slouched over his noodles, stabbing and staring.

"This is the stuff that makes a man, Eryk. You know you did wrong. You can choose to ignore it, or you can face up to the Mamas. I know you've got what it takes to make this right, and if you're patient, I believe you'll come out a better man for it on the other side."

"It seems a little weird to me, Dad. I'm old enough to have a girlfriend, and this is a zero compared to what most of my other friends are doing. I just…I just really value the Mamas. I really care for them, Dad, and when they gave us their blessing to go skiing, I understood what that meant. I've blown it so big; I don't know how I'll ever recover them. And Allie…" Eryk pushed his plate away and broke down sobbing. "How can she want a man like me? I'm not even a man, I'm a little boy!"

Mark's eyes pooled with tears of pride. *How did I raise such a son? How did such a fine young man come from a fool like me?* He pulled Eryk into a hug. "It's your humility that makes this situation hopeful, son. If you don't think the Mamas are going to see that, you're wrong. It's one of the best qualities a man can have."

"I don't know, Dad. I just feel awful!"

"I know, Eryk. But imagine if you didn't? Imagine if you thought the Mamas were overreacting and treating you like a baby. Imagine if you weren't so broken over Allie? How do you think that would go over in winning their hearts again? It's going to take a lot, Eryk. I mean, I have to admit that if I were Allie's father, it would be hard for me to let you date her again, especially because she's so young. But I do believe, if you can be patient, all the Mamas will come around."

What a good man you are! What a God man! Mark cheered for his son in his mind. Eryk had always been kind, but to get to this point was such a victory. Eryk was teachable. He was humble. He was so deeply sorry.

"I believe in you, Eryk. I wouldn't tell you that if it wasn't true. You CAN do this, and I'm going to be right beside you every step of the way. One day, we're going to laugh at this, I promise, but right now, it's about the worst thing you can imagine, right?"

"Yeah… the Mamas are mad." Eryk sighed again, pulled his plate toward him, and started shoving spaghetti into his mouth.

Mark sucked another cold breath of air between his teeth and cringed. He knew they would come around, but imagining Hannie, Kate, Brooklyn, and Wren being angry? It overwhelmed him! All he could see was Hannie's fiery eyes when she was mad, and he squeezed Eryk's shoulder again. Shaking his head, Mark let out a slow whistle and said again, "Man, the Mamas are tough!"

"They're not just tough, Dad." Eryk took his plate to the sink. "The Mamas are mad!"

Chapter 36
Shirts

Kathryn gave Brooklyn the shirt off her back that summer.

Walking on the endless loop at the high school track was the only way Kate and Brooklyn could distract themselves from the fact that the 3M's were taking driver's education. In true 3M fashion, Margaret and Madison had waited a year for Maylee so they could all take it together. The same inseparable girls who still had sleepovers on the trampoline and giggled all night were now sitting behind the wheel of a vehicle that could travel 120 MPH. It made the Mamas nervous.

Walking helped, and Kate and Brooklyn were missing Hannie that week. She was working at a church camp and wouldn't be home until Sunday night.

As they waited at the high school for 3M to complete their practice drives, Kate and Brooklyn walked and chatted the hours away. With the blazing Montana sun beating down on them, they covered miles on the track and in conversation. They aimed to solve their own and the world's problems in that limited time frame saying, "If only someone would put us in charge. We could fix everything!"

Only when Kathryn turned the conversation to Brooklyn's eldest son did their light-hearted chatter fall away.

"How is Jake doing, Brook?" Kate reached instinctively for Brooklyn's hand. Squeezing it hard, she asked, "Have you heard from him?"

Sorrow burst open like stitches trying to constrain a deep wound. Jake was never far from her mind. "I'm losing him, Kate." Brooklyn closed her eyes and lifted her face to the sun. "I can feel it."

Brooklyn lifted the hem of her shirt to wipe the tears and mucus away. There was no disguising the horrible wetness spreading everywhere from Brooklyn's eyes and nose. It was an ugly cry, and Brooklyn was embarrassed.

"Come on, now, Brook." Kathryn soothed, lifting her hand to Brooklyn's shoulder. "He'll be fine. Jake knows what's right, and he's going to be okay."

"It's not what I see on the surface." Brooklyn felt wobbly and bit her lip, trying to stop the tears. "It's what I feel. It's what I know, Kate. He's walking away from Jesus." Brooklyn sniffed hard, trying to stop up her sorrow and snot: useless.

Brooklyn thought about Jake being pulled away by pretty girls, his thirst for adventure, and a desire to be free. Though she knew it was all normal for him, his pulling away from Jesus concerned her.

Several months ago, she and Jake had gone for a drive and for "car talk."

"I don't consider myself a Christian, Mom. I like Christians. I like the Christian lifestyle. But I'm not one of you." Jake, always gentle, held her hand when he told her.

Brooklyn kept trying to deny they'd had that conversation, but as she observed the fruit in Jake's life, she wondered if it was true. If it was, she had to respect his honesty, and she had to accept it. Brooklyn could sense the tension in Jake's folded wings whenever he visited her at home. It was hard to believe he'd been gone for three years already, but Brooklyn could see how hard he worked at being respectful when he was in her home.

Brooklyn was working just as hard at letting all her kids go. "Nobody told me when I had children that it would mean giving birth twice. Once to get your child out of your body and again to launch him into the world! It's not fair, Kate. Why does God set it up like this? Why does he set us up?" The hem of Brooklyn's shirt was soaked, but she wiped her nose again anyway.

"Okay, come here now." Kathryn grabbed Brooklyn by the elbow and pulled her over to the bleachers. "Sit." Stripping her shirt off, Kathryn stood under the sun in only her tank top. She shook her shirt at Brooklyn. "Take this, and BLOW."

"What? No!" Brooklyn said, mortified. "I'm not blowing my nose in your shirt!" She lifted her hem and wiped more tears. More snot. Gross.

"Seriously, Brook?" Kathryn put her hand on her hip, the Mamas' ultimate signal to the end of every conversation. "It will go in the wash. Now, *BLOW!*"

Brooklyn had no choice.

She blew. And blew and blew.

Kate sat down next to her, then placed her long, elegant hand on Brooklyn's knee. Bowing her head, her long, blonde hair fell around her shoulders like a prayer shawl. Now that all the Mamas were practicing praying with their husbands, Brook knew Kate's hair was just that, and she couldn't help smiling.

"Lord, we stand for Jake. Help us trust in your will and plans for that fine, young man. Please, Lord, don't let Jake exchange the truth for a lie." Kate's spiritual sword swung through the air as invisible as her words but filled with power.

Brooklyn sobbed and blew her nose into Kathryn's shirt as she thought of her boy. The distant look in his eyes. The silence of a young gentleman who was afraid to hurt his Mama's feelings. *Say something nice, or don't say anything at all.* Hadn't Brooklyn taught him that? Wasn't it a good thing to teach?

She knew Jake was pulling away, but helping him run away as a little boy hadn't prepared her for this. *At all.* All she could think of was the trembling strings on his little red hoodie and the holy tears in his big, brown eyes. *"Mama, I want to run away."* Brooklyn could still hear his voice, and with it, the tearing sound in her mind. Like two pieces of Velcro being ripped apart, Brooklyn felt like her heart was being torn in two. Her kids were all so close in age, the normal separation felt like an act of violence. It was a lot of letting go, and she didn't know it could hurt this much.

"Jesus," Brooklyn prayed fervently, breathing in big breaths and lifting her sword with Kate's. "Spread your grace on Jake. On us. On our family. Keep him safe from the enemy, Lord. Protect Jake from Satan's cruel lies."

Brooklyn, a timid introvert, was a mighty warrior when she prayed. Prayer gave her courage. It built up her trust in Jesus. It reminded her Who was in control. Brooklyn blew a final blow into Kathryn's shirt. "Cover Jake, Jesus. Keep him safe."

"Amen." Kate ended the prayer and reached for her shirt.

Brooklyn pulled it away. "I'll take it home and wash it. You're not touching this thing! It's gross!"

They giggled and walked the rest of the track until the girls came back from their drives.

"Glad to see you all in one piece!" Kate waved at 3M. "Your instructor looks a little green around the gills though."

"Ha. Ha. Very funny, Mom. *Not.*" Margaret rolled her eyes at Kate.

The Mamas' eyes met. *Seventeen and nature's queen*—was ringing in both their ears. They smiled. If the Mamas had learned anything, it was how much they needed each other. The teen years were tumultuous, and they rolled their eyes at each other.

248

"Same time tomorrow?" Brooklyn lifted a hand to shield her pale skin from the sun.

"See you then." Kate folded her long frame into her car.

"See you tomorrow, Maylee!" Margaret and Madison waved at their friend. 3M really did stick together.

Brooklyn sat for a few minutes watching Kate and the girls drive away. Kate's snotty shirt lay on the floor of her car, and Brooklyn heard those familiar words in her mind.

You are loved. You are loved. You are loved. You are loved.

***

The next day, the Mamas met again at the high school track, and Brooklyn returned Kathryn's shirt.

"I put it through the disinfect cycle, so no more snot. I also brought you this." Brooklyn handed Kate a light-peach sun shirt with tiny, bronze buttons and a ruffle across the back. "I have a blue one, just like it, but this color washes me out."

"That's a great color for me! Are you sure?"

Brooklyn wagged the peach shirt at Kate and put her hand on her hip—end of conversation.

"Okay," Kate laughed, running her hand over the blouse. "Wow, thanks!"

"You don't mind being twinsies once in a while?" Brooklyn winked, loving Kate's big smile.

"Not when I get a great shirt like this. Just look at these adorable buttons! Let me try it on!" Kate slipped the blouse over her tank top. Perfect fit.

"You're right," Brooklyn admired her friend. "That's a great color on you."

"Let the twinning begin." Kate was happy with her gift. As was fitting for a supermodel, she loved clothes.

Brooklyn and Kate wore their matching shirts a lot that summer. Spending hours with the other Mamas in Brooklyn's back yard drinking iced coffee, their tiny, bronze buttons glinted in the sun.

Brooklyn told Hannie and Wren the story of Kate giving her the shirt off her back.

"You gave your shirt up as a snot rag?" Hannie bent forward in her lawn chair to look incredulously into Kathryn's perfect face. "Supermodel, you surprise me!"

Kate took the Mamas' teasing with delight. They were the first women who treated her with respect and who hadn't hurt her because of jealousy. Kate knew the only reason she looked the way she did was because God made her that way. She never thought anything more of it, but Kate often felt her person was cheapened in a world where beauty was worshiped. Being beautiful often left Kate feeling left out and cast aside. Women could be cruel, and Kathryn was often punished for her looks by being ignored. It was hurtful. Did they think she didn't notice?

Kate smiled her enormous smile at her friends. The Mamas calling her "Supermodel" was the lowest thing they could say about her, and it gave Kathryn joy. They knew she was smart. Above all, they knew how much she loved the Lord.

Wren was quiet. Contemplative. "What would the world look like if everyone were willing to give up their shirt like that? What if even we— the Mamas—were more intentional that way?"

Wren was always asking questions like that, calling the Mamas higher.

"Wren, I like that! We could have a little mission statement." Kate loved order. "It wouldn't have to be anything formal, and we're kind of already doing it, anyway."

"Let's keep supporting each other in hard times. Let's always point each other to the cross. And let's stay married, girls." Hannie pulled at the straight edge of her bob haircut.

Brooklyn thought of Jake. Could his pulling away be a gift somehow? "Let's love each other's children too, no matter what. Even if they're seventeen and nature's queen like 3M right now. Even if they walk away from Jesus, and I know we're doing it already, but let's commit to praying for them all our lives."

"We have to encourage each other in the Word, Mamas. Life is always going to pull us away from it. Please, let's hold each other accountable to the Word of God." Wren's voice landed like a small bird on their shoulders. She had a gentle and quiet spirit, and unlike anyone, Wren clung to God's Word.

"Listen, Mamas; I didn't do anything special by giving Brooklyn my shirt. She was just such a mess; what else could I do? I mean, you've seen her in the prayer room. You know what I'm talking about." Kathryn ran an elegant finger around the adored bronze buttons. "But whatever life brings, I do think we should take it hand in hand." Kate sipped her iced coffee and looked at her friends with smiling eyes. "For King and country!" Kate said in her beautiful English accent. "Let nothing in all the world separate us!"

The Mamas raised their coffee. They didn't even need to say the words now.

To the brim.

Chapter 37
Prayer Day 6

The years clicked by, and the Mamas kept meeting to pray on their knees. "To the brim!" was a phrase oft repeated. Brooklyn and Kate's matching shirts with their cute bronze buttons became symbolic of the Mamas' friendships. The fabric faded and frayed, but the shirts stayed favorites. Brooklyn's hair turned gray and started to fall out. Wren helped her brush over the bald spot in the back of her head. Kate fell and broke her leg. Hannie sat by her bed and held her hand. The Mamas took too many trips to the hospital to count—sometimes taking each other's kids.

Brooklyn lost her mom. Then her dad. Kathryn lost her mom. Hannie lost her dad. Wren continued to struggle with grief over the loss of her Matthew, and life rolled onto them. The Wonder Woman cuffs were scuffed with wear, but the friends held. They helped each other hold on.

They held on when one of their men lost his job. When their teenagers fell in and out of love with each other. When they struggled with depression and fought against anxiety. When insecurity, that demon of hell, tried to devour their souls. They held on when their older kids got married, and when it felt like they were watching their life's work walk down the aisle. They held as the culture crumbled away, and when they struggled to hold onto hope.

They hung on to the words Brooklyn had told them about, and they called instinctively to one another in the darkness.

You are loved. You are loved. You are loved. You are loved.

But it was "to the brim" that saved them. It was Jesus Christ obeying all the way to the cross that saved them all.

Brooklyn, Kathryn, Wren, and Hannie stood in the entryway at Kate's house. They took comfort in the familiar ways they took off their shoes and hung their purses on the coat rack. They silenced their phones, putting them on the scuffed, wooden bench.

It was prayer day.

The years had gathered around them, and the Mamas creaked a little going to the floor now. Their hips hurt, and their backs ached. They hadn't slept well the night before.

But Brooklyn still reached for the tissue box.

And Kate still closed the door.

Afterward, there would still be coffee. And laughter and tears and quiet. There would be the love of four women for Jesus, and their friendships as strong as a wall. There would be Brooklyn and Kate and Hannie and Wren.

There would be The Mamas.

There would be love.

Chapter 38
Bandits and Beggars
in the Shepherd's Crook

Brooklyn tapped the words out on her laptop, writing about one of the best days of her life. It had been years ago, and she still remembered every detail. She wrote in story form so that she could give it to her son, Abe, as a wedding gift. Brooklyn could hardly believe how time had passed. She could hardly believe the little boy who had asked her, "Hey, Mama, what does 'haddle' mean?" was going to be a young husband.

Brooklyn prayed as her fingers clacked over the keys, and she recalled the details of the day. How could she ever forget them? It was true her mind wasn't as sharp as it had once been, but Brooklyn remembered that day.

She remembered it all.

***

The shepherd stood at the gate of his sheepfold watching the road.

The Mamas arrived in two vehicles, and their kids burst from open car doors like a massive birth. It was field trip day. The Mamas had driven to a sheep ranch in Wyoming. Brooklyn had befriended the old shepherd who lived there. *(Or had he befriended her?)* He gave all Brooklyn's kids bum lambs for 4-H every spring, and the Wyer family adopted him as their grandpa. He had become a father to Brooklyn.

The shepherd smiled warmly, his brown eyes melting with tenderness as he watched the kids scamper across his field. The newborn lambs couldn't decide if they should run to or away from the children, and they leaped and scampered about on their awkward, long legs. The shepherd spoke softly to them, and the Mamas could see that his flock was comforted by the sound of his voice.

"It's okay, little ones. It's okay, mamas." The shepherd was talking to his sheep, of course—they knew that. But the Mamas were comforted too, all of them thinking about Jesus. The kind shepherd even looked like him.

Kate and Hannie followed the kids to the barn. It was a perfect spring day, and the two beauty queens looked like bright flower blossoms against the backdrop of newly sprouted grass. Their hair lifted in the warm breeze, and they kept their heads close together, talking.

Wren and Brooklyn stayed with the old shepherd, and so did Brooklyn's twelve-year-old son, Abe. The shepherd leaned on his crooked staff and spoke with a gentle voice to the boy.

"You see that little lamb there?" He pointed his crook at a tiny lamb kneeling on his front legs to nurse behind one of the ewes.

"Yes." Abe followed the end of the crook. "He's so cute!"

"That's not his mother." The shepherd looked down at Abe, his face was aglow with the affection of a grandfather. These were not his children, but it didn't matter. The shepherd loved all children.

"How do you know? Why is it getting milk from her if it's not his mother?"

"You see how he's drinking from behind her instead of by her side?"

"Yeah." Abe nodded.

"And can you see that his head is black, instead of white, like the other babies?"

"Yea." Abe nodded again.

"That's because his mother rejected him." The shepherd rested his weathered hand on top of Abe's head. "Or his mother died, or he could a triplet. He might even be one of four."

Brooklyn and Wren were hanging on the shepherd's words. He knew Abe was the fourth of Brooklyn's five, and Brooklyn had written him a long letter asking him to pray for Abe.

"He's stealing milk from all the mamas. He doesn't belong to any of them, so he sneaks in from behind. That black stuff covering his head is urine from the ewes and dirt from the ground that clings to it. They don't know he's back there, so they pee on him."

Abe seemed to lose all self-consciousness and reached to hold the shepherd's hand.

"That's so sad."

"It happens sometimes, but the poor little beggar's going to die, anyway. The ewes don't produce enough milk, and he can't go undiscovered once he gets any size on him." The shepherd looked at Brooklyn's growing boy. He oozed adolescence. The shepherd squeezed Abe's hand with his calloused one. Brooklyn saw honor in the shepherd's eyes that Abe would still hold his hand. The old rancher seemed to understand that it would be the last time. Next year, Abe would be a man.

Lord, Help Abe learn something more of You today. Brooklyn pulled the hood of her sweatshirt up to keep the wind out of her ears.

Abe was Brooklyn's most sensitive child, but he didn't show it. He most often hid his tender heart behind bad behavior. He hid his neediness for affection and affirmation by lying and goading his siblings. He wasn't the only culprit, of course, but Abe was involved in almost all the conflicts they were having in their home these days.

Abe felt things Brooklyn's other kids didn't feel. He noticed everything. He noticed everyone, and he *felt* everyone. Brooklyn could relate. It was something she and Abe had in common. But Abe didn't show his sensitivity in appropriate ways. He felt weak, and it scared him. He didn't know yet that his tenderness was his strength, and Brooklyn and Will were struggling to parent him.

"You're not going to let that happen, right?" Abe looked into the shepherd's warm brown eyes. "You're not going to let him die?" Tears filled his, and he blinked hard to keep them from falling. He was too old for tears now.

"I guess that's up to you. Do you want to take that bum home?" The old sheep rancher looked at Brooklyn. She'd been bringing her kids to his ranch for years, and to him, she was the daughter he'd never had. They'd grown close through correspondence, and he respected the way she and Will were raising their family. The shepherd didn't want to betray her. "Your mom has to say it's okay. If she says no, you need to accept that the lamb will die."

"Mama! Please!" Abe's eyes were as blue as the sky. His voice begged. His body language begged. He didn't say more, though he wanted to, and the shepherd squeezed his hand again.

Good boy.

"Everyone's picked out a bum but you, Abe; he's yours!"

The shepherd smiled at Abe and Brooklyn. He was glad the little lamb would live.

"Okay, Abraham," the old rancher called Abe by his formal name. It sounded so important when he said it, and Abe stood taller. "I know you know what a shepherd's crook is. How would you like to see what it does?"

"Yes! I would like that!"

I would too, thought Brooklyn. She'd been coming to the ranch for a long time, but she'd never seen the shepherd use it.

257

"Watch this."

Brooklyn, Wren, and Abe watched with interest.

As the little lamb nursed as fast as he could, the old man walked toward the ewe. She kept her head down to the ground, ignoring the shepherd for savory blades of spring grass. The tiny lamb knelt behind her, stealing milk, but he tried to scamper off as soon as he saw the shepherd coming toward them. It was obvious the lamb lacked the safety of a mother.

The shepherd's staff, with its crooked end, struck the ground like a rod of wooden lightning. The old man grabbed the animal by the heel with the crook of his staff. Caught by its back leg, the helpless little lamb was dragged across the ground to the shepherd's feet. Bending down, the old sheep rancher picked up the orphan and held him in his arms. With his bare hand, he brushed as much of the sticky dirt and dung from the lamb's head as he could.

"Poor little beggar." He spoke and rocked the lamb like a real baby. "I've got you here. I've got you."

The shepherd turned to Abe. "What are you going to call him?"

"Bandit." Abe's smile split Brooklyn's heart open with joy. They'd been struggling so much; it was wonderful to see him happy! The shepherd smiled, and Brooklyn smiled too—the look of delight on Abe's face was one she didn't see much these days. She could tell by the way Abe leaned his body into the good shepherd how much he loved the old man.

"It's a perfect name." The good shepherd gave the lamb a little squeeze and handed him to Abe. "The other kids have gone to the barn. Why don't you take Bandit in there and mix up a bottle of milk for him? The only one he has to beg from now is *you.*" The old man took Abe by the shoulders and spoke to him man to man. "He needs food, Abraham." The shepherd looked into Abe's eyes and soul. "You need food too, young man. You're growing up, and you need bread. Do you know what I'm talking about?"

Abe looked directly at the shepherd, and they didn't speak for a long time.

Brooklyn was surprised Abe could hold his gaze. Sometimes, the intensity of the shepherd's eyes was almost too much for *her*.

"Do you know what I'm saying to you, Abraham?" The shepherd asked again. "You need food, and that's not something I would say to a little boy."

"Yes, sir. I need to read my Bible."

Brooklyn could tell Abe didn't feel preached at. He was drinking in the shepherd's counsel. This was rare for Abe, who, when he was seven, had told her, "Choose your words wisely, Mama, because I'm going to do the opposite of everything you say." Abe was the most strong-willed, independent child she had ever come across in her life. And he was hers!

"That's right, son." The shepherd smiled at him. "You're coming up to manhood now, and that's a fine thing. The Lord is good at making boys into men. Boys who don't surrender to the Good Shepherd have to steal everything from everyone. They never grow up. A man of The Book, though, that's a man who gets his truth straight from the source. Pure milk. Pure meat. Nothing can take that kind of nourishment away from him. But if he's not taking it in…that man is just like Bandit here." The shepherd pointed to the dung that still clung to the wool on Bandit's head. "The Lord's ways are higher, Abraham. Be a man of The Book. Seek your food from the Bread of Life."

"Yes, sir. I will, sir." Abe cuddled Bandit close to him, but never took his eyes off the shepherd.

"Off you go then. Feed that little beggar."

"Come with me?" Abe shifted the lamb in his arms and reached for the shepherd's hand again. He was twelve years old and terrified of letting people see his need—his weakness. But the shepherd was different. The shepherd already knew.

"Anytime. Always." The old man smiled at Abe, Brooklyn, and Wren. His face was leathered by the Wyoming wind and sun, and Brooklyn loved every wrinkle on his dear face. The old man knew it and winked at her with affection. The shepherd's gaze shifted to Wren, and a softness filled his eyes. "See you ladies at the barn."

The Mamas watched the old shepherd and the boy walk across the field. *Where was Hannie with her camera?* Brooklyn thought, but the sound of Wren's crying grabbed her attention. Turning toward her, Brooklyn caught Wren in her arms. She was sobbing.

"Wren!" Brooklyn held her friend.

"Did you see that, Brooky? Did you see the way the shepherd rescued that poor lamb? Did you see how it went from the crook of his staff right into the crook of his arm?"

"It's okay, Wren. I've got you." Brooklyn held the broken woman in her arms. She, too, was shaken as she replayed the scene in her mind. She saw the helpless lamb being dragged from certain death with the gentle shepherd's crook. *He did it with a piece of wood.* Brooklyn was a writer, and the metaphor left her weak.

She saw herself—a little bum lamb, not belonging to anyone, but begging to be loved. Begging to be fed and cared for. And while Brooklyn had been sinning her youth away, while she'd had her head down just like those ewes—ignoring the voice of the Good Shepherd and smoking grass—Jesus Christ captured her in the crook of His staff.

The cross.

He'd dragged her from her life of sin. He'd held her in His acceptance and washed the dirt and dung of her past away.

As happened sometimes after Brooklyn became a Christian, the Lord downloaded memories from her life like the shuffling of cards, or the changing of channels on the television, or the rapid flipping of the pages in a book. Scene after scene filled Brooklyn's mind in a single moment. She could see how Jesus had rescued her from a dangerous life of sin. And a degrading life of shame.

"Oh, my goodness, Wren! What an amazing Shepherd we have!" Overjoyed, Brooklyn rocked her friend in her arms, but Wren was demolished.

In all their years as friends, Brooklyn had only seen Wren like this the day Matthew left. Brooklyn didn't know what was wrong, but she held tightly to her friend. She thought of her mother holding her in the laundry basket. Brooklyn held so Wren could hold on.

"Oh, Brooky! The shepherd just picked up that little lamb and brushed all the shit off its head." Wren's life had been so changed by the power of the gospel; she never swore. Wholly in love with Christ, she didn't want to do anything that might give Jesus a bad name. She was Brooklyn's best accountability.

"Wren! You swore!" Brooklyn smiled and stroked Wren's head, kissing her hair. "Little Sister!" Brooklyn hugged her tighter, calling Wren by the pet name the Mamas had given her. Wren continued to sob in Brooklyn's arms, leaning into her as if she might fall.

"That's what it was like in my home, Brooklyn. It was just shit." Growing up on the Reservation, Wren had seen her share of neglect and abandonment. Her past rushed toward her like the Wyoming wind.

Her stepfather had beaten her, pulled out fistfuls of her hair, and locked her in the basement. Unable to escape, Wren endured three days without food, and worse, she could hear her stepfather abusing her mother in every possible way upstairs.

When he finally released Wren, her stepfather looked at her lasciviously before leaving the house. "I'll be back." His breath reeked of alcohol, his words slurred together, and bottles of whiskey lay strewn about the kitchen.

Wren ran to her mother's side. "Nuna! Are you alright, Nuna?"

Nuna looked at Wren blankly. All the light had been extinguished from her eyes. "He come back for you."

Wren's mother could speak perfect French and English, but she spoke now in broken tones with a heavy Native accent. An author and a poet, Wren knew she did it on purpose.

"No, Nuna." Wren didn't know she said it out loud as she clung to Brooklyn like a child.

Nuna's name meant *land*. She'd always told Wren, "Someday, we'll move away from this place. Away from him. We'll move to a free land." But Nuna never escaped the abuse of Wren's stepfather, and one day, she just disappeared. Everyone knew the violent husband was to blame, but there was no investigation, no police, no trial. *No fair.*

Like so many Native American women, Wren's mother disappeared like a mist in the sun. She took Wren's heart. She took Wren's will.

"Brooky…" Wren's tiny frame sagged in Brooklyn's arms, but Brooklyn held. "It wasn't only the things done to me. I did some terrible things too. Just awful things!"

"But you're free now, Wren. And you're safe." Tears ran down Brooklyn's face too. "We both are." She hugged her small-framed friend, trying to communicate that.

Wren pulled away from Brooklyn's embrace and took a handkerchief from her pocket. Sopping up tears, she couldn't stop shaking her head. "That was the most incredible thing I've ever witnessed. Thank you so much for bringing me this year." Wren blew her nose. "I mean…did you see that? Did you see how the shepherd did it without any effort? How the lamb didn't have a choice? How it didn't even know what happened until it was up in the shepherd's arms?"

Wren kept shaking her head in disbelief. "That's how Jesus saved me, Brooky! That's exactly what it was like for me!" Wren let the tears flow freely down her Native features. Brooklyn thought she looked more beautiful than ever.

"Whether they admit it or not, Wren, that's how it is for everyone. The only part we have in our salvation is the sinning part." Brooklyn, without a handkerchief, wiped her tears with her bare hand and her snot with the sleeve of her windbreaker. "While I was going all the way with my sin, Jesus was going all the way to the cross for me. The cross! The wood that rescued us, Wren! Just like the shepherd's crook rescued that baby lamb!"

Wren and Brooklyn were facing each other, holding loosely to the tips of each other's fingers. Their eyes locked at the wonder and mystery of salvation.

"But why, Brooky? Why rescue us? Why me?"

"I don't know." Brooklyn looked across the field at the ewes eating grass. *How little I notice The Good Shepherd's voice in my life!* "I'm just grateful He did." She could see Hannie and Kate walking toward them.

Observing Wren and Brooklyn's posture toward one another, Hannie and Kate approached with quiet respect. The women had forged rich friendships on their knees in prayer, and after so many years together, words weren't always necessary. Kate and Hannie didn't need to know the context, they just reached around each other's waists and pulled together in a tight huddle. The Wyoming wind cracked its whip around them, and the Mamas laughed as Kate quoted Acts 2. "And suddenly there came from heaven a sound like a might rushing wind…"

"Mamas, you won't believe what we just witnessed." Wren could hardly wait to tell Hannie and Kate about the shepherd and Bandit. The women held the circle and listened as she spoke.

"Thank you for this special place, Lord, and for my godly friends. Thanks for bringing us together and for being The Good Shepherd to us all." Hannie prayed after Wren told the story.

Wren started crying again. "And thank you, Jesus, for washing the shit off my life."

"Little Sister!" Kate pulled her friend closer. "You swore!"

The shepherd watched the Mamas from the barn door. Abe stayed close. Teaching and encouraging him as they stood in the open air, the old man didn't want this day to end. He loved watching Brooklyn's kids with their arms full of baby lambs, but he kept his eyes on their mother. He could see by the way the four women were holding each other that the Lord was doing His work. *Thank you for answering my prayer today, Father.*

The shepherd smiled a sad smile at what he felt sure the women had been through—especially to have raised such fine children. They were swimming against the current training their kids up in the Lord. He loved seeing all the kids playing together. He smiled as the baby lambs and the Mamas' children ran across the field. It was a good thing to be reminded of what Jesus had done. *Thank you, Shepherd King, for your goodness in this lonely, wind-swept land.*

The old man held Abe's hand in one hand, and his shepherd's crook in the other. His weathered face looked like cracked leather as he smiled his wide, warm smile at the boy.

You are loved, you are loved, you are loved, you are loved.

"Go tell your Mama that you love her, Abraham. Be manly enough to show your emotions sometimes. Tell her you love her. She needs to hear that from you."

The good shepherd took the helpless lamb from Abe's arms and pointed his staff at Brooklyn.

"Run, Abraham!" He wished he could himself.

"GO!"

Epilogue

The kids were all grown and gone, and the house was quiet. Will was at a men's retreat with the Mamas' men, and Brooklyn was alone for the weekend enjoying the fullness of stillness. Her fingers were swollen with arthritis now, but Brooklyn sat by the sliding glass door in the night writing. Like the comfort of home, her stylus sat in its permanent and familiar groove. Ignoring the pain in her hands, Brooklyn listened to the sound of story being born from the marriage of paper and pen—her old friends after all these years. It almost made Brooklyn cry. She didn't know why.

The cuckoo clock ticked in the hallway, so familiar to her, she didn't hear it at all. *Where has the time gone? When did all the children grow?* She gazed at her reflection in the night glass. *And how did you get to be so old?*

Brooklyn could faintly hear the lingering sounds of her children, but her memory warmed them all to life. She thought of Jake and remembered the trembling strings on his red sweatshirt. How manly he had grown to be in his tender-hearted openness! Everyone—her whole family, loved being in his presence, and now that he'd returned to the cross of Christ, they shared more fully in life together.

She remembered Sophie singing worship songs in her bedroom when she didn't know Brooklyn had been listening. Her early commitment to Jesus had survived a near-death test. Sophie was a grown woman now, devoted to Christ. She was an anchor in their family. She was a lighthouse.

Brooklyn smiled at the memory of Derek when he'd found a duck egg by the creek. Bringing it into the house, he'd cooked and ate it. "Delicious!" She could see the butter dripping from his chin, and the pride of his find smeared on his face. The very boy who had peed off the high dive had become not just a good man, but a great one.

Brooklyn remembered when they got a puppy and how Abe had said, "It's a boy's life, Mama.," as the dog nuzzled his chin, making him laugh.

Brooklyn would never forget Abe's laugh, and she thought of him often when she heard the sound of car tires on gravel. *How did he grow to be a man who teaches me, does conflict with me, and who asks me if I'm living up to my potential? How did he become one of my dearest friends?*

Brooklyn could see Maylee, skipping and twirling everywhere she went. She'd been such a happy girl! Maylee had been the chatterbox in the passenger seat on the road to music lessons. She'd been Brooklyn's accomplice in trying to get the boys to leave the house so they could be alone to read. Maylee...*How could she be so grown now? So grown and wise and wonderful?*

Brooklyn wondered how they were doing. *How are you really doing, my loves?*

And then she remembered the Mamas' kids. They were almost as much a part of her memories as her own. Like the ghostly rocking horse boy, she could hear 3M giggling in her mind. She could see their ponytails and their braces glinting in the sun, and her heart ached a little. Brooklyn could hear herself scolding all the boys, "No soccer in the house!" She thought of them on the rope swing and the season of hatchets on tree limbs. It made her smile thinking about the time they'd caught a water snake in the irrigation ditch. They'd dissected it only to discover it had recently swallowed a mouse!

She thought of all the dance parties, sleepovers, and game nights they'd had—all the Mamas' kids joyfully growing up together. She smiled a sad, knowing smile at her reflection as she thought about their fights, the hurt feelings, the broken hearts, and the unrequited loves. Brooklyn could hear the swirling sound of their childhood, and it felt like the wind. She could hear it in her mind. She could feel it in her heart, but she could no longer grasp them in her arms. They were all grown, and all gone, and it was all good. She couldn't help missing them—the way they were. She wondered how they were doing too. *How are you really doing, my loves, and why does growing up have to be so hard?*

Memories of the Mamas came next, and Brooklyn tried to write them, but couldn't. No. The Mamas were beyond words. They were beyond understanding. Words could never capture the sacrifice, the lack of sleep, the chronic worry, or the joy that hurt sometimes. They loved their kids with a passion that even still made them feel as if they might spontaneously burst into flames.

The Mamas.

Kathryn, Hannie, and Wren, with that haunted look of love burning in their eyes, were the friends who wouldn't let Brooklyn go. They grieved alongside her through the hardest times, and they'd rejoiced with her in the happiest times. Brooklyn knew she was rich beyond the world.

After forty years of praying together, the Mamas didn't kneel anymore. Kate broke her hip. Hannie had a knee replacement, and arthritis was Brooklyn's constant, creaking companion.

"Look! It's the Young Mother's Club!" Wren teased them while helping them into their coats, smoothing down their hair, and bending down to tie their shoes after prayer. She'd maintained her youth, and even her long braid was alive with vitality.

"Did you get my bald spot?" Brooklyn turned so Wren could see the back of her head.

"Oh, darling, which one? I did the best I could." Wren wrapped her tiny arms around Brooklyn's now heavy waist. The Mamas stood, as they always had, in Kate's entryway, gathering their things and chatting like schoolgirls.

Her reflection in the sliding glass door caught her attention, and suddenly, there was the memory of her own Mama. How could Brooklyn not cry? She remembered the mother of her childhood, loving and serving and warm and wonderful. The mother of her teens had been confusing, but Brooklyn understood her better now. But it was the Mama who held her on laundry basket day that she would never forget. Her mother had held, so her daughter could hold on, and Brooklyn missed her every day.

Brooklyn smiled as the sound of her grandchildren echoed through her mind. It was their newborn cries and their observations in life that made her feel young again. It was her children asking her, "Mama, how did you do it?" Brooklyn unconsciously touched the wrinkles around her eyes with their scorched expression of love

Coming back to the present, Brooklyn looked up from paper and pen to her reflection in the night glass.

Who are you, old woman? Her image probed. *Do you yet have the answers?*

Brooklyn smiled contentedly.

"I'm me." She answered aloud. "I'm just me. Myself. Old and gray and wrinkled and wise."

Her reflection smiled back. *It's true then, isn't it?*

Brooklyn laughed out loud. Even in the night glass, she could see the wrinkles on her face. She laughed and laughed and wondered how she could get to be this old and not know it until just now.

"At last! At last!" she exclaimed to the old woman in the window. "How good to know in this wonderful and terrible life!"

Her reflection laughed back at her, and they said it aloud and together.

"You are loved. You are loved. You are loved. You are loved."

Other Books By Bernadette Botz

The Mamas
A Companion Study for You and Your Friends

A guide to friendship written by "The Mamas" to help you develop deeper relationships.

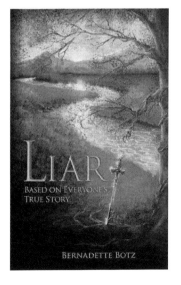

Liar
Based on Everyone's True Story

Liar has been warring against the kingdom of Struggle without opposition and his greatest harvest is truth and freedom. An allegory written for teens and young adults struggling with the goodness of God.

Made in the USA
Middletown, DE
06 January 2023

18738107R00170